As Jersey stepped i

on the back of her neck stir. Something was definitely wrong here.

She flicked on her flashlight and looked around. In the corner was a large commercial-type refrigerator with a lock on it.

She knelt before the door and picked the lock, opening the door to find it filled to capacity with bottles of murky liquid, the tops sealed with paraffin. She reached into the back of the refrigerator and plucked a bottle from the rearmost row, hoping it wouldn't be missed, then relocked the door.

"Anna, come on, let's get out of here," Jersey said, "I've got the goods."

They went out the front door, and were in the process of locking it behind them when a guard appeared out of the darkness. He dove against Jersey, slamming her against the door she was locking. As he raised his hand with a knife in it, Anna chopped across the back of his neck, breaking one of his vertebrae and killing him instantly.

As he slumped to the ground, Jersey turned around with a look of horror on her face.

"Don't worry, Jerse," Anna reassured her. "I took him out."

Jersey's face blanched white as she looked at a wet stain on the front of her shirt. "That's not what I'm worried about," she said in a hoarse voice.

"What is it?" Anna asked, spooked by the fear she saw in Jersey's eyes.

Jersey bent and placed the dog tags with Mingo Higgins's name on them in the dead guard's hand, then looked up at Anna.

"I think we've just loosed the hounds of hell! Stay as far away from me as you can, Anna," she said, pointing to the stain on the front of her fatigues.

"Is that . . . ?" Anna asked, a look of horror on her face as she stared at the dark spot.

Jersey nodded. "Yeah. The good news is, whatever the nasty stuff is those bastards are working on in that lab, we now have a sample of it."

"But that means . . ."

Jersey nodded, and began to move at speed through the jungle toward a stream that ran along the edge of the training fields. "It means I'm probably going to get it."

WARRIORS FROM THE ASHES

William W. Johnstone

PINNACLE BOOKS
Kensington Publishing Corp.
http://www.pinnaclebooks.com

PINNACLE BOOKS are published by

Kensington Publishing Corp.
850 Third Avenue
New York, NY 10022

First Printing: January, 2001
10 9 8 7 6 5 4 3 2 1

Printed in the United States of America

"Let there be light!" said God, and there was light!
"Let there be blood!" says man, and there's a sea!

George Gordon, Lord Byron (in *Don Juan*)

Prologue

If a war had not engulfed the entire world, plunging every nation into bloody chaos, the theory was that the government of the United States would have collapsed anyway. Personal income taxes had been going up for years and the hardworking, law-abiding citizens were paying well over half their income to the government. The left wing of the Democratic Party had taken over and passed massive gun-grab legislation, effectively disarming American citizens; except for the criminals, of course, and about three-quarters of a million tough-minded Americans who didn't give a big rat's ass what liberals said, thought, or did. Those Americans carefully sealed up their guns and buried them, along with cases of ammunition. When the collapse came, those Americans were able to defend themselves against the hundreds of roaming gangs of punks and thugs that popped up all over what had once been called the United States of America. The great nation would never again be accurately referred to as the United States of America.

Slowly, an ever-growing group of people began calling for a man named Ben Raines to lead them. But Ben didn't want any part of leadership. For months he disregarded the ever-increasing calls from people all over the nation, until finally he could no longer ignore the pleas.

Months later, thousands of people made the journey to the northwest part of the nation and formed their own nation out of three states. It was called the Tri-States, and those who chose to live there based many of their laws on the Constitution of the United States: The original interpretation of that most revered document was a commonsense approach to government. Something that had been sadly lacking for years with liberals in control. But after only a few months in their new nation, Ben knew that only about two out of every ten Americans could (would was more to the point) live under a commonsense form of government—a form of government where everyone, to a very large degree, controlled his own destiny. The Rebels, as residents of the Tri-States were named by the press, took wonderful care of the very old, the young, and those unable to care for themselves. But if a person was able to work, he worked . . . whether he liked it or not. There were no free handouts for able-bodied people. If they didn't want to work, they got the hell out of the Tri-States. Very quickly.

The first attempt at building a nation within a nation failed when the federal government grew powerful enough to launch a major campaign against the Tri-States. The original Tri-States was destroyed and the Rebel Army was decimated and scattered.

But the federal government made one major mistake: They didn't kill Ben Raines.

Ben and the few Rebels left alive began rebuilding their Army, and then launched a very nasty guerrilla war against the federal government that lasted for months: hit hard, destroy, and run. It worked.

But before any type of settlement could be reached, a deadly plague struck the earth: a rat-borne outbreak, the Black Death revisited.

When the deadly disease finally ran its course, anarchy reigned over what had once been America. Gangs of punks and warlords ruled from border to border, coast to coast. Ben and his Rebels began the long, slow job of clearing the nation of punks and human slime and setting up a new Tri-States. This time they settled in the South, first in Louisiana, in an area they called Base Camp One. Then they began spreading out in all directions as more and more people wanted to become citizens of the new nation called the Southern United States of America: the SUSA.

Ben and the Rebels fought for several years, clearing the cities of the vicious gangs and growing larger and stronger while the SUSA spread out.

In only a few years, the Rebel Army became the largest and most powerful army on the face of the earth . . . with the possible exception of China's. No one knew what was going on in China, for that nation had sealed its borders and cut off nearly all communication with the outside world.

A few more years drifted by while the Rebels roamed the world at the request of the newly formed United Nations, kicking ass and stabilizing nations as best they could in the time allotted them.

But back home, the situation was worsening: Outside the SUSA, the nation was turning socialistic with sickening speed. The old FBI was gone, in its place the FPPS: Federal Prevention and Protective Service. It was a fancy title that fooled no one. The FPPS was the nation's secret police, and they were everywhere, bullyboys and thugs. Day-to-day activities of those living in the USA were highly restricted. The new Liberal/Socialist government of President-for-life Claire Osterman and her second in command, Harlan Millard, was now firmly in control.

There were border guards stationed all along major crossings in every state. Now, many of the guards had been moved south, to patrol along the several-thousand-mile border of the SUSA.

A bloody civil war was shaping up between the USA and the SUSA. Rewards had been placed on the head of Ben Raines: a million dollars for his capture, dead or alive. But Ben was accustomed to that: He'd had rewards—of one kind or another, from one group or another—on his head for years.

Anna, Ben's adopted daughter, had been kidnapped by the

FPPS. She was to be tried as a traitor against the Liberal/Socialist government and executed. A very highly irritated Ben knew the taking of Anna was to draw him out, for the FPPS was certain Ben would come after her . . . which he did, with blood in his eyes. That abortive move cost the FPPS several dozen agents and accomplished nothing for Osterman and her henchmen. But it further heightened the already monumental legend of Ben Raines . . . and made Claire Osterman and her government look like a pack of incompetent screwups . . . which they were.

After Claire completely lost her temper and what little rational judgment she had, she started a civil war with the SUSA, using hired mercenaries when half of her own USA troops refused to fight their neighbors. All along a battle line that stretched for thousands of miles, from Texas to Georgia in the Old South, federal troops faced Rebel forces across no-man's-lands.*

Once again the SUSA, led by Ben Raines and his team, kicked Osterman's federal troops' butt in battle after battle, driving her into a fury that knew no bounds.

When Sugar Babe Osterman got word from her field commanders that Raines had killed Commanding General Walter Berman, head of her entire Army, in a hand-to-hand combat, she almost had a stroke. In a fit of pique, she notified Cecil Jeffreys, President of the SUSA, that if he and his leaders—especially that bastard Ben Raines—didn't surrender, she was going to launch an all-out missile attack against the SUSA at 0600 hours. The missiles were to contain a highly effective strain of anthrax bacteria developed by a USA scientist named Yiro Ishi. The vaccinations the SUSA had given their troops against anthrax would be useless due to the nature of this new strain.

However, Ishi double-crossed Claire Osterman, and gave the formula for an effective vaccine to Ben Raines and a fake form-

***Standoff in the Ashes.*

ula to Osterman's government. As the plague began to decimate the USA, Otis Warner, one of Claire Osterman's cabinet officers, conspired with General Joseph Winter to have Claire Osterman killed in a plane crash.

When the plane went down, Warner and Winter, sure Osterman was dead, took over the government of the USA, contacted SUSA President Cecil Jeffreys, and began to discuss a peace accord.*

However, Claire Osterman survived the plane crash and was taken in by a family in the Ozark Mountains of Tennessee, whose kindness she repaid by killing the husband and wife. She contacted her old bodyguard, Herb Knoff, and used him to help her establish her own "rebel" government within the boundaries of the USA.

From there, she orchestrated a new war against the SUSA, enticing a rebel leader from Belize named Perro Loco to attack Mexico and head northward toward the SUSA's southern borders, while she hired disgruntled FPPS and Blackshirt brigades to fight the leaders of the USA and try to take back the country she considered her own.

Finally, in a decisive battle, Perro Loco's troops were defeated on the very outskirts of Mexico City and driven back to southern Mexico, just as Claire Osterman succeeded in driving the successors to her presidency, Otis Warner and General Joe Winter, to seek asylum in the SUSA.**

Claire, never one to give up her dream of defeating and killing Ben Raines, hatched another plan for yet another war against the SUSA. . . .

**Crisis in the Ashes.*

***Tyranny in the Ashes.*

One

Perro Loco's army is defeated in its attempt to take Mexico City, and his forces have been pushed back to their stronghold at the old Mexican naval base at Pariso near Villahermosa on Mexico's east coast.*

General Jaime Pena jumped to attention when Perro Loco, followed by Jim Strunk and Paco Valdez, entered the commanding officer's office at the Mexican Army base at Villahermosa. Pena had pulled his troops back to this location after the disaster on the Pan American highway.

"Buenos dias," Pena said, saluting smartly.

Loco gave him a look, his eyes flat as he sat behind the desk in the office.

"General Pena, would you ask your second in command to come in, please."

"Certainly, *comandante.*"

Pena stepped to the adjoining door, which led to the officers' wardroom, and called, "Colonel Gonzalez, would you come in here?"

A tall, swarthy man, with a handlebar mustache and a knife scar on his right cheek that coursed down his face to the corner of his mouth, entered. He nodded at Loco and stood at attention, his back to the wall.

**Tyranny in the Ashes.*

"Now, General Pena, please be so kind as to explain to me why you failed in your mission to take Mexico City," Loco said calmly.

Pena looked from Strunk to Valdez, who were standing behind Loco on either side.

"But, *comandante,* there is only one serviceable road northward through this miserable country, and it was heavily mined and defended." He spread his arms wide. "I needed more air support, but the Mexicans had ground-to-air missiles and shot the few helicopters I had at my disposal out of the air."

Loco nodded, then glanced at Strunk. "Jaime, how much does a helicopter cost?"

"Several millions of dollars, *comandante.*"

"And an APC or a HumVee?"

"Many thousands of dollars, *comandante.*"

"And a portable mine detector?"

Strunk smiled, shaking his head sadly. "Only a few hundred dollars, *comandante.*"

"Why did you not think that the road might be mined, General, and take appropriate precautions? Surely, losing a few men with mine detectors would have been preferable to losing"—he bent his head and studied a sheaf of papers on the desk—"two helicopters, four APCs, three HumVees, and four hundred and fifty-six soldiers, not to mention General Juan Dominguez."

Pena, sweat beginning to bead on his forehead and run down his cheeks to drip off his chin, lowered his head. "We moved so fast, *comandante,* I did not think the Mexicans would have had time to mine the road."

Loco sighed heavily. "That is the truest thing you've said today, General," he said. "You did not *think!*"

"I am sorry, *comandante,*" Pena said, his eyes on the floor in front of him.

Loco slipped a .45-caliber automatic out of his pocket and aimed across the desk.

Pena glanced up, his eyes widening and his mouth opening

to protest as Loco fired. The pistol exploded and the bullet entered Pena's forehead, snapping his head back and blowing the back of his skull out, showering the wall behind him with blood and brains. Pena's body collapsed in a heap in front of Loco's desk.

Loco cut his eyes to Colonel Gonzalez. "What is your first name, Colonel?"

Gonzalez swallowed, the scar on his cheek pulling the corner of his mouth up in a caricature of a grin. "Enrique, *comandante.*"

"Enrique Gonzalez, you are now promoted to general and will be in charge of our forces in Mexico. Is that satisfactory?"

Gonzalez glanced at Pena's body on the floor, trails of smoke still rising from his empty skull. He nodded rapidly. *"Sí, comandante."*

"And you are aware of the penalties for failure?"

Gonzalez continued to nod, unable to take his eyes off Pena's corpse and its right foot, which was still twitching. *"Sí, comandante."*

Loco stood up and holstered his weapon. "Good. Then let us go to the communications room and contact President Osterman of the United States. I fear we are going to need some of her more modern equipment to take Mexico City."

President Claire Osterman hung up the phone after over an hour discussing with Perro Loco how his forces had been stymied on their journey toward Mexico City due to lack of air support and strong resistance from the Mexican forces.

"Jesus," she said, "God save me from Central American desperadoes who think they're generals."

She looked at her team of advisors arrayed before her. General Stevens, Harlan Millard, and Herb Knoff were sitting in chairs in the commanding officer's quarters of Fort Benjamin Harris in Indianapolis.

She winced as rumbling sounds and vibrations shook the ceiling. "Herb, can't we quiet that infernal noise?"

He shook his head. "Madame President, you ordered the removal of the wreckage of the building overhead yourself. The bulldozers cannot do that without making some noise."

"All right, all right," she said testily. She was still pissed off that Otis Warner and General Joe Winter had been allowed to escape the attack on the fort the day before.

"How is everything going with my resuming command of the country?" she asked Stevens.

General Bradley Stevens, Jr., nodded. "Very well, Madame President. The Armed Services have all acknowledged your right to continue as head of the government, and the rank and file of the Army is behind you one hundred percent. A few of the officers whose loyalty was questionable have been replaced with men I can trust, but overall, it's going just fine."

"And the country?"

"A massive propaganda campaign has been undertaken," Millard said. "All of the media are cooperating, as usual. We are informing the people that the coup attempt to overthrow you was orchestrated by Otis Warner with the complicity of Ben Raines and the SUSA. In the absence of any voices telling them otherwise, I think they'll buy it."

"Good," she said. "Now we have two things to do in addition to restarting the war against the SUSA. One, we have to transport some equipment to Perro Loco down in Mexico. He has control of the Navy base at Pariso near his command at Villahermosa. General Stevens, we need to send a transport ship down there with some helicopters, tanks, APCs, and whatever else he needs. I'll leave the coordination of that to you and your men."

"Yes, Madame President."

"The second thing I've got to do is get him some help with his soldiers and command structure. He's just too damned stupid to run a war."

"How do you propose to do that, Claire?" Millard asked.

She glanced at a folder on her desk that read TOP SECRET, INTEL on the cover. "I have here an intel report on Bruno Bottger."

"Bruno Bottger?" Stevens asked. "I thought Raines killed him in Africa a few years back."

She shook her head. "No, as it turns out, Bottger escaped to the island of Madagascar. He stayed there for a year or so, recovering from wounds he'd received in his escape. Then he made his way to South America. Intel has found out he's used his vast fortune to hire an army of mercenaries with the idea of reattacking Ben Raines at some point in the future."

Stevens shook his head. "I don't know, Claire. Getting involved with Bottger will be risky. The man is a zealot and a Nazi. He will be very tough to control."

"That's the beauty of it, Brad. We won't have to control him. He hates Ben Raines so much he'll jump at any chance to get revenge on him. I plan to get him and his mercenary army to join Perro Loco by promising him unlimited access to our weapons and technology. I'll also promise him he may have Mexico as a prize for his new Nazi state if he manages to conquer it."

"But, Claire," Millard protested, "you've also promised Mexico to Perro Loco."

"Yes, I have, haven't I?" she said, a smile curling her lips. "Well, in the event they are successful, they'll just have to fight it out to see who ends up on top down there."

Stevens nodded, seeing where she was headed. "Yeah, and after they've weakened each other fighting it out, we'll step in and take over from whoever's left."

Claire grinned. "Brad, you're a man after my own heart."

Two

Bruno Bottger sat on the terrace of his villa on the Ilha de Sao Sebastiao, a small island off the coast of South America, and watched the sun set over the ocean.

He had a glass of German white wine in his right hand, and used his left to gently massage the massive scar tissue around his eyes and cheeks, while his mind was filled with thoughts of a certain General Dorfmann and the day he was forced to run for his life. . . .

"Tell General Field Marshal Bottger that General Dorfmann is here from Berlin. I must speak to him at oncc."

Bruno Bottger heard the voice through a crack in his office door, which led to a secured waiting area in his underground bunker where his private office was protected from air attack.

Why is Dorfmann here? he wondered, cringing inwardly.

Dorfmann commanded the Gestapo in New Germany. The New Nazi Party governed most of what had once been Europe, now held in an iron grip by Nazi forces.

Dorfmann only answered to Kaiser Wilhelm II, political leader of New Germany. Bruno feared only one thing from Dorfmann . . . that he might discover his racial impurity, his Jewish mother, even though Bruno had made certain all her birth and death records had been destroyed. But Dorfmann was tenacious, always digging to expose enemies of the New World Order.

While Bruno held a higher military rank, and commanded the New World Order Army, he continued to worry that somehow Dorfmann would discover his dark secret, even though Bruno's New World Army was more or less politically independent of New Nazi Germany.

No one told Bruno Bottger what to do, quite simply because he held the power, the military might to crush anyone who stood in his way . . . or had, until this upstart Rebel Army led by General Ben Raines came to Africa.

Raines was proving to be a more difficult adversary than Bruno thought in the beginning. Among the worst bits of news, Raines's forces, headed by that bitch Jackie Malone, had wiped out one of Bruno's elite Special Forces squads in Zimbabwe. The devil woman's troops had killed them down to the last man, including the squad's commander, Major Cheli, a feat Bruno had thought was impossible. Cheli had been among his best recon specialists in difficult terrain. To take him and his Bantu scouts by surprise implied an expertise in jungle warfare Bottger could only envy, and fear.

Bruno's trusted bodyguard, Rudolf Hessner, stuck his head through the doorway. "General Dorfmann is here from Berlin to see you."

"Show him in."

General Dorfmann entered the expansive office where an old Nazi flag adorned Bruno's back wall. Dorfmann saluted, his stocky, muscular body still fit even though he was well past the age of fifty. He wore a copy of the old Nazi uniform, as did all New Nazi soldiers, right down to the knee-high black leather boots and bill cap.

Bruno merely nodded, not returning Dorfmann's salute as a show of superiority. Neither did he stand up behind his desk, giving Dorfmann an indifferent stare.

"What brings to you Pretoria, Herr Dorfmann?" he asked, feigning indifference, as if whatever it was could hold no significance for him.

Without being asked, Dorfmann took a seat across the desk

and removed his cap, pushing a hand through his naturally blond hair, pale blue eyes riveted on Bruno.

"A matter of great urgency," he said in his heavy German accent. "Word of several military defeats for the New World Army has reached Berlin. This Tri-States Army has the kaiser worried, wondering if they will turn toward New Germany sometime in the future."

"I do not intend to let that happen, Herr Dorfmann."

Dorfmann nodded, plainly unconvinced. "We have learned a great deal about this General Raines from a man who fought him in the Western Hemisphere, a Simon Border. Border's mercenary army was soundly defeated by Raines. These Tri-States Rebels grow stronger, acquiring more equipment and more followers. Their so-called Manifesto continues to attract people from all over the world."

"I've heard of this Manifesto," Bruno said, suspecting there was more behind Dorfmann's unexpected visit. He was, after all, Gestapo, not a military field commander. Bruno still wondered why Dorfmann was here, and if he posed a threat to him.

"It has tremendous appeal to the oppressed, to starving men who believe in the foolish tenets of democracy," said Dorfmann. "The SUSA has been built on these principles. But Raines has military power as well as gilt-edged promises to offer believers, and now it appears he has too much military strength for you to contain him. As I said, the kaiser is worried."

Bruno gave Dorfmann an empty smile. "Tell the kaiser not to worry. All is going according to plan. I am luring Raines and his Tri-Staters across the continent toward South Africa. Then we shall cut off all his sources of supply. He is doing exactly what I had hoped he would do."

Bottger yawned, as if bored by the conversation. "I have pulled my most effective troops back to the South African borders, in order to attack Raines after his supplies are no longer forthcoming."

"But the losses? We hear of so many of your defeats at the hands of the Rebels lately. . . ."

"Soldiers must be expendable to serve the cause, General Dorfmann. Most of the men we have lost to Raines have been these simpleminded African natives . . . Bantu tribesmen and especially Zulus. They are continually at war with each other, and when I offered the most powerful of the tribal warlords a handsome sum of money to fight for our cause, the greedy bastards accepted, as I knew they would. They die quickly, and willingly, believing they are making themselves rich. Very few live to collect the wages I've offered, and those who do will be exterminated when we unleash the balance of our chemical and germ weapons on them, as we pull out of Africa, to cleanse it . . . after we destroy Raines and his Rebels."

Bottger waved a dismissive hand, as if the deaths of the natives meant less than nothing to him.

"As you know," Bruno continued, "our ultimate goal is racial purity on this planet, as it was when the great Adolf Hitler unified most of Europe. Had it not been for the damned Americans' intervention against the Führer, we would live in a perfect world where no genetic impurities exist."

Dorfmann glanced over his shoulder. "May I close the door so we can speak privately?"

Bruno felt an adrenaline rush of fear course through him, making his heart pound like a trip-hammer. Was Dorfmann about to reveal something regarding Bruno's own racial mix? Had he discovered Bruno's Jewish lineage?

"Of course, General. Close the door if you wish." As he said it, Bruno pressed a hidden button under his desk to alert Rudolf to the possibility of trouble.

Dorfmann got up and closed the door gently. Bruno noted he was carrying a Luger in a holster tied to his waist. Dorfmann sat back down, giving Bruno a piercing look.

"You mentioned racial purity before," Dorfmann began. "I wanted to inform you of something, in strictest confidence, of course."

"Of course," Bruno said, sensing the direction Dorfmann was headed, wondering how much Dorfmann suspected, and how much he actually knew.

"There have been rumors in high circles having to do with you."

"High circles? Who do you mean? And what are these rumors?"

Dorfmann continued to stare at him coldly. The Gestapo was a place for men with ice in their veins, and Dorfmann fit this mold perfectly. He would have served Hitler well, Bruno thought.

"The kaiser himself has mentioned it to me, as has General Borgdahl. Someone was looking into your past . . . for reasons I do not know. It seems nothing can be found about one side of your family. There are no records concerning your mother. It is as if she did not exist. The kaiser and General Borgdahl wondered if you can explain this, and give me some information about your mother so I can inform those who need to know."

Bruno tensed, but tried not to show it, reaching for a desk drawer. General Borgdahl was head of Schutztaffel, the Blackshirts, a death squad enforcing policies within New Germany by means of executions, killing enemies of the state.

"My mother was a simple woman," Bruno began, a well-rehearsed story he'd told German officials before. "A peasant woman from Bavaria. She was born at home and never registered with the government because the family was so poor, simple farmers who did not understand the Order."

As he spoke he took a counterfeit file from his desk, containing forged records of the birth and death of a Gertrude Fest, his fictitious mother.

"I did, however, finally locate a few documents in the basement of a building in a small village in Bavaria. Here are my mother's documents, what I was able to find."

He tossed the file in front of Dorfmann, waiting, assuming

a bored smile, as if he were totally unconcerned about the inquiry and Dorfmann's veiled threats.

Dorfmann did not bother picking up the file, his eyes still glued on Bruno. "Come now, General Field Marshal Bottger. Those records are false."

"False? Explain yourself." Bruno sat up straight in his chair. He was not used to his word being questioned.

"Your mother was not Gertrude Fest. I know who she was, or should I say, I also know *what* she was?"

"You must explain, and please tell me who else you have told about whatever you suspect."

Dorfmann smiled wickedly, enjoying himself. Bruno's right hand moved closer to the Steyer automatic pistol he kept in the same desk drawer.

"As you say," Dorfmann went on, "there are no records. However, I did find an old woman who knew your mother from childhood. I searched for a good many months to uncover this information."

"What information?"

Dorfmann's smile broadened. "That your mother was a Jew."

Bruno knew what he had to do, what must be done. "I will deny it, of course, since it is not true."

"But it is true, Herr Bottger. I took down a statement from the old woman myself. Your mother was Gertrude Goldman, not Fest as you have claimed. She was even the daughter of a rabbi."

"Utter nonsense. The old woman is lying."

"No. She gave me exact details as to your birth, when and where. However, all records had been removed. I'm quite sure you removed them personally, so no one would know of your genetic weakness . . . impurity, I should say."

"Have you informed the kaiser or Borgdahl of these false charges in order to defame me in Berlin?"

"Not yet. I wanted to strike a bargain with you first. I am sure you will agree."

"What sort of bargain, Herr Dorfmann?" Bruno asked, sitting back in his chair, relaxed now that he had decided what was to happen.

"I want to leave New Germany and join your Army. In the end you will control most of the world, in my opinion, unless this General Raines is your undoing. I wish to be on the winning side when these wars are over."

Now it was Bruno's turn to smile. "You would become a traitor to your own people, Herr Dorfmann?"

"You know precisely what I mean. Calling me a traitor is using the wrong word. You are German, even if you are not of pure blood, fighting for New Germany as well as your New World Order. It is simply that I wish to be a part of what you are doing."

"And you'll use blackmail in order to do it?"

"Again, you have used the wrong word."

Bruno pulled out his Steyer, aiming it across the desk. "I call it blackmail. Where is this statement you were given by the old woman?"

"I left it in Berlin for safekeeping, a form of insurance policy. I am surprised that you feel it necessary to point a gun at me." Dorfmann's eyes showed no fear, as though he was confident of his position in this tendered bargain.

"Where in Berlin, Herr Dorfmann? Your life hangs in the balance."

"In a bank safe-deposit box. Only one person has the key."

"And who might that be?"

"You don't really expect me to tell you, Herr Bottger. I would be at your mercy. And I know you won't shoot me either."

Bruno felt sure he could locate Dorfmann's safe-deposit box and open it, using force if necessary. Few people in New Germany would challenge him, not even the kaiser himself.

"Then I must inform you of your terrible mistake, Herr Dorfmann. You have misjudged me, thinking I could be blackmailed. I will find your safe-deposit box, and destroy the statement you were given. But you will not be here to see it happen."

Now Dorfmann drew back, his cheeks paling. "You cannot think you will get away with killing me."

"I'm quite sure of it," Bruno replied.

As Dorfmann fumbled at the flap covering his Luger, Bruno pulled the trigger on his 9mm automatic.

Seven hollow-point slugs tore through General Dorfmann. His body jerked in the chair seven times. Blood splattered all over the floor of Bruno's office, just as Rudolf Hessner came rushing in with his pistol in his fist.

Dorfmann slumped to the concrete floor, making a wet sound when his body landed in a growing pool of blood, groaning, his legs quivering in death spasms.

"I was listening over the intercom," Rudolf said quietly, lowering the muzzle of his automatic. "But you did not say the code word to come in and kill him."

"Take his body to the lower-level incinerator and cremate him. Wipe up the blood. Contact whoever flew him down here to Pretoria and tell them that General Dorfmann has not kept his appointment with me. Tell them I'm very concerned. Inform all guards to say that General Dorfmann has not been seen entering the compound. If he has a driver waiting, go up there and summon him to the lower level. You can say the general has asked to see him at once. Then kill him and put his body in the incinerator along with Herr Dorfmann."

Rudolf bent down to lift Dorfmann's legs, then hesitated. "He is still breathing."

"What does it matter, Rudolf? Put him in the incinerator anyway."

"I'll have to get a body bag and carry him down. If I drag him he'll leave blood all over the hallway and stairs."

"Do whatever you must," Bruno said, too bored now to bother with details, putting a full clip back in his Steyer. "Make sure you take care of his driver and any aides he brought with him. If you need help, ask Johann to come with you."

"I won't leave anyone alive who came here with him," Rudolf promised.

As Rudolf left to get a body bag, Bruno gave Dorfmann a final glance. The head of the New German Gestapo, the only man in Germany who could discredit him for being part Jew, would be dead in a matter of minutes. Now, all Bruno had to do was fly to Berlin and locate Dorfmann's safe-deposit box. Then he would have Rudolf kill the old woman who gave the statement to Dorfmann about his mother. His secret would remain buried forever. Ultimately, he would have to execute Rudolf for overhearing what Dorfmann said about his mother being a Jew.

Bottger's knuckles grew white around the wineglass and he felt a stirring in his groin at the thoughts of how Dorfmann had looked at the moment of death—killing had always aroused him.

He shook his head to clear the image from his mind. Shortly after disposing of Dorfmann's body, he'd had to flee his headquarters for his very life, and that bastard Raines had shot his helicopter down in flames, burning his face off down to the bone.

Bottger, saved from certain death by Rudolf Hessner, had been too ill for too long to go after the safety-deposit box Dorfmann had hidden. Once its contents were discovered, the kaiser had no choice but to cut off Bottger's funding and brand him an enemy of the state and persona non grata in Germany.

As he remembered that day, Bottger's hand clenched further and the glass shattered, cutting his fingers in several places.

Rudolf rushed from inside, where he'd been standing watching his master. "You've cut yourself," he said, as he knelt next to Bottger and applied a soft cloth to his hand.

"I was thinking of the past," Bottger muttered, his voice hoarse with emotion.

Rudolf glanced up at him. "Better to think of the future and President Osterman's offer."

"You trust her then?" Bottger asked, staring at his only friend in the world.

Rudolf shook his head. "Not for a moment, sir, but I do trust you to use her as long as we need her to get back at Raines and the SUSA." He shrugged, squeezing Bottger's hand to stop the bleeding. "After that, who knows?"

Bottger's eyes flicked back to the setting sun, and the scar tissue around his mouth tightened as he tried to smile. "Exactly, dear Rudolf. After we are done with the bitch president and no longer need her support, we will do with her whatever we wish."

Three

Perro Loco was born Dorotero Arango in a small village in Nicaragua thirty-five years ago. Like so many of the places down there in those times, the area was under the sway of one of the local "rebel" leaders, a man named Santiago Guzman. Guzman was more like a tribal warlord, exacting tribute from the villagers in the form of food, money, and sometimes the young men of the village when he needed them to join his forces. Guzman was known as El Machete, The Knife, because he always carried a long machete he used to execute those who disobeyed his orders.

One day when Dorotero was just entering his teens, El Machete came to his village and called his father out of their hut. He said he needed the boy to come with him. Dorotero's father declined, saying the boy was needed at home to take care of his mother and sister while the father worked the fields. El Machete didn't argue. He simply walked over to the boy's mother and sister and beheaded them with one swipe of his long knife. When the father fell to his knees, cradling his dead wife in his arms, El Machete killed him too. Then he turned to the boy and said, "Now you have no reason to stay in this miserable pigsty of a village."

Instead of following El Machete's orders, the boy told the man he needed to go into their hut and gather his things. When he came out, he walked up to El Machete, pulled a sickle his father used to cut ribbon cane from beneath his shirt, and buried it in El Machete's chest. Guzman had time for one swipe with his machete, and he laid Dorotero's face open with it before he died, giving him a scar he would carry with him until he died.

Dorotero then went on a killing spree, grabbing El Machete's long knife from his hand and killing three of his men before they could draw their weapons. As he stood there in the clearing in the middle of his village, one of the neighbors is said to have whispered, *"Perro Loco,"* meaning Mad Dog. Dorotero took that as his name and vanished into the jungle, where he began recruiting his own gang, which soon became known for their ferocity and viciousness and utter lack of mercy toward their enemies.

Such was the history of the man who now sat behind an admiral's desk at the Mexican Navy's base at Pariso. As his two top assistants entered the room, Perro Loco glanced at them with approval. They suited his needs admirably.

Paco Valdez was a tall Mexican who loved killing, especially with his hands, more than most men liked sex. It was said among the troops that if he went more than a few days without killing, he would get edgy, irritable, and men would make sure to stay out of his sight.

Jim Strunk was a transplanted Englishman with a Belizian wife and four children. As Chief of Security at Comandante Perro Loco's headquarters, Strunk knew what was expected of him, and rarely hesitated to carry out his *comandante's* orders, especially if it involved the shedding of blood.

Strunk was an ex-SAS sergeant from the British Army. The Special Air Service units were specialized forces used for much of the British Army's undercover work, which would range from operating behind enemy lines to the surveillance and infiltration of terrorist groups. They were so well trained and deadly, the Americans had copied their training methods for their own special forces. The Americans' 1st Special Forces Operational Detachment Delta was created with the SAS as a model, the SFOD-Delta intended as an overseas counterterrorist unit specializing in hostage rescues, barricade operations, and high-risk reconnaissance.

When Strunk infiltrated Perro Loco's band of terrorists, he realized he could go much farther and get much richer if he switched sides and allegiance to the man known as Mad Dog. He also got many more chances to use his specialized training in killing, which he enjoyed almost more than the money he was paid.

"Good morning, *comandante,*" Valdez said, touching the brim of his hat with his hand in a lackadaisical salute.

Strunk, standing ramrod straight as always, gave a more formal salute, his flattened palm against his forehead in the British manner. "Good morning, sir," he said in a crisp military voice.

Loco nodded and waved his hand lazily in a semisalute. "Good day, gentlemen," he said, turning his chair to look out the window at the docks and wharves nearby. "Has there been any sign of the tankers President Osterman has sent us?"

"No, sir," Strunk said.

"Perhaps they have been intercepted by either the Mexican Navy or that of the SUSA," Valdez said, a worried look on his face.

Loco shook his head. "No. President Osterman assured me her spies have determined the coward of a president of Mexico wants no further fighting, and is willing to let us stay here in southern Mexico if we do not try to proceed any further north."

"What about the SUSA and Ben Raines?" Valdez asked. "Surely he is not so forgiving."

Loco turned his chair back around, a grin on his face that pulled the scar on his cheek tight. "Fortunately, Raines has his hands tied by the Mexican government's fears. They have forbidden him to take unilateral action, the fools."

Strunk shook his head. "So, he must sit on his hands while Osterman rearms us and sends us more modern equipment by tanker ship."

"Yes," Loco said, his eyes glittering. "It seems we are to

be the beneficiaries of the Mexican president's lack of *cojones.*"

"His lack of balls is exceeded only by his ignorance, I think," Paco Valdez said.

"Now, go and get the soldiers ready to unload the tankers as soon as they arrive," Loco said to Valdez.

He looked then at Strunk. "And you need to get your officers ready and up to speed on the use of the new helicopters and gunships and other hardware Osterman is giving us."

Strunk nodded. "Yes, sir. I'll break out the manuals and start the lessons today. Once the hardware is here, I'll start hands-on training."

"Good," Loco said, an approving look on his face. "I want to be able to renew our offensive by week's end."

Ben Raines called an emergency meeting with his team at the SUSA headquarters near Tucson, Arizona, on the old Davis-Monthan Air Force Base.

As his personal team filed into his office, he reflected on how lucky he was to have such a talented bunch of men and women working with him.

The first through the door, as usual, was Jersey, his personal bodyguard. She was rarely away from his side, and considered his safety her mission in life. Part Apache, she often had visions or dreams that foretold of danger or gave warnings of future happenings. She was tough as nails and somewhat masculine, like a female marine.

Following Jersey, Cooper sauntered in. Coop, Ben's driver, was the nemesis of Jersey, with whom he had a love/hate relationship. Their constant bantering and jibing at each other concealed the real depth of their feelings.

Corrie, the radio tech, and Beth, the team statistician, came in next, talking to each other as usual.

Anna, Ben's adopted daughter, followed the other women into the room. Part Gypsy, she, like Jersey, could see into the future on occasion, a heritage of her Gypsy ancestors. Currently, she was under the spell of a strong infatuation with Harley Reno, and could barely keep her eyes off him.

Harley Reno and Scott "Hammer" Hammerick filed in last. Late of the SUSA's special forces, they'd recently joined Ben's team as weapons experts and tactical strike team leaders. Harley was well over six feet tall and had flaming red hair, tied in a single braid that hung to the middle of his back, and ice-blue eyes, inherited from his Karankawa Indian ancestors.

Hammer Hammerick stood six feet three inches tall, an inch shorter than Harley, and had dark hair and brilliant green eyes. There wasn't a weapon made that he didn't know intimately, and his command of Spanish had been very useful in the fight against Perro Loco's forces in Mexico over the last few months.

"Have a seat, guys," Ben said, waving at the array of chairs around his office.

Hammer stood aside with a smile as Anna hurriedly jockeyed for position next to Harley so she could sit next to him during the meeting. Her infatuation with Harley was well known by the team, and looked upon with some appreciation.

"What's up, Boss Man?" Jersey asked, sitting in the chair closest to Ben.

"Mike should be here any minute to give us the latest intel on Sugar Babe Osterman and her latest endeavors."

Mike Post was the Rebels' Chief of Intelligence, and often acted as Ben's second in command when Ben was in the field.

Seconds later, Mike entered the room, his ever-present pipe sending clouds of aromatic smoke into the air.

He nodded at Ben and the team, then took center stage, standing next to Ben's desk where he could address the entire group.

"I have some good news and some bad," he started off. "The bad news is Osterman and her team have finally switched from using the old Unitel model 602 scramblers on their transmitters, so we are currently unable to monitor their talks as we used to be able to."

"You mean the old National Security Agency satellites can no longer pick up their transmission?" Corrie asked.

"Oh, we can pick them up," Mike replied. "We just can't make head nor tail of what they're saying. The computers are working twenty-four hours a day to decode the new scrambler codes, but unless you guys can come up with one of their units, it doesn't look too hopeful."

"You said there was some good news," Ben observed.

"Yeah. Before they switched scrambler units, we managed to intercept a few transmissions."

"And?"

"She made two calls yesterday. The first was to Perro Loco at his base at Pariso. Sounds like she's planning to resupply him and continue the fight for Mexico City."

Ben nodded. He'd expected nothing less from Osterman. She was a lot of things, most bad, but she was no quitter.

"What about the second call?"

Mike shrugged. "All we got on it was the location she called. It was to an island off the coast of South America. She didn't use any names, and it was during this transmission she was warned to switch scrambler codes, so we lost the rest of the conversation."

"Do we have any idea who she might have been calling down there?" Coop asked.

Mike nodded. "Well, there have been rumors for some time of a massive buildup of mercenary troops in the region. We've had reports some bigwig down there is hiring all the men he can get his hands on, as well as acquiring a lot of matériel and weapons."

"Any clues as to who this big man is?" Ben asked.

"None. We've sent a couple of men down there undercover, but they haven't been heard from since, so I assume their cover was blown and they were killed."

"Sounds to me like Osterman is calling in reinforcements

to supplement Perro Loco's rather inept military leaders," Hammer observed.

"I think you're right," Ben said, rocking back in his chair. "Maybe it's time we sent a team down there to see what's going on."

"Why not just intercept the shipment of weapons to Perro Loco and be done with it?" Harley asked.

Ben shook his head. "Politics," he answered. "The president of Mexico is sticking his head in the sand and thinks this will all go away if we ignore it. He's refused us permission to conduct any military operations in his country."

"A couple of jets with air-to-ground missiles could take out any tankers heading down that way before the Mexican government could object," Harley said, his expression showing this was the way he would do it.

Ben smiled. "As much as I'd like to do just that, Harley, Cecil Jeffreys, the President of the SUSA, has 'requested' that I do nothing to jeopardize our relationship with Mexico. He thinks the Mexican government will soon wake up to the dangers of leaving Perro Loco in place and then we'll have our chance to take him out permanently."

"Of course, by then he'll be much better armed and it will cost us a lot more men to do it," Hammer said.

"Can't be helped," Ben said, a look of disgust on his face. "Reminds me of when the politicians were running the war in Vietnam. They got a lot of young men killed who didn't need to be."

"Have you decided who you're gonna send down to South America to check up on this unknown hirer of the mercenaries?" Coop asked.

Ben glanced at Mike Post. "Yeah. I'm going to send you guys. Mike here has been working on some papers showing you to be disgruntled ex-Army people from here and the USA. With your obvious skills, I don't think they'll have too many second thoughts about hiring you for the mercenary forces."

"You mean all of us are going to go in undercover?" Jersey asked, her eyes lighting up at the prospect of action.

"Not exactly," Ben replied. "Corrie and Beth will go with you partway. They'll break off just short of the mercenary camp and set up a communications post in one of the villages nearby so Corrie can keep them apprised of the situation."

"What good will that do us if we get in trouble?" Harley asked.

"My son Buddy is going to be there with Corrie and Beth, along with a squad of scouts, ready to go in on a moment's notice to pull you out if need be."

"That's a lot of folks to have hanging around without the mercs finding out about," Hammer said.

"Mike," Ben said.

Mike Post pulled a sheaf of papers from his briefcase and glanced at them. "The mercs' headquarters are on an island off Brazil, near Sao Paulo. It's called Ilha de Sao Sabastiao and it's about twenty miles square. I've had intel do some research, and there's a small village on the coast south of there called Santos. It's pretty remote and there is no real communication with the other cities in the area. The team will be sent there on a freighter we've leased from Rio de Janeiro, which is about a hundred miles to the north."

"You don't think twenty new faces will cause attention in Santos?" Harley asked skeptically.

Mike shrugged. "Not as much as you'd think. The town, though small, has an active port and is always full of seamen coming and going from freighters that run up and down the coast. We'll have the freighter outfitted with state-of-the-art communications equipment and the scouts will be dressed as ordinary seamen."

Hammer grinned at Harley, both of whom were ex-scouts. "I'd like to see them make a scout look like a scruffy sailor."

"I agree, the cover won't be perfect," Mike said, "but hopefully, it won't have to last too long. The team's mission is to get in and out quick as soon as they find out who's heading the mercs and how dangerous they really are."

"Hammer," Ben interrupted, "I know you and Jersey are both fluent in Spanish, but they speak Portuguese in Brazil. Mike has arranged for a language tutor to work with you two for the few days it'll take for us to set this up. By then, you should be able to get by in the native tongue."

Hammer looked at Jersey and winked. "Good. I was really impressed with the way Jersey operated in Mexico. I'm looking forward to working closely with her on this mission."

Jersey stared back at the scout, wondering if he was making an oblique pass at her and if she should shut him down now or later.

She was saved from making a decision when Ben stood up. "All right, guys. Mike has some info from intel for you to study while you get your gear together. I'm leaving the choice of weapons in Harley's and Hammer's hands, as usual."

Four

The trip to Rio de Janeiro was uneventful. There, Ben's team met up with a contingent of Navy SEALS who worked with Buddy Raines's scouts to man the tramp freighter they would use as cover on their trip to Santos on the Brazilian coast.

Buddy introduced the leader of the SEALS to the team. "This is Captain Matt Stryker, guys, and his men are going to be teaching us how to look and act like real sailors on this little jaunt."

Coop stuck his hand out and the two men shook, followed by Harley, Jersey, Hammer, and the others.

Stryker looked at them. "I understand you are going into the mercs' camp undercover as mercenaries for hire," Matt said.

Harley nodded. "Yeah."

Stryker grinned, looking the six-foot-four redheaded giant up and down. "Well, you certainly look the part."

Harley glanced around at the SEALs team. "You men do too," he observed, taking in their ragged denim shirts and jeans and worn sneakers. "I'd never take you for Navy men."

Stryker smiled. "That's the whole point, Harley. We're supposed to be low-level sailors on this rust bucket Ben Raines provided as our cover." He looked around at the dilapidated ship. "I just hope we don't run into any heavy weather."

Coop's face screwed up in alarm. "You mean it might sink?" Coop was a notoriously poor sailor. He'd been rumored to get seasick in a swimming pool.

"Not to worry, Coop," Stryker said. "It's a relatively short run down to Santos and the seas shouldn't be too rough, short of a tropical storm."

"There aren't any in the forecast, are there?" Coop asked, letting his eyes roam across the horizon, looking for clouds or other signs of storms.

"Naw. The meteorologists tell me it's gonna be smooth as a baby's backside for the next week."

"Good," Coop said, unconsciously feeling his pocket where he kept a bottle of dramamine Doc Chase had given him.

"Don't worry, Coop," Jersey said, a smirk on her face. "I brought along an extra pillow for your knees to rest on as you hang your head over the side while you feed the fishes."

"Thanks, Jersey," he said sarcastically, "that's the old team spirit."

"While your boys get us cast off," Harley said, "I'll take my team to the meeting room and go over our weapons."

Harley stood before the team with an array of weapons on the table before him. "We're pretty much going with the same armament we uscd against Perro Loco our last time in the field," he said.

He reached down and picked up a small machine gun from the table. "Jersey, you and Anna will be carrying these Mini-Uzis. Fully loaded, they weigh only four kilograms, have forty-round detachable box magazines, and can fire six hundred fifty rounds per minute on full automatic."

He put the machine gun down and picked up a shotgun with a pistol grip on it. "Coop, Hammer, and I will be carrying the SPAS Model 12. SPAS, as you probably remember, stands for Special Purpose Automatic Shotgun. It's twelve-gauge, weighs four-point-two kilograms, has a seven-shot tubular magazine, and on full automatic can fire two hundred forty rounds per minute." He gestured at a couple of boxes of ammunition. "As usual, we will have a variety of slugs available, from light bird shot to heavy metal slugs that'll penetrate steel plate at a hundred yards."

Coop interrupted. "How about side arms? Are we gonna go with the Berettas again?"

Harley nodded. "Yeah, as you know, I prefer the Beretta Model 93R over the old Colt .45's. It fires a nine-millimeter parabellum bullet, has a twenty-round magazine, and can fire single-shot or in three-shot automatic bursts. Remember, on automatic fire, a small lever drops down in front of the trigger guard for the left hand to grab and steady your aim." He held up a metal box of cartridges. "I want the entire team to spend the time on our voyage down to Santos practicing with these weapons."

"You don't think we got enough practice using them against Perro Loco last time?" Jersey asked.

Harley glanced at her. "Yeah, but we're gonna have to show whoever's in charge of the mercs that we're worth hiring, and that may mean a test of just how good we are with our weapons."

"I'd think they'll be hiring anybody who's warm," Coop said.

"You're probably right, Coop," Harley explained, "but I don't want us to be grouped with the rest of the grunts. We need to be with the elite troops if we're going to get any useful intel out of this trip."

Jersey glanced at Coop, and couldn't resist one more jibe. "Harley, do these guns shoot okay if they're covered with vomit? 'Cause otherwise, Coop won't be able to practice till we get off the boat."

"Keep it up, Jerse," Coop said, his face turning red.

"Oh, I don't have any problem keeping it up, Coop, unlike what some of your women friends tell me about you."

"Okay, guys, that's enough," Harley said, unable to keep a smile off his face. "Let's get our gear together and get settled into our cabins."

"Put my cabin as far away from Coop as possible," Jersey

said, grinning. "The sound of retching keeps me awake at night."

"Since you have no male friends, it's a sure thing nothing else will keep you awake," Coop shot back.

Hammer stood up, a sheet of paper in his hand. "Here are the cabin assignments." He handed the paper to Jersey. "And, Jersey, you got your wish. Your cabin is on the opposite end of the corridor from Coop's."

Jersey glanced at the paper and noticed Hammer had put her in the room next to him. She looked at him, but his face was straight, with no hint of any ulterior motive in the assignments. She wondered again if she was going to have trouble with him coming on to her . . . not that it would be all that hard to take, she thought, noticing again his heavily muscled body and handsome face. In fact, it might not be bad at all.

Coop was miserable. In fact, if he'd had his side arm with him as he hung his head over the rail and vomited repeatedly into the choppy waves of the Atlantic, he would most assuredly have used it to end his misery.

To make matters worse, the rest of the team seemed to have no problem whatsoever with the roughness of the seas. Jersey would stand behind him and offer helpful suggestions, such as why not eat some greasy bacon and eggs so the fish would have something substantial to eat rather than the pure bile he was pouring on them with some regularity.

Other suggestions, such as watching the shoreline, barely visible on the horizon, or fixing his gaze on clouds overhead, seemed to do nothing but make his misery worse.

Finally, just before lunch, Matt Stryker approached the gray-faced Coop, still on his knees at the rail.

"Come on, Coop. You've got to put something in your stomach or you're going to be too weak for the mission."

Coop glanced back over his shoulder. "Are you kidding? It wouldn't stay there for more than a minute."

Stryker squatted down next to him. "Listen, I've got some suppositories in my duffel bag that will help. Phenergan will take most of the vomiting away, though you'll probably still be nauseated."

"Suppositories?" Coop asked weakly.

"Yeah. You couldn't keep a pill down, so it's either suppositories or a shot."

Coop, who hated needles almost as bad as traveling by sea, shook his head. "I'll take the suppository."

Stryker put his hand under Coop's arm and helped him to his feet. As they walked toward Stryker's cabin, Jersey began to walk alongside them.

"Tell you what, Coop," she said, smiling broadly. "Since you were so nice to me when we were marooned in the jungle last year, I'll be glad to insert the suppository for you."

He cut his eyes to her, sweat beading his forehead. "No thanks, Jerse," he mumbled.

"Really, it wouldn't be any trouble at all," she said sweetly.

He managed to give her one of his trademark smirks. "You just want to get my pants down, hussy," he said, "so you can have your wanton way with me."

Jersey gave a mock shudder. "I think I'll pass, Coop. Puke on my face has never been much of a turn-on for me in the way of foreplay."

"Foreplay?" he rejoined. "What's that?"

"Oh, I forgot for a minute, you're a man. Naturally, you don't know the first thing about pleasing a woman."

Coop jerked his head toward Hammer, who was watching them from a distance. "Why don't you head on back to Hammer, Jerse? From the looks of things, he's got some ideas along that line for you."

Jersey raised her eyebrows. "Is that jealousy I hear in your voice, Coop?"

He hung his head and dry-heaved a time or two. "No, dear, it's nausea at the thought of you with your clothes off trying to tell someone how to make love in your own bossy way."

"Well!" Jersey said, irritated by Stryker's smile at Coop's statement. "As if you'd know anything about how I make love."

"The thought never crossed my mind, Jerse. I'm more into women a bit more . . . feminine," Coop flung back at her as he and Stryker entered Stryker's cabin and shut the door behind them.

Jersey whirled on her heels and stalked back out onto the deck, muttering, "Feminine, huh? I'll show him feminine."

She walked over to stand at the rail next to Hammer, who was looking out over the sea, watching dolphins as they raced through the bow wave of the freighter.

He glanced at her, then said, "Something I'd like to know."

"Yeah?" she replied without looking at him.

"Is there . . . anything between you and Cooper?"

Now she did look at him, a slight smile on the corner of her lips. "Not now, not ever," she said. "Why do you ask?"

"Just wondering if I'd be wasting my time if I gave it a shot."

She looked back out over the sea, excited by the closeness of the man. "You'll never know unless you try, Hammer."

Anna and Harley were sitting in the wardroom of the freighter, drinking coffee. The mug looked like a demitasse cup in Harley's huge hands.

"Is it true you're descended from the Karankawa Indians?" Anna asked.

Harley nodded. "Yeah, indirectly. They interbred with some prisoners they took from a tribe of Mexican Indians who were descended from the Vikings, which explains the red hair and blue eyes."

"Is it true the Karankawa were cannibals?"

He shook his head. "Not really. Like the Aztecs, they would occasionally eat the heart or brain of an enemy they respected, in order to capture their cunning or bravery, but it was more of a ritual thing, like Catholics eating the crackers and drinking the wine which symbolize the body and blood of Christ."

She smiled at him. "So, you've never . . ."

He laughed. "No. I've never been that hungry . . . at least not yet."

They were interrupted by the rest of the crew filing in for lunch.

Anna saw Coop walking slowly into the room, his face still gray and his eyes sunken and hollow-looking.

"Coop," she called, patting the seat beside her. "Come sit over here."

He sat down as she reached over and poured him a cup of coffee. "You up for this?" she asked.

He nodded. "Yeah. The medicine Stryker gave me seems to be working, at least for now."

"Once you get something in your stomach, the sickness will pass," Harley advised, a sympathetic look on his face.

"I hope so," Coop said. "I feel like such a damn fool."

"Hey, man," Harley said, "seasickness is nothing to be ashamed of. I heard back during the Second World War one of the admirals of the fleet suffered from it, and it didn't keep him from kicking Jap ass."

"Really?" Coop said, his expression brightening a little.

"Sure enough," Harley replied. "Matter of fact, my first few weeks in jump training I was sick as a dog from air sickness, so I know what you're going through."

"How'd you get over it?" Coop asked.

Harley shrugged. "With time, you just get used to it, I guess. Maybe being shot at while you're flying takes your mind off your stomach."

Coop grinned. "If that's true, you have my permission to unload a few rounds in my direction next time you see me at the rail."

Five

Bruno Bottger sat behind his desk, drinking his German wine, as Sergei Bergman and Herman Bundt gave their report on the New World Order mercenaries' readiness for battle.

Bergman, who had been with Bottger since the African campaign and was in charge of the mercs' training facility, took a deep drink of his scotch whiskey, then dipped the end of his cigar in it before taking a puff. As he let smoke trail from his nostrils, he shook his head. "I don't know, Bruno," he said in answer to Bottger's question about the mercs. "We've had plenty of men answer your ads in *Soldier of Fortune* magazine, but only about half of them are really battle-experienced. The rest are wannabes who are dirt poor and looking for an easy way to make some money."

Sergeant Herman Bundt, Bergman's second in command, sneered over his bottle of beer. "Those can be useful too, Sergei," he said. "We can always use them for cannon fodder if the need arises."

"That's true, Herman," Bergman agreed, "but at some point, we're going to need men who can give as well as follow orders. My experienced line officers are too few to be everywhere at once, and it doesn't do any good to have good weapons and matériel if the men don't know how or when to use them."

"I thought we were on schedule with our training," Bruno said, a scowl on his face.

"We were, Bruno," Bergman said, "but the schedule was

advanced by over a year when President Osterman offered you the chance to attack the SUSA earlier than you'd planned."

"Well, then we need to accelerate the training," Bruno said, as if his ordering it would make it possible. "This chance is too good to pass up. That crazy bitch Osterman has practically given us the keys to her country as well as the means to defeat that bastard Raines and his mongrel country. Whatever it takes to get more men who are acceptable must be done. Increase the ads if you need to or offer more money, but get me some troops that are worthy of the New World Order."

Bergman finished off his scotch and stuck his cigar in the corner of him mouth as he got up from his chair. "I'll do what I can, Bruno, but don't expect miracles."

"That is exactly what I do expect, Sergei," Bruno said, his expression dangerous, "and you know the price of failure."

Bergman glanced at Rudolf Hessner standing off to the side, wishing their leader's second in command would try to talk some sense into him. "Yes, sir," he said, snapping off a quick salute and leaving the room, Bundt right behind him.

"Do you think Bergman is up to the task?" Bruno asked Hessner.

Rudolf nodded. "Do not let Sergei's trying to warn you of the facts mislead you into thinking he is not fully committed to our war, Bruno," he said. "Sergei is one of the best men I've ever seen at motivating and training mercenaries. He will get the job done if it is at all possible to do it."

"He'd better," Bruno growled. He rubbed the scar tissue on his face with his fingertips. "I've waited a long time to pay Ben Raines back for what he did to us in Africa, and I don't intend to let him off the hook now."

Sergei Bergman walked out of the villa and got into his personal HumVee, waiting only a moment as Herman Bundt followed. He started the engine and squealed the tires as he raced out of the driveway toward the mercenaries' training facility on the other end of the island. "Goddamn generals, they're all the same," he muttered to himself. "They think if they order it, it will magically happen, like I'm supposed to make good soldiers out of riffraff overnight."

He drove over winding roads through heavily jungled terrain until he arrived at the camp. He pulled to a stop and sat in his vehicle for a moment watching his officers put the mercs through their training exercises.

Shaking his head at the inexperience some of the men showed, he climbed down and walked to the officers' billet to check and see if any worthwhile candidates had come in recently.

Sergeant Herman Bundt walked around to sit behind his desk. He pushed a button on the intercom and said, "Send in the new arrivals."

A moment later, a group of men and women stood at attention before him.

Bundt glanced up and smiled at Bergman. "These are the latest arrivals, Sergei," he said. "From their records, I think you'll be pleasantly surprised.

"I hope they're better than the last bunch," Bergman replied, looking over the new recruits. There were a couple that looked interesting. Two men who were well over six feet tall and had the look of battle-hardened veterans about them, along with another man who was leaner and less muscled, but whose eyes were hard as flint.

"What have we got here?" Bergman asked, shifting his gaze from the men to two women who were standing with them. "Are these women applying for jobs as cooks, or hostesses?"

The taller of the two women, a pretty, dark-haired female who looked as if she had some *indio* blood in her veins, turned her eyes to him. Her look made the hair on the back of his neck stir, and he thought maybe he'd misjudged this one. She certainly looked dangerous enough. He glanced at her companion, a fresh-faced younger woman with close-cropped blond hair and a trim build. *This one looks much too soft to be a mercenary,* he thought. *She looks more suited to sharing a man's bed than a foxhole.*

"These applicants all have battle experience, Sergei," Bundt commented, looking down at the papers the recruits had filled out. "First with Claire Osterman's Army in the U.S., then with Raines's forces in the SUSA."

"You've all fought together before?" Bergman asked, waiting to see who answered as the leader of the small group.

The tall redheaded man turned to speak. "Yes, sir," he said crisply.

"Why did you switch alliance from the U.S. to the SUSA?" Bergman asked, stepping in front of the desk and sitting his hips on the desktop.

The red-haired giant shrugged. "More money, less hassle with poor officers who were trying to get us killed."

"So, money, not ideology, is what is important to you, huh?" Bergman asked.

"Staying alive to spend the money is the most important thing, sir. From what we've seen, Raines's forces don't have the will to win this war, or they'd have finished Perro Loco off in Mexico when they had the chance. We prefer to be on the winning side, for all kinds of reasons."

Bergman nodded. He could understand that, all right. It was the main reason he'd decided to fight with Bruno Bottger himself.

"I don't have any quarrel with that," Bergman said, "if you can earn your keep. Just how good are you?"

The big man's lips curled in a half smile. "Good enough to take anyone you've got with you now."

Bergman pursed his lips as he thought. He liked this man's confidence. In fact, it reminded him of himself when he was younger and full of piss and vinegar.

"Herman," Bergman said, "bring me those laser flak jackets. We're gonna have a little war game action today."

* * *

Bergman handed out the jackets to Harley Reno and his team.

"What are these?" Coop asked as he examined the strange-looking garment.

"Specially constructed flak jackets with laser-receivers built in," Bergman answered. "They're used with these special laser rifles. If you're hit with a beam, the jacket begins to beep and you're classified as a kill."

Harley slipped his jacket on and took a laser rifle from Bergman. "So, what's the deal?"

Bergman thought for a moment. "I think I'll send you and your team out into the jungle. Give you about an hour head start, then send my best team of commandos after you. Whoever comes back with the most live men is the winner."

"And if we lose?" Jersey asked.

"Then obviously, we won't be needing your services," Bergman answered with a grim smile.

Harley started to leave, then stopped and faced Bergman. "You want us to kill your team or bring them back alive as prisoners?"

Bergman laughed. "You're awfully confident you won't be the ones brought back."

Harley shrugged. "Let's just say we capture the entire force. What then?"

"I'll make you my lead commando group and send the others back for more training," Bergman said, his expression showing he doubted very much that would happen.

Once out of sight of the camp, Harley shifted into double time, practically jogging as he moved through dense jungle overgrowth as if it weren't there. It was all the rest of the team could do to keep up with him as he moved silently and swiftly down narrow jungle trails.

After thirty minutes, he stopped when he found an area he liked. Squatting, he and Hammer stuck sticks in the soft earth just off the trail and strung thin, almost invisible wire across the path. The wire they connected to slam-bangs, percussion grenades that exploded with a loud bang and a brilliant flash of light when triggered.

Harley then moved back down the trail the way they'd come, whispering directions to Coop and Jersey as he positioned them in undergrowth off the trail and handed them a handful of plastic tie-downs, such as cops use in place of handcuffs.

Taking Anna by the arm, he and Hammer ran on ahead, jumping over the wire as they passed it.

Fifteen minutes passed, and then a group of ten men appeared on the trail, passing between Jersey and Coop without seeing them. Evidently, Bergman hadn't kept his word about giving them an hour's head start, Coop thought as he ducked down behind his bush and waited for the scout group to pass.

The leader of the commandos, a tall black man with broad shoulders and old burn scars on his face, walked in a semi-crouch, sweeping his laser rifle back and forth as he moved silently up the trail.

The men behind him were good, for they kept their attention on what they were doing, with little chatter or unnecessary talk. They were strung out in single file, five yards between them, as they walked.

When the leader tripped the wire, causing the grenades to explode, all ten men hit the dirt facedown, yelling and groaning from the pain in their ears.

Coop and Jersey jumped from their cover, reversed their K-Bar assault knives, and coldcocked the last two men in the line in the back of their heads, knocking them unconscious. Then Coop and Jersey slipped back under cover.

Up ahead, just before a bend in the trail, Anna stepped into view and fired off several rounds with her M-16 laser rifle, making sure not to hit anyone.

The laser rifles were fitted with blank cartridges so they would sound like real combat weapons.

The black leader managed to get off two rounds, which

missed, before Anna disappeared around the bend and out of sight.

"Come on, men, they're up ahead!" he yelled, jumping to his feet and taking off in pursuit. His men scrambled to their feet and followed him, none noticing that the last two men in the group remained facedown on the jungle ground.

After the group ran out of sight, Jersey and Coop emerged from hiding and wrapped the hands and feet of the unconscious men with the plastic tie-downs, then followed the scouts up the trail.

As the commandos rounded the bend in the trail, two dark figures dropped from trees next to the path onto the last two men in the group, slapping the back of their necks with vicious karate chops as they landed.

Jersey and Coop caught up with them just as Hammer and Harley finished securing the men's arms and legs with tie-downs.

"Four down, six to go," Harley grunted with a smile as he tightened the final tie-down.

"What about Anna?" Jersey asked.

"She's okay," Hammer said, consulting a map of the region Bergman had given them. "She's waiting for us up ahead, near where the trail splits and goes in two different directions."

"How'll we get to her?" Coop asked. "The commandos are between us and her."

"We go this way through the jungle," Harley answered, pointing to the left. "The left-hand trail bends back this way and we can cut straight across and meet her ahead of the enemy force."

Coop glanced at what looked like impenetrable jungle. "We're going through that?" he asked.

Harley smiled. "No pain, no gain," he said, as he melted into the undergrowth.

* * *

Ronald Watanabe, the leader of the commandos, stopped and looked behind him. "Where are the others?" he asked.

His men glanced around. Lieutenant Johnson, his second in command, shook his head. "We're missing four men, sir."

"I can see that, you imbecile," Watanabe almost shouted. "Where are they?"

Johnson, sweat beading on his forehead in the thick humidity of the jungle, shrugged. "I don't know, sir. If they'd been shot, we would've heard their flak jackets go off."

"Damn!" Watanabe exclaimed. "These recruits are better than I thought. Keep together and let's move slower. I don't want to lose any more men."

They moved less than a hundred yards before coming to a wide, shallow river flowing sluggishly through the undergrowth.

"Be careful, men," Watanabe said as he held his rifle over his head and waded out through rushes and weeds into the stream. "These rivers are full of crocs and snakes."

On the opposite bank, Anna stepped out and fired a quick burst, then turned and ran away again.

"Go, go, go!" Watanabe shouted, splashing and firing his M-16 as he struggled against the slow current to cross the river.

With his men's attention in front of them, none noticed the four figures rise silently out of the water behind them, bamboo breathing tubes in their mouths.

Four hands rose and fell, knocking four more commandos unconscious and taking them back into the rushes at the water's edge.

Watanabe and Johnson scrambled out of the water onto the opposite bank, their rifles held before them, looking for the elusive Anna, who was nowhere to be seen.

"Goddamn!" Watanabe said, wiping water out of his eyes as he turned to check his men.

"Shit!" he almost yelled, seeing no one behind him except

Johnson. "What the hell's going on here?" he asked his lieutenant.

Johnson looked around, his eyes widening in fear at the sight of the empty water behind them. "You think crocs got 'em?" he asked.

"If it wasn't, those bastards are gonna wish they had been eaten when I get through with 'em."

Watanabe slammed a fresh clip in his M-16 and began to move up the trail, his eyes searching the bushes for enemies, his finger itchy on the trigger.

Johnson followed, his head swiveling as he continually checked his back trail.

Twenty minutes later, they heard what sounded like the deep growl of a jungle cat, followed by the high-pitched scream of a woman in danger.

"Shit!" Johnson said. "That sounded like a panther, an' all we got with us are blanks."

Watanabe nodded. They'd lost two men to the big cats during training, and he wanted no part of facing one without live ammo in his rifle.

"Let's get the hell out of here," he said. "I ain't gonna get killed for no training exercise."

They began to jog back down the trail, looking back over their shoulders as the sound of a panther again rang out through the jungle.

As they rounded a bend, Harley and Hammer jerked on a vine they'd laid across the trail, sending Johnson and Watanabe sprawling onto their faces. Before they could look up, they were knocked unconscious by blows to the back of their heads by Jersey and Coop.

Anna strolled up to the group just as they were finishing placing the tie-downs on their victims.

"Jesus, Anna," Coop said. "That cry sounded so real it made the hair on the back of my neck stand up."

She smiled. "Fooled you, huh?"

"Damn straight!" Coop said.

Harley stood up from immobilizing Johnson and Watanabe. "It fooled them too. Now, let's get back to camp and see what Herr Bergman has to say about our performance."

"Are we just going to leave these men out here in the jungle with their hands and feet tied?" Anna asked, a worried look on her face.

"Yep," Harley answered. "Maybe it'll teach 'em not to fuck with us in the future."

"That's if the snakes and jungle cats don't eat them first," Coop said, looking around at the dense undergrowth with a shudder.

Six

Otis Warner and General Joe Winter sat down across from Ben Raines in his office.

"Good morning, gentlemen," Ben said. "Can I offer you some coffee?"

"No, sir," Otis said. "We've already eaten breakfast."

Ben leaned back in his chair and crossed his hands behind his head. "Then, what can I do for you?"

"We want to know what you plan to do about Claire Osterman's illegal takeover of the USA," Otis said, a challenging note in his voice.

Ben smiled and shrugged. "Nothing."

"But, General Raines," Winter began.

"Hold on a moment, General," Ben interrupted. "In the first place, what Claire did was not illegal. As far as I've been able to find out, she is merely performing the job to which she was legally elected by the people of the United States."

"But . . ." Otis said.

Now Ben leaned forward, his elbows on his desk. "No buts, Otis. The only illegal act I'm aware of is the one in which you and your general here attempted to assassinate the elected leader of your country and take over her position."

"But, General Raines, we did it for the good of the country . . . and the world. You know what Claire was up to. If she'd stayed in office she would have continued the war against you and the SUSA until the United States was completely destroyed," Otis said.

"The woman is a complete psychopath!" Winter added, a look of extreme distaste on his face.

Ben smiled and nodded. "Oh, I agree with you, gentlemen, and I must say I agreed completely with what you did when you took her out and took over her presidency. But, now that she's managed to take it back, it's not my job to rid your country of its elected leader. If the people of the U.S. are too spoiled by the welfare state she's set up to see what kind of woman is leading them, then I think they deserve what they get."

"It's not the people's fault, General," Otis said. "She has a massive propaganda machine in place that misleads the people as to what is going on in the world."

"Bullshit!" Ben exclaimed. "President Lincoln said it best over a hundred and fifty years ago . . . you can't fool all of the people all of the time—not unless they want to be fooled."

"What do you mean, want to be fooled?" General Winter asked, a puzzled look on his face.

"You know exactly what I mean, General. In your country, men and women don't have to work if they don't want to, 'cause your government is predicated on the principle that everyone is completely equal and deserves the same share of the country's wealth."

"What is wrong with equality?" Otis asked belligerently.

"Nothing," Ben said shortly, "except it's not true now and never has been. Men are not created equal, except under the law. There are workers and there are slugs who prefer to live off the sweat of other people. Your country has chosen to treat them all as equals, and that is why your productivity has fallen to record low levels since Osterman and her socialist/democratic government took over."

"What do you do with your citizens who are unable to work?" Otis asked. "Let them starve?"

Ben shook his head. "No. Those who because of sickness or ill health cannot work are taken care of. But those who refuse to work out of laziness or perverseness, are not. Usually, when they get hungry enough, they find the inner strength to go back to work. We haven't had anyone voluntarily starve themselves to death since I've been here."

"That's barbaric," Otis said.

"No, Mr. Warner, it's realistic. It's the reason my country, a tenth the size of yours, outproduces yours every year and has kicked your butt every time you've attacked us."

General Winter laid his hand on Otis's arm to shut him up. "We're getting off the subject here, General," he said to Ben. "Do you plan to help us get rid of Osterman or not?"

Ben once again leaned back in his chair and tried to calm himself. He always got overexcited when he heard the same tired old arguments supporting socialism, a form of government that had never in the history of the world worked for very long.

"Of course I'll help you, General Winter," he said. "I will give you all the logistic support you require to attempt to take your government back from the crazy lady."

"What do you mean, logistical support?" Otis asked.

"I'll see that you are taken back to the U.S. and set up with funds and equipment to start a revolutionary movement within the country. If, as you say, the people are truly tired of the way Osterman has been running the country, you shouldn't have any problem getting recruits to join your movement. But, on the other hand, if the citizens are satisfied with the status quo, then you will fail, as you should."

Otis glanced at General Winter and shrugged. "That's fair enough."

"Good. Then I'll arrange to have one of my pilots fly you into the country under their radar and put you down wherever you want, along with some money and whatever else you need to get started."

After Warner and Winter left his office, Ben asked his secretary to get Mike Post to his office as soon as possible.

Mike entered a few moments later. "Hey, Ben. What's up?"

"I've changed my mind about the supplies Osterman is sending down to Perro Loco."

Mike grinned. "You mean you've decided to take out the freighter?"

Ben pursed his lips. "Not exactly. That would cause too much political backlash between us and Mexico."

"Then just what've you got in mind?"

"I thought we might send a SEAL team in, under cover of darkness."

"Boss, it doesn't matter if we sink the freighter with a missile or with a SEAL team," Post argued. "The president of Mexico is still gonna be pissed off."

"I don't want the SEAL team to sink the ship," Ben said. "Get them in here and I'll explain."

Captain Michael Kevin Fitzpatrick had been sailing on ships for most of his fifty-one years. Called Fitz by everyone on shipboard, he had promised to share with the crew the bonus Claire Osterman was paying them to sail into Mexico. They'd been loaded down with aircraft, munitions, vehicles, and just about every other type of war weapon he'd ever heard of—and some he hadn't—at Portsmith, Virginia.

The plan was for them to sail around the southern coast of Florida, turn west, and cut across the Gulf of Mexico toward the Mexican Navy base on the eastern coast of Mexico. When Fitz had initially refused to put his ship in danger by sailing into a war zone, the president had laughed and told him she had it on good authority there would be no attack.

"The Mexican president doesn't have the balls to do his job," she'd said with a sneer. "He thinks if he ignores us, we'll go away quietly and not bother him anymore, the stupid bastard."

"The Mexican president may be chickenshit, but Ben Raines isn't," Fitz had countered. "How do I know he won't send his planes after us?"

"Raines will do what President Jeffreys tells him to do," Claire had said, "and my spies say he's ordered Raines to lay off for the present."

After some haggling back and forth, Claire finally promised Fitzpatrick and his crew a bonus of fifty thousand dollars for the trip, if they got the matériel to Mexico safely.

It was just after midnight when Lieutenant Jerry Roberts, who went by the nickname Water Dog, loaded his five-man crew of Navy SEALS into a Zodiac fitted with an electric motor. They were all dressed in rubber wet suits, and had Scuba gear ready in the boat, along with six limpet mines and other assorted assault weapons.

The moon was covered by a scattering of low-lying clouds, and there wasn't much ambient light to spoil their attack on the freighter they'd picked up on radar from the patrol boat that had carried them into the Gulf of Mexico from Corpus Christi, Texas.

The motor hummed as it pushed the Zodiac over the six-foot swells of the Gulf at five knots. Unless the men on the freighter were very alert, they'd never know what hit them.

The attack had been planned for the hours between midnight and four in the morning, the dog watch when men were typically least alert.

The Zodiac homed in on the ship at a forty-five-degree angle until the rubber sides of the small craft brushed up against the rusted iron of the freighter.

Tommy Harris leaned over the bow of the Zodiac and affixed a magnetic clamp to the iron sides of the freighter, letting it hold the Zodiac in place alongside the ship as it slowly made its way through the darkness toward Mexico.

The SEALs donned their Scuba gear and made ready to drop over the side, the most dangerous part of the mission. Each man had a line attached around his waist to the Zodiac, for they were going to be working in almost total darkness very close to the huge twin propellers of the freighter, which would try to pull them into their turbulence.

"Remember," Water Dog advised in a hoarse whisper before they dropped into the sea, "we need to make sure the mines take out the propeller shaft and the rudders without making a hole in the ship's belly. We don't want to sink the bastard, just disable it."

His men nodded, their grins visible behind the Plexiglas of their masks. This was just the sort of dangerous task they lived for, and had trained for months to carry out.

Once in the water under the ship, where they couldn't be seen from above, the men snapped on underwater lights and fanned out, kicking furiously with their fins against the turbulence of the props.

Three of the men swam toward the port rudder and propeller shaft, and three toward the starboard ones. Once in place, they clung to the metal like so many water bugs, looking tiny against the size of the propellers.

Limpet mines were taken from pouches and placed against the metal shaft and rudders, the magnetic clamps in the mines holding them fast.

Finally, when he saw all of his men ready, Roberts blinked his light three times, a signal to set the mines.

Each man reached up and twisted a knob on his mine in three complete circles, setting the timers for a forty-five-minute delay.

Now came the trickiest part of the mission, trying to fight against the turbulence and return to the Zodiac. Even the strongest swimmer couldn't make headway against the pull of the big bronze propellers, so the SEALS pulled themselves along their lines toward the Zodiac.

All went well until the line connected to Harry Parrish got snagged on a cluster of barnacles growing on the bottom of the ship. When he tried to jerk it loose, the razor-sharp edge of one of the barnacles sliced through the nylon line as if it were kite string.

Water Dog turned his head when he heard Parrish scream, just in time to see his body tumbling head over heels through the water, unable to fight the awful pull of the propellers.

Water Dog reached down to disconnect his own line and go to Parrish's aid just as the SEALS's body hit the propellers and was shredded into a thousand pieces, sending scarlet blossoms of blood that looked black as ink into the water.

The lieutenant choked back bile as he turned back toward the Zodiac and continued on his way, thankful that he'd only lost one man to this job.

Captain Fitzpatrick came out of a dead sleep when he felt the jolt as the limpet mines detonated, followed by the sudden horrible vibration that shook the ship the way a cat shakes a mouse.

Fitz jumped out of his bunk and rushed to the phone on his wall. He dialed the engine room and shouted, "Shut the engines!"

After slipping into his clothes, he rushed up the metal ladder to the deck of the ship and leaned over the aft-side rail, trying to see what was wrong with the propellers.

As he stared into the inky blackness, the captain of the watch ran up to his side.

"What the hell happened?" Fitz asked. "What did we hit?"

"I dunno, Cap'n," Tom Johnson answered. "There was nothing on radar or sonar to indicate a reef or another ship. We were just cruising along when suddenly there was this bump and everything went to hell."

Fitz glared at him. "There aren't any reefs in the middle of the Gulf of Mexico, you idiot! The only thing we could have hit was another ship."

"Cap'n, I promise you, there hasn't been another ship anywhere near for over an hour."

Fitz turned to another sailor standing nearby. "Jimmy, get

below and make sure we're not taking on water, see if the hold was breached."

As the freighter slowed without power and began to drift on the prevailing winds, rocking heavily as the swells hit it broadside, the captain shook his head.

"The only thing I can think is you must have run over a sailboat too small to show up on radar and fouled the propellers and rudders," he said to a skeptical Johnson.

"What do we do now, Captain?" Johnson asked.

Fitz shrugged. "We'll just have to radio for assistance and hope we don't drift all the way to Cuba before it gets here."

"But, Captain, there ain't no way they're gonna be able to fix our rudders and props at sea," Johnson said.

Fitz frowned. "I know. It looks like we may have to be towed all the way to Mexico."

"But the port at Corpus Christi is closer."

Fitzpatrick glared at the seaman. "You really want us to make port at Corpus Christi fully loaded with war matériel for an army they're at war with?"

"Uh, I guess not," Johnson replied.

"Good, then get on the horn to Claire Osterman's office and tell them what's happened. If they want this shit delivered, they'll just have to get someone out here to tow us the rest of the way."

Seven

Claire Osterman was in bed with Herb Knoff when her phone rang. She reached across his body to pick it up.

"This better be damned important!" she said harshly into the mouthpiece.

After listening a moment, she fairly screamed, "That son of a bitch Raines is behind this, I know it!"

She listened another few seconds, then slammed the phone down.

Herb, his breathing slowing a bit from the exertion of a few minutes earlier, asked, "What's wrong, Claire?"

"Our freighter to Mexico has been sabotaged," she answered. "It's drifting dead in the water toward Cuba."

"Raines?"

She stared at him for a second, then shook her head. "The captain says not. He thinks they ran over a sailboat and damaged his rudders and propellers."

Herb's eyebrows knitted. "That doesn't sound very likely, does it?"

"No. I'm sure as hell that Raines had something to do with this, but without proof, it won't do any good to argue about it."

"So what now?"

She shrugged as she pulled on a robe to cover her nakedness. "I guess we'll have to hire another boat to go and pull him the rest of the way to Mexico."

Herb frowned. "That's gonna be kinda expensive, isn't it? I thought the treasury was down to nothing."

She gave an evil smile. "It is."

"But, you've already promised Captain Fitzpatrick fifty grand to take the stuff there."

"Who says he's going to live to collect any of it? I cabled Perro Loco yesterday and told him he could have the freighter for his own use after it docks. All he has to do is . . . convince Captain Fitzpatrick he has no further use for it."

"How's he gonna do that?"

"At the point of a gun, I suspect." She left the room and headed for her desk to make the necessary calls to get someone to tow the freighter to Mexcio.

Herb shook his head and lay back on his pillow. *Damn if she's not the meanest bitch I've ever known,* he thought. He glanced down at his privates. *Better not ever let her down, big guy,* he whispered, *or she'll have you in a jar on her shelf.*

The Boeing V-22 Osprey dropped through the clouds over Columbus, Ohio, like a stone. Inside, Otis Warner and General Joe Winter held their breath, certain the plane was going to crash.

"Take it easy back there," Captain Joe Gonzales called on the intercom. "We're just trying to get below their radar as fast as we can."

Once the Osprey fell below five hundred feet, Gonzales leveled off, rotated the twin turboprop engines to the vertical arrangement, and the craft operated like a helicopter.

It dropped as easily as a bird settling to the ground with hardly a jolt.

"Are we there?" Otis asked, unbuckling his seat belt.

Winter glanced out the window. "Yeah, looks like."

"Here we are, gentlemen," Gonzales said as he strolled down the aisle. "Right where you asked to be delivered."

"Clinton Army Base?" Winter asked.

"Yeah. Intel says it's been abandoned since you guys took over from Osterman last year. Word is she hasn't gotten around to restaffing it yet."

Winter and Warner hurried between the seats to the door as Gonzales opened it and extended the ladder to the ground.

"I can give you half an hour to get your people and your gear unloaded. Any more than that would be pushing our luck," he said.

Ben Raines had supplied Winter and Warner with fifty thousand dollars in gold coin, a staff of ten men and women from the intel division to help them recruit and train guerrillas to take back the government from Osterman, and assorted communications and weapons supplies to use until they could steal or buy more of their own. Ben and Mike Post had picked the location of the U.S. rebels' new headquarters near Columbus, Ohio. It was near enough to Osterman's base camp at Indianapolis to be of use, but not so close they'd be noticed.

Once Warner and Winter's crew and supplies were unloaded, the Osprey took off again. To escape notice, Gonzales kept it under five hundred feet until it was miles away from Clinton Army Base, and then pointed the nose at the sky and took off like a shot.

Otis Warner wasted no time. He appropriated the commanding officer's office in the base headquarters, and had his people begin setting up the long-range radio and other equipment in the adjacent offices. They patched into nearby phone lines, using the SUSA's newest technology so their lines wouldn't be detected or traced.

General Winter, meanwhile, was consulting his files for friendly names to contact to begin building a guerrilla force to combat Osterman's Armed Forces. He had over two thousand names of men and women who'd been supportive of their own short-lived government and the peace process they'd started before Osterman seized back control of the government last year.

As he combed his files, he made marks next to the men

and women he would contact first, people who had contacts in Osterman's Armed Forces. It would be important to have men on their side who could keep them informed of Claire's plans and warn them if she became aware of their activities.

The new war for freedom was just beginning.

Eight

Harley Reno and his team strolled back into the mercs' camp, as if they'd been out for a walk in the jungle. Sergei Bergman was in his office reading over their resumes when Sergeant Herman Bundt stuck his head in the door.

"Hey, Boss, you gotta see this."

Bergman glanced up. "I'm kind'a busy here, Herman."

"I'm telling you, you don't want to miss this," Bundt persisted.

Bergman threw his pencil down and got to his feet. When he walked out the door, he saw Harley's team depositing armfuls of weapons in a pile in the center of the camp.

"Reno, what the hell's going on?" Bergman asked, striding over to the big man.

Harley grinned. "We figured these were easier to carry than the men themselves," he answered.

"What do you mean?"

"Your men are all out there in the jungle, tied up and waiting for you to send someone to cut them loose."

"You mean you killed them all?" Bergman asked, an astonished tone in his voice.

"No," Hammer answered, stepping up next to Harley. "We captured all of them. They weren't good enough for us to have to kill them."

Bergman shook his head as if he couldn't believe his ears. "They were my best scouts."

"If they were your best men, sir," Coop said, "then you're in a world of hurt."

Bergman looked over his shoulder at Herman Bundt. "Herman, send some men to pick 'em up."

"Yes, sir," Bundt answered, a grin on his face. It seemed he appreciated the audacity of this new group of recruits more than Bergman did.

Bergman stood there, face-to-face with Harley Reno. Bergman was almost as tall as Reno, but his shoulders were narrower and his muscles were leaner, like a long-distance runner's. With short-cropped blond hair and blue eyes over a fair complexion, Bergman looked like a poster-child for the Aryan ideal of Bottger's New World Order.

"All right," Bergman finally said, his hands on his hips and his eyes boring into Reno's. "I can see you people are good at tactics. How are you at hand-to-hand combat?"

Harley shrugged. "Try us and see."

"I will." Bergman whirled around and walked over to a cleared area used for hand-to-hand combat training. There was a large circular area of mulched soil surrounded by bleacher-like stands for others to watch. The rest of the mercs were already gathering to see what the newcomers had.

Bergman glanced over the crowd until he spied one of his drill sergeants. He gestured to him to come forward.

A huge man, over six feet four inches in height and heavily muscled, stepped forward. He had the face of a bulldog, with heavy brows over a nose that looked as if it'd been broken more times than it'd been fixed.

"This is Helmut Gundarson," Bergman said. "He's my combat instructor in martial arts."

Harley looked at Helmut and shook his head. "Is this the best you've got?" he asked, a sneer in his voice.

"Yes," Bergman answered. "I think he'd make a fitting opponent for you. You two are about the same size."

"It ain't about size, sir," Harley said. He looked at his team. "Jersey, you want to take a shot at this one?"

"Sure, Harley," she answered as she stepped up to the man. Her head barely came to the level of his chest and he outweighed her by two hundred pounds.

Helmut grunted and glanced at Bergman. "Sir," he said, his German accent thick, "I would not want to hurt this small one."

"Are you sure this is the one you want to fight Helmut?" Bergman asked skeptically.

Harley nodded. "How far are we going with this? Is it a fight to the death?" he asked seriously.

Bergman looked surprised at the question. "Uh, no, just tell her to try to win the fight."

Harley called to Jersey. "Jersey, try not to kill this one, okay?"

She looked disappointed. "Is it okay if I break him up a little?" she asked, her face innocent.

Helmut growled. "You will be the one broken, bitch."

Jersey wagged her finger in his face. "Now, don't try and make this personal, Helmut baby," she cooed in a soft, feminine voice. "The first rule of combat is to keep your cool. Otherwise you get your fat ass kicked."

Helmut's face flamed red as the soldiers around all laughed at Jersey's comments at his expense. He ripped off his belt and holster and walked to the center of the circle, flexing his massive muscles as he stretched and paced the area.

"Better give me your K-Bar, Jerse," Coop said, holding out his hand. "Wouldn't want your reflexes to take over and have you gut the bastard."

Jersey took out her K-Bar assault knife and flipped it end over end to land stuck in the ground millimeters from Coop's foot.

She glanced at Bergman. "You want this over fast, or do you want a show for the boys in the back row?"

Now even Bergman had to grin at the audacity of this small woman. "Oh, by all means, dear girl, give us a show," he answered as he joined the others around the edge of the circle of combat to watch.

Jersey bent and untied, then slipped out of, her heavy combat boots, before walking barefoot to the center of the circle.

Helmut crouched in the classic martial-arts stance, his feet apart with his left foot slightly forward, his hands held up before him with index and middle fingers extended.

"Hah!" he grunted, shaking his arms in the typical greeting before combat.

"Oh, Jesus, Helmut," Jersey said, standing flat-footed, her hands at her sides, "cut the crap and let's get it on."

Helmut's face blazed even redder and he began to dance around her on his toes, waving his arms up and down slowly, like snakes weaving before striking.

Jersey just stood there, letting her eyes follow him without moving her body at all. She looked completely unprepared for an attack.

From the edge of the circle, Coop called, "Any bets? I'm giving two to one on the little lady."

At least twenty of the men crowded around him, holding out wads of currency and shouting out they'd take his bet.

In the circle, Helmut suddenly leaned to the side with his weight on his left leg, and his right leg flashed out in a sidekick aimed at Jersey's head.

It flashed by, missing her by inches as she leaned slightly to the right and let the leg pass harmlessly by.

Helmut continued his spin and swung a stiffened right arm backward at her.

Jersey again leaned her head back, allowing the blow to miss her by less than an inch. As Helmut's face came around after his arm, she took a short, quick step forward and her right hand shot out, palm first.

The base of her palm hit Helmut flush on the nose, flattening it and sending a shower of blood and mucus spraying outward as his head snapped back and he grunted in pain, tears flooding his eyes.

Jersey didn't follow up her advantage, but stood there, her hands again at her side as she grinned at Helmut.

"Had enough, big guy?" she asked. "From now on, all you have to look forward to is more pain."

Helmut sleeved blood off his face, his eyes glittering hatred. "You bitch!" he growled.

Jersey's face darkened. "I told you not to get personal, Helmut. You don't know me well enough to call me bitch," she said calmly.

Helmut raised his hands and danced forward on his toes, just as Jersey dropped onto her outstretched right hand and swung her left leg in a sweeping arc at Helmut's feet, knocking them from under him.

Without slowing her movements, Jersey bent her leg at the knee and imbedded her heel in Helmut's chest as he went down. Everyone in the crowd heard the crack as one of his ribs snapped and he screamed.

When they rolled to their feet, Helmut was bent slightly to the left, favoring his aching rib, while Jersey stood there watching him.

"I could take your eye next," she said, an appraising look on her face, "but that would make you useless to Mr. Bergman. So, I think I'll just take part of your left ear instead."

Helmut's eyes widened for a second, before Jersey stepped in, dodged his chopping right hand by letting it slip off her shoulder, and buried her left fist in his solar plexus just below his sternum.

Helmut doubled over and Jersey slashed at the side of his head with a flattened right hand in a move so quick only a few of the bystanders saw it.

Helmut grunted again and jerked his head back. His left ear was hanging, partially torn off at the top, blood spurting down the side of his face.

Jersey turned to look at Bergman. "Have you seen enough? I really don't want to cripple the big guy."

Helmut yelled in anger and jumped at her exposed back, his arms outstretched to strangle her.

Without looking, Jersey ducked and backed into his charge, grabbing his right wrist as it passed her head and yanking down on it, catching his right elbow on her shoulder and breaking it with a loud snap.

Helmut didn't scream this time. He fainted from the shock and pain of his broken arm, slipping quietly to his knees, then toppling over onto his face, out cold.

The men watching the exhibition were silent. All too many of them had been manhandled by Helmut in their combat training, and they knew he was no easy mark. Yet this small woman had made him look like a clumsy oaf.

Coop held up the wad of money in his hand. "Thanks, gents. It was a pleasure doing business with you."

Bergman walked out to stand over Helmut, shaking his head. "Herman, get two or three men to carry Helmut to the medical tent and have the doc look at that arm."

"Yes, sir," Bundt said, winking at Jersey as he pointed to a couple of men to come and help him with Helmut.

Jersey wasn't even breathing hard, and had barely broken a sweat when Bergman spoke to her.

"You made that look easy," he said.

She shrugged. "He made the mistake of judging me by my size," she said. "In combat, it's not size that counts, it's ability, and the easiest way I know to get killed is to underestimate the ability of your opponent."

Bergman nodded. "Very well said, Jersey."

He turned and waved at Harley. "Bring your team into my office after lunch. We need to talk."

As Harley and the others moved toward the mess tent, Harley spoke in low tones. "Spread out while we eat and try to get some of the others to talk. We need to find out who's ramrodding this outfit and just how dangerous they really are. Concentrate on amounts and types of weapons and matériel, as well as strength and training of the other troops."

"From what I've seen so far, they don't look all that dangerous," Coop said.

"Don't judge them all by what we've seen here," Hammer said. "This is just the training ground for the new recruits. There's no telling what kind of troops have already passed through here."

"Yeah," Anna said. "There can't be more than a few hundred men here at this camp. We need to find out the strength of the rest of this army, 'cause I know Claire Osterman wouldn't be asking this group for help unless there are a hell of a lot more of them somewhere else."

They filed into the mess tent and went through the line to pick up their trays, then dispersed to sit among the other trainees and gather what intel they could through casual conversation.

When Jersey got to the end of the line with her tray, men at several tables stood up, all trying to get her to sit with them. Anna received a similar reception from the men.

Coop snorted through his nose. "Huh, guess it's been a while since these guys had any female company."

Harley grinned. "Yeah, an' the ones they got here don't exactly set a man's loins on fire either," he said, inclining his head at some of the other women mercs in the room, all of whom had faces that would stop clocks.

After lunch, the team proceeded to Bergman's office, where he sat waiting for them, looking over their papers on his desk.

When they were seated, he went through their applications one by one.

"Harley, I see you were an officer in Ben Raines's Army," he said.

Harley nodded. "Yeah, until I slugged an officer and got court-martialed."

"Oh?"

"Yeah, I didn't like Buddy Raines's attitude, so I decked him one night in the officers' club."

"Buddy Raines? Any relation to Ben Raines?" Bergman asked with upraised eyebrows.

"His son."

"Shit. No wonder you got canned," Bergman said.

"He's an arrogant little pissant who's gettin' by on his daddy's reputation," Harley said with a sneer.

Bergman nodded, going on to the next sheet. "Cooper, it says here you were on Raines's personal team . . . as a driver."

"I was, until I porked his main squeeze," Coop said, sticking to the story Mike Post had put in his file. "Then I found myself pulling every dirty job in the business. Figured I'd better get out before I got fragged by one of his friends."

The interview went on like this, with each of the team having a story that would account for their leaving the employ of the Army of the SUSA.

Finally, Bergman leaned back, sticking a cigar in his mouth and lighting it as he looked at the group. "Well, other than your obvious discipline problems, you seem like soldiers who will do us some good."

"It'll be a pleasure to get our licks back against Raines and his soldiers," Harley said with feeling.

"I think I'll have your team take over as my drill sergeants here at the training camp," Bergman said. "You obviously have some special skills we can use in our training program."

"Before we sign on, we'd like a few questions answered," Harley said. "Like, just who are we working for and what kind of action can we look forward to."

"That's on a need-to-know basis," Bergman said, dismissing the question. "All you need to know is the pay is excellent, especially for staff personnel, and that we'll have the best equipment money can buy when we go into combat."

Harley nodded, too cautious to press his questions now. He'd wait until later, when he could do some snooping around the office without being observed, to find the answers he needed.

"How long do we have to get these troops combat-ready?"

Hammer asked. "From the looks of those we've seen, it's gonna take a while."

"Less than a month," Bergman said. "So, you'd better get busy whipping them into shape."

"Yes, sir!" Harley said, standing up.

As they filed out and headed to the barracks to find their places, he asked each of them if they'd found out who the head man was. None had.

"It's like none of the troops know who the boss man is," Coop said. "They're as much in the dark as we are."

"Well," Harley said, "keep digging. We can't leave here until we find the answer."

"I did learn there're a hell of a lot of troops already finished with basic training," Jersey said. "Several battalions at least."

"Shit," Harley said, "and from what Bergman says, they've got modern equipment and lots of it to use against us when the time comes."

"Why not just have Ben call an air strike against this place?" Anna asked.

" 'Cause he's not ready to start a war with South America," Harley answered. "No, we're gonna have to wait until they start to move out and get in neutral territory before we can do anything offensive against them."

"Did you catch that comment Bergman made about having the troops ready within the month?" Jersey asked.

"Yeah," Harley said, "and that's some info we need to get back to Ben as soon as we can. I don't think he has any idea things are moving that fast."

Coop nodded. "That probably means Perro Loco's gonna start his offensive in Mexico any day now."

"Jerse and I'll get out to the communications gear tonight and try and let Ben know what's going on."

"Why don't you tell him we're gonna line these bastards up and let Jersey kick the shit out of 'em one at a time?"

Coop said with a grin. "That way he wouldn't have to worry about them helping Loco out."

She cut her eyes at him. "I know just who I'd start with too," she said, giving him a flat look.

Nine

Bruno Bottger, Rudolf Hessner, and Sergei Bergman made their way to the scientific lab Bottger had built on the outskirts of his mercenary training facility.

"Have there been some new developments by Dr. Krug?" Hessner asked as they wound their way down several flights of stairs to the subterranean basement where the scientist he spoke of did his work.

Bottger nodded. "Yes, he says he's solved the problem of the new anthrax biological weapon he's been working on for the past three years."

Bergman shook his head. "I don't know why he's continued to work on anthrax," he said. "We tried that in Africa and the SUSA's vaccines made it worthless as a weapon. All it succeeded in doing was to kill a lot of animals and aborigines."

"Wait until you hear what he's accomplished," Bottger said with a sly grin as they entered the laboratory through double-sealed pneumatic doors, a precaution against accidental infection of the training facility.

As they walked into the room, a tall man with an acne-scarred face and wild hair looked up from a microscope he was peering into.

"Ah, Herr General Bottger," Krug said with a smile, wiping his hands on his white lab coat before shaking hands all around.

"Doctor," Bottger said, "perhaps you can explain your most

recent breakthrough to my associates. They seem to have some doubt as to the efficacy of your bacteria as a weapon."

"Follow me, gentlemen," Krug said, leading them down dark passages into what appeared to be a prison section, walled off with two-inch-thick glass.

He stepped up to the window and pointed inside. There were six beds in the room, upon which lay four men and two women with the dark skin of South American Indians. Their skin was covered with large, pustular sores and they were soaked with sweat, shivering and shaking as they coughed and hacked until blood ran from their mouths.

"I sprayed my anthrax into the cell of the man on the left four days ago. He initially developed flulike symptoms which lasted only thirty-six hours, then apparently recovered. I then exposed the others to him. Twenty-four hours later, all were sick and are now as you see them."

Bergman shrugged. "So what, Doctor? I see nothing here to indicate any difference in the results from what we had several years ago."

Krug shook his head. "Ah, but there are several differences. Notice the animals in the cages around the room? They are unaffected by the bacterium, unlike the previous weapon, which left a barren area desolate of mammalian life forms. In addition, all of these subjects were previously vaccinated with the vaccine in the possession of the SUSA and the U.S. As you can see, it had no preventive effect on the sickness."

"Tell them the other part," Bottger urged.

"I have been able to make the anthrax infective from a spray that can be released by either bombs or missiles, and, unlike traditional respiratory anthrax, it is infective from person to person, so that the spray does not have to be everywhere to do its work. Once a segment of the population is infected, they stay healthy for several days, long enough to travel and infect hundreds of other unsuspecting citizens."

"Let me get this straight," Bergman said, "we now have a biological weapon that the SUSA and the U.S. have no vaccine against, and it can be delivered by aerial bombs or missiles, and it will spread throughout the country person to person?"

"Yes," Krug said with a maniacal gleam in his eye. "Wonderful, isn't it?"

"Is there no conventional treatment for the illness?" Hessner asked as he peered at the Indians who were near death.

Krug shrugged. "Yes. If the patients are caught very early in their illness, massive doses of antibiotics will slow or even reverse the illness. But the amount needed will quickly use up the available supplies of even the richest country in a matter of days, leaving the rest of the populace at its mercy."

"And you have a vaccine I can use to inoculate my troops against this respiratory anthrax?" Bergman asked.

Krug nodded. "It is being manufactured on a large scale even as we speak."

"Will the SUSA scientists be able to duplicate this vaccine?" Hessner asked.

"Certainly, given enough time," Krug answered. "But the rapidity with which the illness spreads means they will lose at least fifty to sixty percent of their fighting forces before they can make enough to do any good."

"By that time, our armies should have been able to take control of all of the major cities and facilities in the country, forcing Raines to sue for peace," Bottger said, his eyes aflame with insane excitement.

After they'd returned to Bottger's office, he poured them all brandy and handed out fat cigars to celebrate Dr. Krug's accomplishment.

As Bergman puffed his stogie and sipped his brandy, he had a thought. "General Bottger, I have a suggestion," he said.

Bottger waved his hand in an expansive gesture. He was feeling good enough to take advice from anyone at this point. "Go ahead, Sergei."

"The last time we fought Raines, he learned of our bacterial weapons in time to formulate a vaccine against them. I suggest we keep Krug and his workers completely isolated from the rest of the troops, just in case there are spies around who might tell Raines of our new weapon."

"Excellent idea, Sergei," Bottger said. "Anything else?"

"Yes. I further suggest that we hold off vaccinating our own troops until the last possible moment to keep any hint of our having new biological weapons from leaking out."

"I had already anticipated such a move," Bottger said. "Dr. Krug assures me the vaccine only takes about a week to do its job, so we'll plan to vaccinate our troops on the day they move out. At that time, we'll initiate saturation bombing of Mexico City and points up to the southern border of the SUSA."

"Why not bomb the SUSA itself?" Hessner asked, smoke from the cigar trailing from his nostrils.

Bottger shook his head. "The SUSA is too well guarded, especially from an air assault. I fear none of our planes or missiles would get through." He paused to drink the remainder of his brandy in one large draught. "No, if we manage to infect a significant portion of the Mexican citizens, they will travel to the SUSA looking for help and thus spread the infection almost as fast our bombs could, and without wasting any of our precious aircraft on a futile assault."

Bergman nodded, smiling. "And additionally, in the initial stages of the plague, the SUSA will think their troops are protected from the anthrax, not knowing it is a new bug."

"Exactly," Bottger agreed. "For now, the most important thing is to keep the secret of our new weapon from being discovered by the SUSA or anyone else."

"That brings up an interesting point, General," Bergman said.

"Yes?"

"I fear it will be impossible to keep the secret if we start to vaccinate Perro Loco's troops, or Claire Osterman's Army in the U.S. Raines would be sure to find out, perhaps in time to develop their own vaccine."

Bottger smiled once again. "Who said anything about giving the vaccine to either Loco or Osterman?"

"But, we're gonna need their troops to help us in our takeover of the SUSA. We only have about twenty thousand mercenaries in our ranks," Bergman argued. "Hardly enough to form an assault on Mexico and the SUSA at the same time, even if a large percentage of their troops are becoming sick from the plague."

"I know that," Bottger said. "That is why I intend to hold off on the biological weapon until Perro Loco has taken or is very close to taking Mexico City. Once that has occurred, to hell with him and his troops, we will no longer need them."

"What about Osterman's Army?" Hessner asked.

"The plan at this point is for her to harass Raines and the SUSA from the north, to divide his attention between her and Mexico. While I don't plan to bomb the U.S. itself, the disease will invariably make its way northward once it's gotten a hold in the SUSA. By that time, Osterman and her Army will likewise be of little use to us. Once the entire continent of North America is reeling under the influence of the plague, I will offer the vaccine on condition I am appointed lifetime ruler of the entire continent."

"What is to keep them from going back on their word once they have the vaccine?" Hessner asked. "We can't possibly hold the entire continent with only twenty thousand men."

"Don't worry, my friend," Bottger said, leaning back in his chair and puffing on his cigar. "If there is one thing I've found in all my years as a general, it is that there are plenty of people in every country who are willing to switch sides to the winning side in time of war. Just look at the history of World War II, when many of the most idealistic Frenchmen joined the Vichy government and helped Germany rule their conquered country. I have no doubt the SUSA and the U.S. will be little different. I don't think we'll have any problem identifying and recruiting men to help us rule, once we've attained power."

"So, what is our next step?" Bergman asked, stubbing out his cigar in an ashtray.

"Assign men you know are completely reliable to guard Dr. Krug's lab and his records," Bottger said. "I'd suggest you use only men who have been with us from the start, back during the Africa campaign or before."

Bergman nodded. "Anything else?"

"Yes, you must get our men in fighting shape as soon as possible. It is my understanding Perro Loco is going to start his assault on Mexico City within the month. We must be ready to step in as soon as he's done all the hard work. I want our army amassed on the southern border of the SUSA at the time the bombings with our plague organism commence, for it will only be a matter of days after that when the SUSA will begin to feel the effects of the plague, and our army must be ready to invade on a moment's notice."

Ten

Ben Raines stopped for a moment outside the hospital room and tried to rearrange his face into a hopeful expression to replace the sorrowful one it now held.

He knocked on the door and entered.

In spite of knowing how sick he was, Ben was still surprised by Dr. Lamar Chase's pale, drawn face. It had been almost twenty-four hours since Ben's doctor and longtime friend had had his heart attack while playing golf on the headquarters' course. This was the first time Chase's doctors had allowed anyone to visit the ailing physician.

"Hi, Doc," Ben called as he entered the room, trying to sound cheerful.

Lamar rolled his head to the side and smiled wanly at Ben. "Howdy, Ben," he said, even his voice sounding weak and tired.

Ben knew the man, who was in his sixties, had been slowing down of late, but he'd had no idea his friend was so sick. He took a chair next to the bed and put his hand on his friend's arm.

"So, what happened, old friend?" Ben asked.

Lamar smiled, and Ben could see some of his old personality shine through.

"Well, first of all it was hot enough to fry eggs on the greens, and I should've known better than to try and play on such a day," Lamar said. "On the next to the last hole, I hit my ball into a sand trap . . . a really deep bunker. After I hit it out—right next to the pin, by the way—I started to climb out of the bunker and felt like a mule kicked me in the chest."

Ben nodded. "Your doctors said it was a minor heart attack."

Lamar grimaced. "There ain't no such thing as a *minor* heart attack, podna," he said. "I'm afraid I won't be much use to you in the upcoming war with those bastards down in Mexico."

"Sure you will, Doc," Ben tried to reassure him, though he knew he spoke the truth. "The doctors say you're gonna be fine."

Lamar nodded. "Sure, if I take it easy and don't do anything stupid, like playing golf in a hundred-and-ten-degree heat, or traveling to Mexico where a hundred and ten is considered a nice fall day."

"Well," Ben said, "we'll make do somehow."

"That's what I want to talk to you about, Ben. There's this new young doctor I want you to assign to take my place. He's a little green, but I've never met a smarter or better all-around doctor."

"And just what is this young hotshot's name?" Ben asked. He knew Lamar was a hard taskmaster, and anyone who got such praise from him had to be the real deal.

"Larry Buck," Lamar replied. "He's top-notch, and not afraid to get in there where the action is if need be. He just got off a tour with the scouts as a field medic." Lamar smiled grimly. "Said he wanted some field experience with gunshot wounds and such."

"Sounds like just the sort of man I need on my team. Have you spoken to him about it?"

"Yes. As soon as I was out of ICU, I called him on the phone and we talked it over. He's all for it if you'll have him."

"Doc," Ben said seriously, "I've known you almost twenty years. When was the last time I neglected to take your advice?"

"When I told you to stay out of the field and give up those hand-rolled cancer sticks of yours."

Ben laughed. Doc had indeed told him he was getting too old to be traipsing around the world fighting battles. He'd said it was a younger man's game. In his heart, Ben knew his old friend was right . . . that he was slowing down as he got older and it would be sooner rather than later when he would finally have to resign himself to doing his generaling from a desk instead of a HumVee in the field.

"All right, so I still smoke occasionally. But other than that, I'll take your advice and hire this Dr. Buck on as my team physician and the Surgeon General of the entire command."

Lamar rested his head back on his pillow, a smile on his face. "Good. Now get the hell out of here and let me rest. Don't you know I've had a heart attack and need my sleep?"

"Okay, pal," Ben said, ruffling the gray hair on Lamar's head. "I'll see you later, all right?"

"If you're lucky," Lamar slurred, already beginning to fall asleep.

Dr. Larry Buck stepped up to Ben's desk and snapped to attention. "Dr. Buck reporting as ordered, sir!"

Ben smiled. The man was indeed young. He looked to be no more than thirty on the outside. He was also remarkably fit for a doctor. Standing almost six feet tall, with broad shoulders and a head of unruly black hair that fell in a comma over his right eyebrow, he was a good-looking man who looked more like the scouts he'd trained with than an M.D.

"First off, Larry, we don't go in much for salutes and formality around here. As a member of my team, you'll be family. I can't abide yes-men or sycophants. When I ask for your opinion, I don't care whose ox gets gored. I want your honest thoughts."

"Yes, sir . . . uh, Ben."

"That's why Lamar and I got along so well and why he did such a good job of keeping my team and the Army healthy.

He's the type that'd walk right up to the devil and tell him he wasn't drinking enough water."

Larry laughed. "You got that right, Ben. That's one of the reasons I asked to be assigned to his command when I graduated from the military academy medical school."

"Most of the rest of the team is on assignment in South America right now, so you'll have to wait to meet them."

"I've already familiarized myself with all of their medical records, Ben."

Ben eyebrows raised. "That include mine?" he asked.

Larry grinned. "Especially yours. Doc Chase told me if I let anything happen to you, he'd personally kick my ass from here to there."

"How do you think he is, really?" Ben asked, becoming serious.

Larry nodded. "Looks like he's gonna be okay. They did a cath on him this morning and he only had a partial blockage of the left main coronary artery, the one they call widow-maker. Dr. Polukof did an angioplasty on him and cleared the blockage completely, so he should do fine unless he overdoes it before he's healed."

"I take it you'll make sure that doesn't happen, correct?" Ben said pointedly.

"Yes, sir. I've got two of the toughest nurses on the ward watching him twenty-four hours a day. They're both ex-marine nurses, so even Doc Chase won't be able to scare them off."

"Have you had a chance to go over Lamar's records to see if there's anything about his chain of command you want to change?"

"Yes, and the only suggestion I'd make is to have a few more female doctors assigned here. Lamar was something of an old-fashioned doc who didn't think women belonged in battle situations."

"And you disagree?"

"Yes. From what I've seen, women are able to handle the emotional stress of combat surgery and battlefield medicine better than men, and the men patients are less likely to give women docs the guff they do the male docs."

"Then go ahead and make whatever changes you deem necessary. It's your command now, Larry, so make the best of it."

"Yes, sir."

"Eagle One to Nest, Eagle One to Nest," Anna said into the microphone. She was crouched in the ruins of an old plantation where her team had stashed the communications gear on the way to join Bottger's mercenaries. Jersey was outside the rotted walls of the main house, keeping watch to make sure they weren't being observed. It was close to midnight, and they'd sneaked out of the barracks to give their first report to Corrie, who was maintaining a twenty-four-hour-a-day watch on the radio back at the freighter.

"Eagle Nest to Eagle One, come in," Corrie's voice replied in the earphones. The communicator was fitted with the latest in scrambler technology, so they were able to speak in the clear without using code.

"We've made it into the merc training program," Anna said. "In fact, they've made us DIs."

"Drill instructors?" Corrie asked.

"Yeah."

"Have you gotten any idea about how large their forces are?"

"From what we've picked up talking to other troops, it appears to be about twenty to twenty-five thousand mercs."

"And any indication who is behind the training camp? Who the number-one man is?"

"Not a clue yet. He must stay pretty much in the background, 'cause no one we've spoken to has ever even seen him, much less met him to talk to. And the higher-ups in the training program won't say a word about who's footing the bill for all this."

"How well equipped are they?"

"Extremely well. They have the best and newest weapons and seem to have plenty of ammunition to waste on training exercises. The other trainees tell us they've also got planes, choppers, and other heavy equipment and matériel stored and ready to go at any time."

"Still, twenty-five thousand troops doesn't sound like enough to get too worried about," Corrie said.

"That's what *we* thought. It's certainly far less than Perro Loco has in Mexico already."

"Keep digging. I'll check with Ben and see if he needs anything else. When he hears how small the forces are there, he may just say the hell with it and pull you out."

"You'd also better let him know they want us ready to move out in one month."

"One month. Wow, that's a lot sooner than Ben thought."

"Yeah, so tell him he'd better keep a close eye on Loco in Mexico, 'cause that means the offensive there is going to be starting real soon too."

"Okay, will do. You and the others watch your back and we'll get this info to Ben ASAP."

"There is one other thing, though," Anna said, almost as an afterthought.

"What's that?"

"There's a rumor going around among the troops about some sort of secret weapon. Something that's supposed to be really big."

"You think it's nuclear?"

"No, I doubt it. Tactical nukes are old hat to these mercs. They wouldn't get excited about those. It must be something else, something that makes whoever runs this place think he's got a chance to stand up and run with the big dogs."

"Well, see what you can dig up and I'll talk to Ben. Eagle Nest out."

Anna packed up her gear, put it back under the rotted wooden flooring of the main room in the old house, and with Jersey started back toward the camp.

As they moved easily down the trail through the jungle under a half-moon, they heard voices ahead of them. Jersey tapped Anna's arm and pulled her aside into the underbrush just as two camp guards walked up the trail, M-16's cradled in their arms.

"I'm tellin' ya', I heard 'em pass this way not more'n twenty minutes ago," one of the guards said.

"You sure it wasn't an animal?" the second man asked.

"No, I told you I heard 'em talkin' on the audio sensor plain as day."

Shit, Jersey thought to herself. They had audio sensors planted around the camp. She should have thought of that.

"Could you hear what they was sayin'?"

"Somethin' 'bout a radio, an' it sounded like it was women talkin'."

Uh-oh, Jersey thought. *Now we've got to take them out. They know too much.*

She slipped her K-Bar from its sheath and nudged Anna's arm, making a cutting motion across her throat with her index finger. Anna nodded and slipped her knife out, a Canadian Army Stiletto model.

After the men walked past their hiding places, the girls stepped out onto the trail, their knives held down low next to their thighs.

One of the men must have sensed something, for he turned and looked back up the trail. His eyes widened in the moonlight as he saw the two dark figures behind them. He started to raise the M-16, but he was far too slow.

Anna was on him like a cat, burying her stiletto up to the hilt in his chest. The point entered just under the ribs on the left and proceeded upward at a forty-five-degree angle and pierced the heart muscle, killing him instantly.

As the second man whirled around, Jersey did a spinning side-kick into his groin. He dropped his rifle and doubled over, clutching his balls and groaning. She stepped to his side and ran the razor-sharp blade of her K-Bar across his throat, jerking it back quickly so it wouldn't get splattered by the gush of blood from his severed carotid arteries.

After the two men had quit moving, Jersey and Anna trotted back up the trail, being careful not to make too much noise this time lest someone else hear them on the audio sensors. They could only hope the two guards hadn't told anyone they'd heard two females on the mikes, or Jersey and Anna were in deep shit.

Eleven

The freighter carrying supplies and matériel finally pulled into the harbor at Villahermosa, pulled by two giant seagoing tugboats. As it was being unloaded by huge cranes dockside, Perro Loco stood on the wharf, talking with the captain.

"Did you find out what caused the damage to your rudder and propellers?" Loco asked.

Captain Fitzpatrick nodded, his eyes angry. "Yes. Once we were docked, I sent a couple of divers below to survey the damage. There's no question. Someone planted limpet mines on the hull next to the propeller shafts that took out both rudders and both propellers."

"Limpet mines? How could they do that without you knowing it?"

Fitzpatrick shook his head. "It must have been Navy SEALs. I don't know of anyone else who could do that while we were under way without getting themselves killed in the process."

Loco turned his head and stared northward toward the SUSA. "That bastard Raines is behind this."

"Well, whoever it is, my company's not going to be happy about it," Fitzpatrick said. "The cost of the repairs will have to be added to my bonus for bringing you this equipment."

"Oh, your bonus," Loco said, as if he'd forgotten all about the arrangement Osterman had made with the captain. "After the ship is unloaded, bring your crew to my headquarters on the Navy base and you'll get your money."

"How about you just bring me the money here to the dock and we'll be on our way."

"But, Captain Fitzpatrick, wouldn't you and your men like a day or two of . . . recreation after your long voyage? I promise you, the Mexican *señoritas* can be very entertaining."

Fitzpatrick glanced at the ship, where his men were sweating under the hot Mexican sun as they supervised the unloading of the equipment. "They could use a couple of days of rest," he said, as if to himself. "All right, General Loco."

Loco patted him on the shoulder. "I'll see that you have first-rate accommodations on the base while you enjoy a few days of relaxation," he said.

The captain nodded his thanks and walked back toward his ship.

Loco turned to Paco Valdez, a sly smile on his face. "Once the captain and his men arrive at the base, have them put in the brig."

"Why not just kill them and be done with it?" Valdez asked, his hand caressing the hilt of the long knife he carried on his belt.

Loco shrugged. "I have a feeling we may be needing the good captain and his men in the future. His freighter will make an excellent transport for some of our troops, once we've captured the northern ports of Mexico. We can use them to move up the replacements we're going to be sent from Nicaragua next month."

"Good idea," Valdez agreed.

"And, Paco, treat them well, plenty of food and water. Sick men don't sail well."

"Yes, *comandante.*"

Loco turned back and watched as several more helicopters and airplanes and tanks were unloaded from the ship. He was going to use this equipment to make Raines pay for all the trouble he'd caused him, after he took Mexico City.

The Mexican troops would not be able to stand against his soldiers once they began their march up the Pan American

Highway toward the north. The tanks and helicopters were much better than the antiquated equipment the Mexican Army used.

Harley Reno was having lunch with his team, after a morning of putting the merc trainees through the hell of basic training.

He spooned up the navy beans and ham, and washed it down with iced tea with lime. One thing he had to give the mercenary training center. The food was as good as any he'd ever tasted in the Army.

Coop, his elbows on the table, spoke in a low voice so men at surrounding tables couldn't hear. "Scuttlebutt has it a couple of guards were killed last night. Word is getting around there might be some spies in the camp."

Harley nodded. "Yeah, I heard the same thing."

Jersey's face turned red. "We didn't have any choice. They knew the voices they heard on the audio pickups were female."

"I know," Harley said. "It can't be helped now. Problem is, security's gonna be doubled around the camp, making it almost impossible to sneak out and report back to base."

"Speaking of security," Hammer said from the end of the table, "you guys notice that area off to the north, past the firing range?"

"You mean that cluster of buildings on the edge of the jungle?" Anna asked.

"Yeah. A couple of days after we got here, I noticed they put guards all around the place, along with signs saying, 'Off Limits.' "

"What do you think's going on?" Harley asked.

"I just wonder if that's got anything to do with the rumors we've been hearing about a secret weapon of some sort," Hammer said between mouthfuls of beans and ham.

"You think it might be some sort of nerve gas?" Jersey asked.

Harley shook his head. "Naw. If we were gonna be using gas of any type, they'd have us training the men with masks and gas gear. Even mercs aren't crazy enough to go into the field where gas has been used without masks and chem gear."

"What kind of weapon would make them think twenty thousand men are gonna make a difference in Mexico?" Coop asked. "Hell, that crazy bastard Perro Loco had over two hundred thousand, and he only got halfway to Mexico City before he got his ass kicked."

"I don't know," Harley said, "and that's what bothers me. Bergman and the other leaders are pretty damned confident of their success, so it must be something they think will make the difference."

"Then, it's up to us to find out what's in that building," Jersey said.

Harley cut his eyes at her. "You think you can do it?"

She nodded. "The problem won't be getting in. The problem's gonna be doing it without leaving some trace we've been there. If they suspect their secret's been compromised, they'll be a lot more thorough in the background checks, and we'll be found out."

"Then we need two things," Harley said. "First, a diversion to allow you to get in and get out of that building without being seen, and second, we need a scapegoat to take the fall as a spy to take the heat off us."

"How are we gonna do that?" Coop asked.

"I'll get into the records room tonight and go through the paperwork to try and find a likely suspect," Harley said. "Coop, you and Hammer get together tonight and figure out a suitable diversion to give Jersey and Anna time to search the building."

Coop looked at Hammer and grinned. This was the kind of thing he loved to do, throw a monkey wrench into someone else's machinery.

"We'll set it up for Saturday night, after everyone's gone to town for weekend passes."

* * *

Saturdays in the camp were called "half-days," and in theory were supposed to be short so the men could get cleaned up and go into a nearby village for what little entertainment existed in the area. In fact, the days usually lasted almost as long as the other days, due to Sergei Bergman's insistence that the schedule be worked overtime to get the men trained as soon as possible.

So, it was almost dusk when the final exercises were over and the DIs dismissed the men to their barracks with twenty-four-hour passes.

Harley and the team gathered in the mess shack, which was almost deserted since most of the soldiers planned to eat in town later that evening.

"You come up with someone we can put the blame on if we're caught?" Jersey asked Harley.

"Yeah. His name's Mingo Higgins. He was one of the men who supported the takeover when Osterman was ousted and had to flee the country when she took over again. He'll be perfect, 'cause he's got ties to someone friendly to Ben Raines."

"But, Harley, if he was against Osterman, doesn't that make him one of our friends?" Coop asked.

"Not this guy, Coop. He's already been up on charges twice for raping Indian girls out in the jungle. The only reason he wasn't prosecuted was the families were too afraid to come in." Harley got a look of extreme distaste on his face. "And get this. Bergman has the guy's record marked as a good candidate for their interrogation squad. Seems he's always looking for men with a taste for violence."

"Lends a whole new meaning to the phrase 'looking for a few good men,' doesn't it?" Anna asked, a grim smile on her face.

"Yeah, and remember, he'll only be needed if they discover

we've been snooping around the off-limits area," Hammer added.

"Any idea why they haven't said anything about the two guards we offed on the trail the other day?" Jersey asked.

Harley shook his head. "No, but I figure they're aware there are spies in camp and are watching and waiting for us to make a mistake and give ourselves away.

"I figure we'll set off Coop's diversion around 2100 hours, so you and Jersey should be ready to make your move then," Harley continued.

The ammunition bunkers were set on the edge of the camp, away from the barracks and other living quarters of the officers in case of explosion. Just before nine o'clock that night, while Harley and Hammer were in town establishing alibis for the team, Coop snuck into one of the smaller bunkers and made a pile of M-16 ammo, hand grenades, and mortar rounds in the center of the bunker. When his watch showed exactly nine P.M., he put a flash-bang phosphorous grenade in the center of the pile and pulled the pin, then bolted from the bunker as fast as he could run.

Five seconds later, the grenade exploded, the heat from the phosphorus set off the other munitions, and the bunker exploded, sending slugs and shrapnel slicing through the surrounding jungle with a tremendous explosion of fire and sound, flames shooting a hundred feet into the air.

Bergman and some of the other officers, who rarely went into town, along with everyone else remaining on the base, came running from their houses to try and fight the blaze.

When Jersey and Anna heard the explosion, they waited for the guards that were always in front of the buildings to run toward the disturbance. Then they slipped through the area marked OFF LIMITS, and crept up to the large, stucco building covered with signs saying ABSOLUTELY NO ADMITTANCE.

Jersey took a pick-set out of her pocket and went to work

on the locks on the door. It took her less than two minutes to open the door, and she and Anna slipped inside the darkened room.

They pulled small flashlights from their pockets, and proceeded through the maze of rooms until they came to what looked like a laboratory in the rear of the building.

The room was filled with long counters covered with bottles and Bunsen burners and microscopes, all the equipment of a well-appointed college chemistry lab back in the States.

"Jesus," Anna whispered, "they must have spent a fortune on this stuff."

"You look around here and see if you can figure out what they're working on. I'll roam around and see if I can find an office with some papers that might tell us more," Jersey said.

Anna continued to search the room, looking in all the microscopes, but finding nothing that would give her a clue as to what was going on.

Jersey went through the house room by room, until she came to another locked door made of metal. "This looks interesting," she mumbled to herself as she once again got out her picks.

When she opened the door, she noted it was surrounded by a rubber seal. "Uh-oh," she said, "this doesn't look good." The only times she'd ever seen doors like that were in biological warfare centers.

As she stepped into the darkened room, she felt the hair on the back of her neck stir. Something was definitely wrong here.

She flicked on her flashlight, and almost gagged at what she saw through a large glass partition in the rear of the room.

Six bodies were lying on cots. Two of the people were obviously dead, the others as close to death as it was possible to be and still be breathing. Their bodies were covered with sores and pustules, and seemed to be rotting away as she watched.

She quickly turned away from the grisly sight and looked around the rest of the room. In a corner was a large commercial-type refrigerator, also with a lock on it.

She knelt before the door and again picked the lock, opening the door to find it filled to capacity with bottles of murky liquid, the tops sealed with paraffin.

"Shit," she whispered, "this must be the bad stuff that caused whatever it was in that other room."

She reached into the back of the refrigerator and plucked a bottle from the rearmost row, hoping it wouldn't be missed, then relocked the door and left the room, relocking that door behind her also.

She found Anna in the lab, still trying to find some clue as to what the men were working on.

"Anna, come on, let's get out of here," Jersey said. "I've got the goods."

"What is it?" Anna asked.

"I don't know, but it causes a hell of a reaction in whoever is exposed to it," Jersey answered.

They went out the front door, and were in the process of locking it behind them when a guard appeared out of the darkness and attacked them. He dove against Jersey, slamming her against the door she was locking. As he raised his hand with a knife in it, Anna chopped across the back of his neck, breaking one of his vertebrae and killing him instantly.

As he slumped to the ground, Jersey turned around with a look of horror on her face.

"Don't worry, Jerse," Anna reassured her. "I took him out."

Jersey's face blanched white as she looked at a wet stain on the front of her shirt. "That's not what I'm worried about," she said in a hoarse voice.

"What is it?" Anna asked, getting spooked by the fear she saw in Jersey's eyes.

Jersey bent and placed the dog tags with Mingo Higgins's

name on them in the dead guard's hand, then looked up at Anna.

"I think we've just loosed the hounds of hell!" Jersey said through a throat closing with dread.

Twelve

Claire put down the microphone and turned to General Bradley Stevens, Jr., with a grin on her face.

"That was Perro Loco. The equipment and matériel we sent finally arrived. He's unloaded it and is in the process of beginning his assault toward Mexico City."

"Have you heard anything from Bruno Bottger?" Herb Knoff asked from his chair in front of her desk.

She shook her head. "No, but I'm expecting a call any day now. When we last spoke, he was in the final process of training some new recruits. He should be about ready to add his men to those of Loco's for the move against Mexico City."

"How are you going to set up their cooperation?" Stevens asked. "You know they're both egomaniacs. They'll probably end up fighting each other more than the Mexicans."

Claire leaned back in her chair, an enigmatic smile on her face. "I thought I'd set it up as a contest."

"Contest?" Herb asked.

"Yes. I'll simply suggest to Loco and Bottger that they keep their respective troops under their own control, and that they should each take a different route to Mexico City, one up the coast and one inland. That way, the first troops into the city will get the majority of the spoils and credit for taking the city."

"That's brilliant, Madame President," Stevens said, a smile of appreciation on his face. "It also serves the additional purpose of keeping the two leaders from getting too close personally, and will prevent them from having the time to conspire against you."

Claire nodded. "Oh, I have no illusions, General," she said. "I'm quite certain both of these men have designs on betraying me eventually. They both have too much ambition to be satisfied with merely ruling Mexico."

"If you believe they plan to betray you, why use them?" Stevens asked.

"They are merely a means to an end, Brad," she answered. "Attack dogs to take some of the heat off our troops and keep us from having to divide our forces in our attack on Raines and the SUSA."

"But, isn't that dangerous?"

"Life is dangerous, Brad. I'm counting on the two of them destroying each other long before they can become a threat to us here in the U.S."

"And if they don't?" Herb asked.

"The fighting to take Mexico City will weaken both of them, and the subsequent fight against Raines's southern border will weaken them even further," she answered, "if not destroy them completely. What is left should be easy pickings for our forces after we destroy Ben Raines."

"Why are you so sure we'll beat him this time?" Herb asked.

She glared at him. "Having doubts about my plan, Herby?" she asked, venom in her voice.

"No, it's just that every time we've gone after Raines, he's managed to survive. I don't want to underestimate how difficult this is going to be."

"I'm not underestimating the bastard," she said irritably. "Whatever I think of him personally, I have come to believe he is a brilliant field commander when it comes to waging war. But"—she held up her hand—"never, in the history of combat, has a country been able to successfully prosecute a war on two fronts. Even the Germans in World War II couldn't do it."

"Speaking of the second front, when do you want our forces to attack the SUSA's northern borders?" Stevens asked.

"I think we should now begin to move them into position, very slowly so as not to attract too much attention, but hold off our offensive until Raines is forced to commit some of his battalions to his south, probably after Mexico City itself comes under attack."

"Will do, Madame President."

After the general left the room, Claire turned to Herb, a gleam in her eye. "Well, Herby, now that business is taken care of, do you have any suggestions for how we can while away the time until Bottger contacts us?"

Herb smiled, and glanced toward the door to Claire's bedroom on the opposite wall. "Oh, I think I can come up with something, if I'm pressed."

Claire began to unbutton her blouse. "Consider yourself pressed," she said with a lascivious grin.

Sergei Bergman stood at attention before Bruno Bottger's desk, his neck red with worry about how the man would receive the news he was about to give him.

"Yes, sir," Bergman said. "I'm certain the fire and explosion in the ammunition bunker was a diversion so the laboratory area could be broken into and searched."

"Do you think this ties in to the killing of the two guards several days ago?" Bottger asked, leaning forward with his elbows on his desk.

"Yes, sir."

"Go on, Sergei," Bottger said, leaning back in his chair and reaching into the humidor on his desk for a cigar.

"Although the scientists say they can find nothing disturbed in the lab, the guard that was killed at the front door did have a set of dog tags clenched in his fist."

"So, you think that possibly the guard attacked the burglars before they managed to get inside the facility?" Bottger asked.

"Yes, sir, that is my presumption."

"And who did the dog tags belong to?"

"A recent trainee named Mingo Higgins."

"His history?"

"He was involved in the abortive rebellion against President Osterman's rule. When she came back, he was forced to leave the country and seek other employment with us."

Bottger pursed his lips around the butt of the cigar, then removed it and stared at the red-hot ash on the end. "And did it not occur to you that a man who was at least sympathetic to Ben Raines and the SUSA might be a danger to us?" Bottger asked, steel in his voice.

"No, sir. The man's record is replete with instances of cruelty and criminality that make him completely unsuitable in Ben Raines's eyes."

Bottger slammed his hand down on his desk and stood up. "Records can be doctored, you fool!"

Bergman dropped his eyes to the carpet in front of him. "Yes, sir, I'm well aware of that. But this Higgins was given no access to sensitive material. In fact, he was in training as a simple foot soldier."

"Even a flea can cause a dog trouble, Sergei," Bottger said. "Are you sure this man acted alone?"

"No, sir. In fact, I would be surprised if he didn't have accomplices."

"Are you taking measures to ferret out these traitors?" Bottger asked as he turned his back and walked to stare out of his window.

"Yes, sir. I'm personally reviewing all the records of the recruits that have come to us since we moved here."

Bottger turned around, the cigar sticking out of the corner of his mouth. "Sergei, I want results on this, and I want them fast. Pick up Higgins and take him down to interrogation."

Bottger cut his eyes to Rudolf Hessner, who, as usual, was standing in the corner of the room observing everything that went on. "Rudolf, I want you to personally go to the lab and interrogate the scientists. Make them go over everything in the lab to make sure nothing was disturbed."

"Yes, sir," Hessner said, nodding his head quickly.

"If the secret of the plague we're working on gets out, it could ruin my entire plan to take over the North American continent."

"I will make sure nothing was taken, Herr Bottger," Hessner said as he walked rapidly out the door.

Thirteen

As soon as she realized she was contaminated with the biological weapon they'd found in Bottger's lab, Jersey stepped away from Anna and held out her hands.

"Stay as far away from me as you can, Anna," she said, pointing to the stain on the front of her fatigues.

"Is that . . . ?" Anna asked, a look of horror on her face as she stared at the dark spot.

Jersey nodded. "Yeah. The good news is, whatever the nasty stuff is those bastards are working on in that lab, we now have a sample of it."

"But that means . . ."

Jersey nodded, and began to move at speed through the jungle toward a stream that ran along the edge of the training fields. "It means I'm probably going to get it," Jersey replied shortly, her voice showing none of the terror she felt.

Anna followed Jersey through the thick undergrowth as close as she dared.

Finally, when they reached the sluggishly moving water, Jersey stripped out of her clothes, even removing her dog tags, and threw them in the water.

"What are you doing?" Anna asked, puzzled by Jersey's strange actions.

"Remember the phrase they taught us in Biological Warfare class? 'The solution to pollution is dilution.' That means the only chance I've got to prevent this BW from spreading throughout the entire camp is to dilute whatever bug is in there with plenty of water."

As she finished speaking, Jersey slipped off the bank and into the stream.

"Cover me with your side arm," she called softly to Anna, looking around for crocs as she scrubbed at her skin under the water to try to wash off the chemical solution, though she knew in her heart it was impossible to decontaminate herself in such a manner.

Anna pulled her Beretta out and searched the water for any signs of life. "You think that's going to work?" she asked.

Jersey shook her head as she climbed from the stream, water coursing down her naked body. "Naw, it won't help me keep from getting sick, but it may keep you guys from getting it."

She took off through the jungle, still naked. "Come on, we haven't got long before they discover that body in the lab. We've got to get the hell out of here."

When they got back to the base barracks, Anna slipped inside and quietly woke Coop, Harley, and Hammer, whispering to them to come outside.

She led them around the side of the building to where Jersey was waiting, standing naked in the shadows.

"What the . . ." Harley said as they saw her condition.

"Keep your distance," Jersey said. "I've been contaminated with whatever biological weapon these guys are working on. Our only chance to prevent them from using it is to get me back to Santos and the ship before I die so the doc can use me to make some sort of vaccine."

Coop noticed her shivering in the cool night air and walked over to her, slipping his T-shirt off.

"Coop, stay back!" she said.

"Screw that," he said, his lips curling in his trademark grin. "You're cold and you're naked. Here," he said, handing her his shirt.

After she slipped it on, he stood there with his arm around her, trying to warm her and stop her chills.

She looked up at him. "But you'll get it too," she said softly.

He shrugged. "Then Doc'll have two specimens to work with. It'll double his chance of getting enough blood to make a vaccine."

Harley and Hammer stepped over to Anna and asked her what had happened at the lab. She told them everything, including the fact they'd left Mingo Higgins's dog tags on the dead guard.

Harley nodded. "Good. That may give us a few extra hours. As soon as they discover those tags, they're gonna come for Higgins."

"While they're wasting time interrogating him, we can be making tracks for Santos," Hammer added.

Harley glanced at Coop and Jersey. "Hammer and I will gather up what clothes and weapons we can for the trip and we'll meet you out here in five minutes."

"It's gonna take us a day or two, so bring some rations too," Coop advised.

Harley nodded, and he and Hammer and Anna disappeared into the barracks.

After they were gone, Coop squeezed Jersey's shoulder. "How long do you think we have before we get sick?"

"Most BWs are designed to work fast. I'd say we'll begin to experience our first symptoms within twenty-four hours."

"Any idea just what it is we're dealing with here?" he asked.

"No, there wasn't a clue in the lab. But," she added with a shiver, "you can bet it'll be bad."

"You think we'll be able to make it twenty-five miles through the jungle if we get sick?"

"We'll have to," she answered. Then she looked up at him and caressed the side of his face with her hand. "Coop, thanks," she said.

"For what?" he asked, a surprised tone in his voice.

"For the shirt, and for being with me," she said.

Even in the moonlight, she could see him blush.

"Oh, well, I couldn't have those horny bastards looking at you like that. It wasn't right."

She smiled. "I noticed you didn't turn your eyes away."

He glanced down at where her breasts pushed against the thin cloth of his T-shirt, her nipples clearly visible.

"Hell, no," he said. "I'm a gentleman, but I'm not completely stupid."

She looked over her shoulder and saw no one watching them. She turned her body into his and put her arms around him. "Did you like what you saw?" she asked, her face turned up to his, her breasts pushing against his chest.

As he returned her gaze, she felt his answer as his body responded to her closeness.

"More than anything I've ever seen," he said, leaning his head down to kiss her gently on the lips.

After a moment, she drew back with a deep sigh. "Better quit, while I still can," she whispered.

"You think they'd miss us if I picked you up and carried you off into the jungle," Coop asked, his voice husky with desire.

Jersey was saved from answering by the approach of Hammer, Harley, and Anna, their arms full of clothing and weapons and other gear for the trip.

Jersey and Coop quickly slipped into their BDUs and boots while the others kept watch.

"I figure they'll be here for Higgins any minute, so let's make tracks outta here," Harley said.

"Wait a minute," Jersey said. "Won't they notice we're not here when they come for Mingo?"

Anna shook her head. "No, we fixed up our bunks with pillows to look as if we were still in them."

"Let's travel, people," Harley whispered, his voice urgent as he turned to lead them into the jungle. "We've got a lot of ground to cover," he said, glancing over his shoulder, "and we don't know how long until you two get too sick to travel."

As they moved off into the darkness, with Jersey and Coop well back from the others, Coop asked, "Any chance of getting the communications gear and having them pick us up in a chopper?"

Harley shook his head. "Too risky. They could track the chopper and it'd lead them right to the ship. No, we're gonna have to do this the old-fashioned way and walk home."

"Just what I was looking forward too, a leisurely traipse through the jungle at night," Coop said, glancing nervously around him at the thick underbrush surrounding them.

Jersey quietly reached out and took his hand as they walked. She idly rubbed at the spot on her chest where the BW had stained her shirt. Her skin was already beginning to itch, but she thought that was probably just her imagination.

Mingo Higgins's head lolled on his chest, blood dripping from his shattered nose onto the concrete floor between his bare feet. His hands were tied behind the back of the chair he was sitting on.

Bruno Bottger stood before him, his eyes glittering hate as he questioned the merc. "Who sent you here?" he shouted, slapping Higgins awake again.

Higgins answered through swollen, split lips. "No one," he said, his voice barely intelligible.

"Why did you break into my lab?"

Higgins shook his head, the movement making him wince as waves of pain shot through every part of his body. "I already told you, I don't know what you're talking about."

Bottger scowled and stepped back, allowing Sergeant Herman Bundt to step forward. Bundt's hands were covered with padded black gloves, and he delivered two quick blows to Higgins's face, snapping his head back and shattering his two front teeth.

Bottger took a handkerchief out of his pocket and wiped away blood that splattered onto his boots.

"I think it is time for the chemicals," he said.

"But, Herr Bottger," Sergei Bergman said, "they will turn his mind to mush. He will be useless to us afterwards."

Bottger cut his eyes to Bergman. "He is already useless. Do you think I would trust him again? Do whatever you have to and make him talk!"

Bergman nodded his head at Bundt, and the sergeant picked a syringe up off a nearby table and filled it with a colorless liquid from a vial. He bent next to Higgins and jabbed the needle into his arm vein, depressing the plunger and sending the liquid coursing through Higgins's body.

As his eyes clouded over under the influence of the truth serum, Higgins began to mumble and laugh to himself, as if he were sharing a private joke in the recesses of his mind.

Again, Bottger put the question to him. "Who sent you here to spy on me?"

Higgins's eyes rolled back in his head as he tried to focus on the man standing in front of him.

"No one sent me. I came on my own to find work," he answered, his voice slurred as if he were drunk.

After another fifteen minutes of this, Bundt finally said, "It is of no use, Herr Bottger. Either he is innocent, or he is so well trained we will never get the truth out of him."

Bottger threw his bloodied handkerchief into the wastebasket.

"You want me to have him shot?" Rudolf Hessner asked.

"No, send him to the lab. The scientists can always use another subject for their experiments."

He hesitated, thinking of what to do next. "And while you are there, tell them to conduct another search of the lab to make sure nothing is missing."

"Yes, sir," Hessner said as he bent to untie Higgins's hands and help him to his feet.

"Rudolf," Bottger said.

"Yes, sir?"

"When you're finished at the lab, go with Sergei and Sergeant Bundt and have all of the trainees assembled in the squad yard. It's time to find out just who is loyal and who isn't."

"Yes, sir," Hessner said.

Fourteen

Mike Post knocked and entered Ben Raines's office just after breakfast.

"Hey, Ben," he said, as he took his usual seat opposite Ben's desk.

"Mornin', Mike," Ben said over the brim of his coffee cup. "What've you heard about Osterman and her current plans?"

Mike looked at a sheaf of papers in his hand. "Lot of reports of troop movements to the north. Nothing on a large scale, but lots of small units seem to be on the move, and all of them are heading south."

"You think she's getting her troops in position to make a move against us?"

Mike nodded. "That'd be my first guess. That, combined with the intel from Harley Reno's group saying the mercs in South America are gearing up for an offensive within one month, suggests that she's planning on hitting us from the north simultaneously with the offensive from the south in Mexico."

Ben smiled. "I guess she thinks she can keep us so busy defending ourselves here we won't be able to help the Mexican Army stand off Perro Loco and whoever is fronting the mercs from South America."

"Yeah, and I've gotta say it's not a bad idea. It's gonna be real hard to manage a war on two fronts."

Ben's face grew reflective. "She's certainly studied her history. No major power has ever been able to do it successfully."

"What do you think our chances are?" Mike asked, stuffing the papers back in his briefcase.

"If you mean keeping Mexico free as well as fighting off Osterman from the north, I'd say about fifty-fifty."

"That low?" Mike asked, his expression becoming worried as he contemplated the idea of the SUSA losing a war.

Ben nodded. "In fact, if we expended a major effort to save Mexico City, the odds would be even lower than that."

"So, what do you plan to do?"

"Since the president of Mexico is being so stubborn about accepting our help before the fact of an invasion, I think we're gonna have to let him do it his way and defend his capital city on his own."

"You think he can pull it off?"

Ben shook his head. "Not a chance," he said. "The man is a complete imbecile where modern warfare is concerned. Mexico City is far too large and spread out to defend in the usual manner, and Perro Loco has too much sophisticated weaponry to be held off the way the Mexican president wants to."

"So, you think Mexico City is doomed?"

"Yeah, sooner or later, and probably sooner, Loco with the help of the mercs will take the city."

"Then what?" Mike asked.

"Mexico City is five to seven hundred miles from our southern border, which we control. I'm going to send a couple of battalions down there to beef up our forces there, as well as sending in as many scout teams as I can spare to the northern parts of Mexico. I'm going to make Loco and his mercs fight for every inch of territory between Mexico City and our southern borders. It's going to be a war of attrition so devastating that Loco may have to be content with having Mexico City."

"Then, you're gonna cede Mexico to Loco and his minions?"

Ben nodded. "Essentially, yes."

Mike shook his head. "That doesn't sound good."

Ben grinned. "Oh, it won't be a permanent situation. I'm hoping at some point the citizens of Mexico will rise up and revolt against the carpetbagger leadership of their country. As soon as a credible revolutionary leader emerges, we'll give him our full backing and help him take back his country."

"That means a lot of Mexicans are going to die."

Ben leaned forward, his elbows on his desk. "Mike, I've said it a hundred times. A country gets the kind of leader they deserve. The Mexican president is an idiot, but he's the one the people down there wanted to lead them. If he fails to protect his people, then they're going to have to pay the price for electing him in the first place. It is not our place to spend the lives of American men and women to shore up his deficiencies of leadership."

"You think he'll agree to letting our scouts into his northern regions to protect our southern borders?"

"Not a chance," Ben replied.

"But you said . . ."

Ben nodded. "I'm going to send them in and have them dig in down there, but he's not going to know anything about it," Ben said with a smile. "Every road that can carry tanks or other heavy equipment is going to be mined, and every hill or mountain high enough is going to have antiaircraft batteries on it to help protect us against any bombing raids."

"But, with a force that size, he's bound to find out about it," Mike protested.

"Oh, I'm sure at some point he's going to realize what's going on," Ben replied. "That's when I'm going to sit down and talk some turkey with him. I'll simply say if he ever wants to trade with us again, or if he wants any help in saving his country from those madmen from South America, he's going to have to accept the way we do things."

"And if he's too dumb to see the light?"

Ben's face became hard. "Then, I'll simple put his lights out permanently."

"That's playing hardball."

Ben nodded. "Like they say, Mike, war is hell."

As Mike got up to leave, Ben asked him, "By the way, have you got any hints on who may be leading the mercs down in South America?"

Mike shook his head. "No, they've been keeping it pretty tight down there. Whoever it is must have spent a lot of money on the South American government to keep his secret, 'cause no one's talking."

"Okay, maybe Harley and his people will be able to find out for me."

After Mike Post left the room, Ben sent for Georgi Striginov, a big bear of a man and the leader of Bat 505, and for Ike McGowen, the commander of Bat 502 and one of Ben's dearest friends.

The two men entered the office at the same time, making it seem suddenly smaller by virtue of their large size. Ike, who weighed close to three hundred pounds and was in a continual battle to try to lose weight in spite of his penchant for sweets, flopped down in a chair across from Ben's desk, making it groan with his weight.

Ben smiled. "Ike, if you get any bigger, I'm going to have to special-order some chairs for you to sit in."

"Bigger?" the big man protested. "Why, I'll have you know I've lost almost ten pounds on my latest diet."

"Yeah," Striginov laughed, "a seafood diet. If you see food, you eat it."

Ike glanced at Striginov, who weighed over 250 pounds. "I don't see where you have any room to talk, Georgi. You look even bigger than you did last time I saw you."

Striginov stuck out his chest and pounded it with his hands. "Yes, Ike, but the difference is my weight is all muscle, while yours is fat."

As Ike started to reply, Ben held up his hand. "All right, you two, cut it out."

The two men leaned back in their chairs and gave Ben their full attention.

"Intel says Perro Loco is fixing to make his move down in Mexico," Ben said. "I want your two bats down there on the border to get ready for anything."

"How soon can we expect to be attacked?" Striginov asked.

Ben shook his head. "That depends on how long it takes the Mad Dog to take Mexico City. He won't dare try and leapfrog to attack us with the Mexico forces behind him, so he'll have to conquer Mexico City first. That'll give us plenty of warning."

"So, we just sit and wait?" Ike asked with distaste.

"No," Ben answered. "I want you both to field as many scout teams as you can and have them infiltrate Mexico without anyone knowing."

Striginov grinned. "In other words, that horse's ass of a president in Mexico has not approved this plan?"

"You got it, Georgi."

"How do you want us to divide it up?" Ike asked.

Ben shrugged. "Work it out between the two of you."

The two generals looked at each other and smiled. "The troops are gonna love this," Ike said. "They've all been complaining things have been too quiet since Osterman was deposed last year."

"Spread your scouts out," Ben advised. "I want them to harass and slow Loco as much as possible while I'm busy with Osterman's forces to the north."

"Who's going to take care of our northern border?" Striginov asked.

"I'm going to station Dan Gray and his Bat 503 along with Pat O'Shea and the 510 along the border."

"That'll be a hoot," Ike said. "An Englishman and an Irishman cooperating to screw Osterman."

"What about Jackie?" Striginov asked, referring to Jackie Malone, leader of the 512 Bat. "She's been bitching for months now that her command is getting sloppy from inactivity."

"Jackie's going to have a special treat," Ben said with a grin. "I'm gonna leapfrog her and her command up north of Osterman's forces. I intend to show Osterman just what fighting on two fronts means."

Striginov rubbed his hands together. "This is beginning to sound like fun."

"I don't think Sugar Babe Osterman is going to think it's much fun when she finds Jackie Malone breathing down her ass," Ike said with a wide smile.

Bruno Bottger stood before the assembled troops with Rudolf Hessner, Sergei Bergman, and Herman Bundt at his side. The mercs gathered there were apprehensive, not knowing exactly why they'd been mustered out at such an early hour.

Bundt went among the mercs, stopping and asking several of them questions before he came back to the front of the group and stood before Bottger.

"Well?" Bottger asked him.

"It appears that several of our newest recruits are missing. Their beds had pillows stacked on them under the covers to conceal the fact they weren't there."

"Who are the ones missing?" Bergman asked.

"Harley Reno and his friends, sir," Bundt answered.

"And just who are these missing mercs?" Bottger asked, turning to Bergman.

"Some of the best recruits I've ever seen," Bergman answered. "They claimed to be ex-soldiers from Ben Raines's SUSA Army. They were so good I made them drill instructors after their first days here."

"And you think they had something to do with the lab break-in?"

Bergman shrugged. "They must have. It's the only reason I can think of for them to be AWOL."

"Send a team of your best men after them immediately,

Herman. I do not want them to escape with whatever information they managed to get from the lab."

"Yes, sir," Bergman said.

"If they manage to get off the island, they will undoubtedly head south, since going north would merely take them farther into the jungle and it is much too long a trip to Rio de Janeiro on foot. Fill one of the helicopters with a team and have it take them south to the mainland. Then set up an ambush there while another team follows from the rear," Bottger said, turning on his heel and striding rapidly toward his office without waiting for Bergman's reply.

"Herman," Bergman said, leaning close to his friend.

"Yes, Sergei?"

"If you don't want to end up like Higgins, I'd suggest you bring us the heads of these traitors, or don't bother to return."

Bundt swallowed as his face blanched as pale as the underbelly of a slug. "I understand, Sergei."

As Bergman stalked away after his boss, Bundt turned back to his men. He pointed to the team Harley and his group had humiliated on their first day in the camp, and motioned them to come forward.

The tall, broad-shouldered black man with extensive burn scars on his face stood at attention before Bundt.

"Ronald Watanabe," Bundt said.

"Yes, sir!" the man snapped back, his spine straight as an arrow.

"Would you like a chance to avenge yourself on the traitors who humiliated you last week?"

Watanabe grinned, exposing several gold teeth in his mouth. "Yes, sir!"

"Good, 'cause you're going to get your chance. Assemble your team and report with full weapons and gear to the airport. You will be transported ahead of the traitors by helicopter. You will set up an ambush on the mainland and stop them from escaping. You will then bring me back the heads of the bastards. Do you understand?"

Watanabe's grin faded, replaced by a sneer. "Yes, sir. I guarantee you it will be done."

"It had better be, Ronald, or you might as well stay in the jungle and let the cats and crocs eat you, because that will be an easier death than the one you'll face here if you fail."

As Watanabe gestured to Lieutenant Johnson to gather their team together, Bundt began picking other men to lead the chase of the traitors. He wasn't as concerned with the quality of the men who would be sent, for he planned to send such a quantity of men that it wouldn't matter how good they were. Their only job was to chase and hound the deserters into the ambush being set up by Watanabe and his team.

When he had twenty men picked out, he gathered them around the big table in the mess tent and spread out a detailed map of the area in front of them.

"The only chance the deserters have is to make it to the coast and find some native fishing boats for the trip across the strait to the mainland. They won't dare make the crossing in the daylight, so that will give you almost twenty-four hours to find and kill them."

He looked around as the men nodded they understood. "Let me make myself clear," he added. "These men are the best I've ever seen. Take no chances. You will have superior firepower, so do not be afraid to use it. Blast the bastards to death from as far away as you can, 'cause if you get close to them, they will surely kill you first."

Fifteen

Bruno Bottger sat in his office with Rudolf Hessner and Sergei Bergman, making plans for the upcoming war.

"Sergei, we cannot afford any more time for training of our mercenaries. It is time to move the men and equipment out and head for Mexico."

"But, Herr Bottger," Bergman said, "the men are not ready."

"We have no choice, Sergei," Bottger said impatiently. "If these traitors manage to get the information about our plague weapon to Ben Raines, it will give Raines time to try and develop a vaccine. We must press the attack on Mexico immediately, and keep our enemies so busy they have no time for defensive measures against our biological weapons."

"But what about this Perro Loco who is to fight with us?" Bergman asked. "Will he be ready?"

"I will contact Osterman in the U.S. and tell her the timetable must be advanced."

"She will want to know why, Bruno," Rudolf Hessner said, "and we dare not tell her of our plans to use the plague as a weapon."

"I will merely tell her that some spies from Ben Raines have found out about our mercenary force and we need to strike before the Mexicans can ask Raines for reinforcements."

"Do you think that will work?" Hessner asked.

Bottger nodded. "Yes. Osterman is so paranoid about Raines that any mention of his name will cloud her mind to our real reasons for advancing the date of the attack."

"Then I will begin preparations for an immediate departure," Bergman said, standing up.

"We have five of the C-130 troop transport aircraft at our disposal," Bottger said. "Send a few thousand of our best troops in those, and put the rest of the twenty thousand men and our equipment on the troop transport ships. They should be able to make it to Perro Loco's base within a week."

"I'll see to it immediately, Herr General," Bergman said, and left the room.

"Get me President Osterman on the scrambler," Bottger said to Hessner.

Claire Osterman was in a strategy meeting with her top advisors when her phone rang.

"President Osterman, this is Bruno Bottger."

"Hello, General," she said.

"I am advising you that I am sending my men and equipment to Mexico today. I feel it is imperative we advance the attack date on Mexico."

"Is there some reason for your haste?" she asked, tapping a switch on the phone and putting him on the speaker so her advisors could hear the conversation.

"Yes. I have just found out that Ben Raines sent a team of spies into my camp. I'm afraid they now know of the strength of my forces and our plans to aid you in your attack on Mexico."

"And you let them get away with this information?" she asked, steel in her voice.

"Not yet, Madame President," Bottger answered. "They are still in the jungle and haven't been able to communicate what they found out to Raines. However, if he does find out how large our force is, he may be able to convince the Mexican president to allow his SUSA forces to join the Mexicans. That would make it very difficult for us to succeed in our attempt to take Mexico City."

Osterman hesitated a moment, then nodded as she answered. "Yes, General, I see your point. Better to make a quick strike before Raines has a chance to reinforce the Mexican troops."

"That is what I thought," Bottger said. "Do you think Perro Loco will have any trouble getting ready earlier than anticipated?"

"No. He has been pushing me to move the attack date forward. There should be no problem at all."

"How about your forces?" Bottger asked. "Will you be able to attack Raines from the north in conjunction with our attack from the south?"

"I have already started moving my men into position," she said. "We will be able to start by the time your men and equipment get to Mexico."

"I believe we will be in place and ready to move within one week, Madame President."

Osterman consulted a calendar on her desk and marked the date. "One week it is, General."

After she hung up, Claire glanced around at the men in her office. Herb Knoff, Harlan Millard, Major General Bradley Stevens, Jr., and his second in command, Colonel James King, were all watching her intently.

"What do you gentlemen make of that?" she asked.

Stevens shrugged. "It doesn't matter to me when we attack. Our forces are almost in place and will certainly be ready within the week."

"I'm a little concerned, Claire," Harlan Millard said, his eyes narrowed.

"Why is that, Harlan?" she asked. Though she had little respect for Harlan as a man, she knew him to be a shrewd thinker and politician.

"His reasons for advancing the date of the attack don't make any sense. We always knew Raines was going to find out about Bottger and his mercenaries sooner or later. Why the sudden panic when it happens?"

She glanced at Herb Knoff. "What do you think, Herb?"

Herb shrugged. "I agree with Harlan. I don't think Bottger is telling us the whole truth about his reasons for advancing the attack date. I've never trusted him."

"Nor have I," Claire said. "There's something he's not telling us, but until we can discover what it is, I can see no harm in moving up the attack. He's right about one thing. We can't afford to let Raines talk the Mexican president into allowing the SUSA to send troops to aid him before our attack."

"Our intel says that's not going to happen, Claire," Stevens said. "From what our spies in Mexico City say, the president is a vain, stupid man who thinks his Army can handle Perro Loco without letting the SUSA help."

"By the time he finds out differently," Colonel King added, "it'll be too late for Raines and his Army to make much difference in the battle for Mexico City."

"What about after we take Mexico City?" Claire asked.

"Raines won't dare counterattack then, Madame President," Stevens said, " 'cause we'll have the ten million citizens of the city as virtual hostages. We'll just let Raines know if he interferes, we'll raze the city and he'll have the deaths of millions of innocent civilians on his conscience."

"That bastard doesn't have a conscience," Claire said spitefully.

"No, but the United Nations does," Millard said. "Once we've taken the city, we'll appeal to the U.N. to intervene and keep the SUSA from doing anything to help."

"Do you think they're dumb enough to fall for that?" Claire asked.

Millard grinned. "You'll never go broke underestimating the stupidity of the U.N., Madame President. Their only function seems to be to maintain the status quo. Once we're in a position of power in Mexico City, they will do everything in their power to stop further warfare."

"But Raines has shown he has nothing but contempt for the U.N.," Claire argued.

"If it were up to Raines, the U.N.'s opposition would mean

less than nothing," Millard said. "But the president of the SUSA, Cecil Jeffreys, is more of a political animal. I feel if the U.N. strongly opposes intervention, he will keep Raines under control to prevent it."

Claire slammed her hand down on her desk. "It's settled then. General Stevens, inform your commanders we attack the SUSA in one week all along its northern border."

"Yes, ma'am," Stevens said with a smile.

"Harlan," she said.

"Yes, Claire?"

"I want you to start to work on the U.N. Call in some debts, bribe whomever you have to, but make damned sure that once we've taken Mexico City, they keep Raines and the SUSA out of it."

"That shouldn't be a problem, Claire."

"Okay, gentlemen, you've got your orders. Now, get to work."

After the men filed out of her office, Claire put her head in her hands. "All this has given me a headache," she moaned.

Herb Knoff got to his feet and walked around behind her chair. He put his hands on her shoulders and began to knead the muscles there.

"I know a great cure for a headache," he murmured in her ear.

She leaned her head back and kissed him on the lips. "You must have read my mind," she said in a soft voice.

Sixteen

Jersey's body shook with a chill, and sweat broke out all over her body. She glanced to the side, and saw Coop wasn't much better. His skin was pale and pasty-looking, and he was breathing heavily through his mouth as they made their way through heavy jungle undergrowth.

Harley was keeping them off the main trails to prevent their being ambushed, but it was heavy going. He was constantly checking his maps and compass as he led them toward the coastline of the island.

Anna looked back over her shoulder as Jersey stumbled over a root and almost fell.

"Jerse, you all right?" she asked worriedly.

Jersey nodded, accepting Coop's arm to help her stand up. "Just keep your distance, Anna," she said.

A cough started deep in her chest and exploded from her mouth, causing a deep, burning pain in her lungs that almost made her faint. She sleeved her face off, and noticed flecks of blood on the cloth when she looked at her arm.

"Trouble breathing?" Coop asked from her side.

She nodded. "Whatever the hell this bug is, it must attack the lungs, 'cause I feel like a truck is sitting on my chest."

He reached over and wiped sweat from her brow. "You're burning up, Jerse," he said. "Your fever must be up to a hundred and four."

"You don't look so hot yourself, Coop," she answered with a wan smile.

"I'm still in the early stages," he answered. "You were exposed before me."

"How much farther till we can rest?" she gasped through the mucus clogging her throat.

"Hey, Harley," Coop called. "How soon 'fore we can take a break?"

Harley stopped and turned to look at them in the slight light from a half-moon. His eyes widened when he saw how bad the two of them looked.

"Jesus," he whispered. "We've got another couple of hours to the coast, but we can take five now if you need it."

Jersey flopped down on the ground and lay on her back, breathing heavy, her BDUs saturated with sweat.

Coop broke out his medical bag and opened a bottle of aspirin. He poured several into his palm and handed them to Jersey along with a canteen.

After she swallowed them, he took a handful and did the same, wincing at the bitter taste they left in his mouth.

As they sat there, munching on MREs to keep their strength up, the *whoop-whoop* of a low-flying helicopter sounded over their heads.

Harley glanced upward. "Looks like they've found out we're missing."

Hammer nodded. "They'll be sending teams ahead of us to set up ambushes."

"If we can make the mainland, it'll be tougher for them to figure out which way we're going," Anna said.

Harley shook his head. "Not really, Anna. The Pariba do Sul runs parallel to the coast a few miles inland."

"What the hell is a Pariba do Sul?" Coop asked irritably.

"It's a wide river flowing to the sea," Harley answered, looking at his map. "Several hundred yards wide and filled with crocs and snakes and other goodies, I imagine. The leader of the mercs has got to know we won't be able to cross it, so we'll be trapped in a corridor a few miles wide. He'll also know we're bound to head south, 'cause there's nothing north except more jungle."

"That means we're gonna have to fight our way to Santos," Hammer added unnecessarily.

Jersey had another shaking chill as the aspirin began to lower her body temperature. Some of the aching in her joints eased a bit, and she felt well enough to try to force down an MRE, knowing she had to keep her strength up as much as possible or she'd never make it back to the ship.

Harley glanced at his wristwatch. "Time to saddle up," he called.

"Do we have to?" Coop groaned.

"Only if you want to live," Harley replied with dry humor.

Coop helped Jersey get to her feet, concerned when he felt how weak she was. If she got much worse, he was going to have to carry her.

Harley, seeing that Jersey was not going to be able to make much speed, pulled Hammer to the side.

"Hammer, we're never going to make it at this speed, not with men on our tail."

Hammer followed his glance at Jersey and Coop, both barely able to stand. He nodded.

"I need a rear-guard action to slow them up a bit," Harley said. "You think you can manage it?"

Hammer grinned without speaking.

Harley squatted and shined his flashlight on the map. "Here's where we'll rendezvous, just before first light. Once we get there, I'll scout up and down the coast until I find a boat suitable to take us across the strait. You just be there by 0400 and we'll cross then."

"If I'm not there, go without me," Hammer said.

"No way, pal. We *all* go, or none of us goes," Harley replied grimly. "So, be careful not to get your ugly butt fragged or you'll do us all in."

Hammer held out his fist and they touched knuckles. Then he whirled and disappeared into the darkness of the jungle.

* * *

Hammer made quick time back the way they'd come, coursing back and forth until he found a trail leading toward the coast. This was most probably the way their pursuers would come.

He followed the trail until he came to an area to his liking. Squatting, he dug several small holes in the humus of the path and placed fragmentation grenades in the dirt. He pulled a spool of twine from his backpack, tied it to the rings on the grenades, and stretched it across the trail, tying the ends to a bush there.

Once the grenades were covered with leaves and twigs, he ran up the trail to a large banyan tree and scurried up into its branches. He pulled his SPAS shotgun out and checked the loads, replacing the buckshot with flechette rounds. Each shell was filled with hundreds of tiny razor-sharp shards of metal that would shred a man like a scythe would grass. Once the SPAS was ready, he pulled out his Beretta automatic and placed it on the branch near him, ready for use.

Lieutenant Jean LaFite was a Frenchman who'd hired on with the mercenaries after being kicked out of the French Foreign Legion for raping and killing an Arab girl. The only reason he hadn't been hanged was he'd heard of his impending arrest and managed to leave the country ahead of the gendarmes.

He was leading a squad of twenty men through the jungle after the deserters. He knew a promotion was in it for him if it was his troops who killed the deserters their leader wanted so badly.

Even though he was markedly ambitious, LaFite was no fool. He led his men from the rear, having six or seven other men take the point ahead of him. He remembered how Harley Reno and his team had taken out Watanabe's squad with seemingly little trouble, and he didn't intend to make the same mistakes the black man had.

Gunter Held was an eighteen-year-old German boy who was full of the ideals of Bruno Bottger's New World Order and had volunteered to walk point. He was sure this was the fastest way to get a promotion in Bottger's army.

He felt a slight tug as his leg tripped the string attached to the fragmentation grenade, and he looked down just as the grenade exploded, taking his head off and the upper half of his body down to the waist. He didn't even have time to scream as the shrapnel passed through him and shredded the next four men in line, sending body parts, blood, and brains showering through the jungle.

Lieutenant LaFite reacted with lightning reflexes at the sound of the explosion, throwing himself facedown in the moldy humus of the jungle trail just as the second grenade went off.

The bloody stump of an arm hit LaFite in the back, and he screamed as blood and mucus showered his face. He rolled over once and brought his M-16 up and squeezed the trigger, ripping off a full clip of twenty rounds in two seconds.

Six more of his men danced a macabre dance of death as their lieutenant shot them in the back in his terror.

Sergeant Blandis jumped on LaFite's back and ripped the M-16 from his arms, shouting, "Stop it, Lieutenant, you're killin' our own men!"

"Oh, God . . . oh, God, help me!" LaFite screamed, completely out of his mind with fear and loathing at the sight of the carnage around him.

Sergeant Blandis stood up, sneering down at LaFite. "You yellow bastard," he hollered, and aimed his own weapon at LaFite.

LaFite held his arms out as if they could stop the bullets, but before Blandis could pull the trigger, a booming echo of an automatic shotgun shattered the sudden quiet of the jungle and Blandis was blown off his feet, his head shattered and almost decapitated as he slumped and flopped down on top of LaFite.

What remained of LaFite's command all started firing blindly into the jungle, some screaming and some moaning in fear at the horror of their first firefight.

Several more loud explosions of the shotgun took more men down, and caused the others to bury their faces in the ground and cover their heads as they saw their comrades blown apart before their very eyes.

After a few minutes, when no more shotgun blasts came, one of the braver men crawled over to LaFite and pushed what was left of Blandis's body off him.

"Lieutenant, what'll we do now?" he whispered in the stillness of the early evening darkness.

LaFite tried to gather his thoughts as he stared wildly around the semidarkness, looking for whoever was killing his men.

The young soldier shook LaFite's shoulder. "Lieutenant, I said what'll we do next?" he asked again.

"Fall back! Let's get the hell outta here!" LaFite said as he scrambled on hands and knees back into the heavy undergrowth surrounding his position.

"But, sir, what about the wounded?" the soldier asked to his back.

"Fuck the wounded!" LaFite whispered hoarsely over his shoulder. "We're obviously outnumbered. We'll regroup later," he added as he cowered under a banana leaf plant, his empty M-16's barrel sticking out uselessly.

Of the twenty men in his command, LaFite had only six that were unmarked by the battle, including himself.

When Hammer saw the men crawling away in the underbrush, he climbed carefully down from the banyan tree and quietly made his way in a semicircle around their position. Moving in a semicrouch, he never made a sound as he circled behind the group and then got down on his belly and crawled the rest of the way.

Within a few minutes he found two men lying side by side, whispering to each other next to a low-lying bush.

"Who the hell attacked us?" one asked.

"I dunno," the other answered. "It was only supposed to be four or five men we were after."

"Hell, there must've been fifteen or twenty that let down on us," the first replied.

Hammer rose up on his knees, his K-Bar in his hand. "Try one, you stupid sons of bitches," he growled.

As the two soldiers turned to look over their shoulders, Hammer slashed to and fro, opening both their necks to the bone.

The two men grabbed their throats, trying without success to stop the spurting blood with their fingers as they gurgled and strangled their lives away.

Hammer wiped his blade on one of the men's shirt, and stuck it back in the scabbard tied to his leg. Then he got to his feet and began to trot through the jungle toward the coast to join up with Harley and his group.

"If this is the caliber of men in the merc army," he muttered to himself, "then we ain't got nothing to worry about."

After an hour passed, LaFite got to his feet and began to gather his men around him.

"Hey, Lieutenant, look at this!" a private called from the bushes next to the trail less than twenty feet from where LaFite had gone to ground.

He walked over and shone his flashlight on the bodies lying there, gaping wounds smiling up at him from their ruined throats.

"Jesus," one of his men whispered, and crossed himself.

LaFite sighed. There was no way he was going to go after someone who could do this.

"Listen up, men," he said to the wide-eyed boys and men around him. "We'd better get our stories straight before we head back to camp."

Seventeen

The heat was like a giant fist that beat down upon the soldiers and made the metal parts of the equipment they were driving too hot to touch as Georgi Striginov moved his 505 Battalion into place in deep west Texas on the border with Mexico.

His area of coverage stretched from the city of Del Rio above the Mexican state of Coahuila, westward across the Big Bend National Park area, to El Paso, Texas, above Chihuahua, Mexico.

The land was beautiful in its stark, desertlike terrain, containing both sandy, alkali flats and mountains that had to be traversed. The average daily temperature was in triple digits, and the humidity was so low the air would suck the moisture out of a body almost faster than it could be replaced.

"It's like that old war called Desert Storm all over again," he complained to Ben Raines via scrambled radio transmission. "The sand gets in everything from food to equipment, an' I've got soldiers dropping like flies from the heat."

"Then do like the commanders in Desert Storm did," Ben advised. "Keep your daytime activities to a minimum and move your troops during the cooler evening hours."

"That's easy to say," Striginov answered testily, "but there ain't no roads down here, and you haven't lived till you've buried a fifty-ton Hemic or tank in sand up to the turrets 'cause some private ran it into a sinkhole in the dark."

Ben laughed, knowing that Striginov, like most of his Russian forebears, liked nothing more than to bitch and complain before buckling down and getting the job done.

"Well, if you're having that much trouble, maybe I'd better send one of the other bats down there to help you out," Ben suggested, tongue in cheek.

"Did I say I couldn't handle it?" Striginov asked in a hurt tone of voice. "I'll get it done, Ben. I just wanted you to know how difficult the terrain is here."

"Have you seen any sign of Mexican troops yet?" Ben asked, to change the subject.

"No. I suspect they're mostly stationed to the south of Mexico City where the action is going to be."

"Good, then don't be afraid to . . . um . . . advance your line southward as far as you like to get a better stronghold."

"All right!" Striginov answered happily. "I was hoping we weren't going to have to worry overly much about borders and such down here in the wasteland."

"I think by the time we'd be faced with any objection from the Mexican government, they're going to have their hands full with Perro Loco's army, so get as far south as you need to set up a good defensive perimeter for your troops."

"Will do, Ben."

As the big C-130 aircraft began to land one after the other on the airfields of the Pariso Navy base in Mexico, bringing Bruno Bottger's most elite troops to join Perro Loco's army, Loco met with Paco Valdez, Jim Strunk, and General Enrique Gonzalez, head of his armed forces.

"Before the soldiers of our new 'ally' from South America get here, I want to make a few things clear," Perro Loco said.

The men sitting before him in his office nodded, and he continued. "First of all, General Gonzalez, you will be in overall command of the campaign to take Mexico City. General Bottger's men will take orders from you. Is that clear?"

"Sí, comandante," Gonzalez said. He was a lean man, with-

out the paunch and sloppy habits of the men who'd preceded him in the job. He was hard as nails, and Loco knew he would stand his ground against any encroachment of his authority by Bottger or his minions.

"Secondly, when the battle plan is drawn up, I want our troops to advance on the eastern side of the country. Assign Bottger's troops to the western front. All of the passable roads are either centrally located or follow the eastern seaboard."

Valdez smiled grimly. "Also, most of the western coast consists of jungles and mountains. His men will be bogged down for weeks just trying to make headway through the country, even if there is little resistance from the Mexicans."

"What if Herr Bottger's commanders balk at following our orders?" Strunk asked.

Loco shrugged. "They are dependent upon us for their logistical support, are they not? If they don't get fuel for their vehicles or ammunition and food to replace what they use, how can they fight?"

"A good point, *comandante,*" Strunk said, nodding and smiling.

They were interrupted by a buzzing of the phone on Loco's desk. He picked it up, then said, "Of course, send them right in."

The door to his office opened and several men walked in. They stood at attention, and one stepped forward.

"Comandante, my name is Sergei Bergman, and this is Helmut Bundt. We will be commanding the forces of the New World Order sent by Bruno Bottger to aid you in your fight for Mexico."

"Good morning, gentlemen," Loco said. He waved his hand to the side. "And this is General Enrique Gonzalez, Commander in Chief of the People's Liberation Army of South America. He will relay my orders to you concerning the battle plans."

Bergman glanced at Bundt, then back at Loco. "I understood this was to be a joint operation, *comandante,* with shared command."

"Then, I'm afraid you understood incorrectly, Herr Bergman," Loco said, his voice becoming hard. "I have spent many months advancing this far, and we've suffered many casualties to push the Mexican soldiers back to Mexico City. I told President Osterman that I did not need your help, but she suggested I take it to speed things along. At no time did I offer to give up my sole command of the armies that are to fight here."

"I see," Bergman said. "I will have to discuss this with General Bottger."

"You may discuss it with anyone you wish to, but it will not change things. Either your soldiers fight under my command, or you may get back on your planes and fly back to the South American jungle where you came from."

Bergman nodded, snapped off a quick salute, and he and Bundt left the room.

Sergei used the scrambled radio in one of the C-130's to call Bruno Bottger, who had remained in South America to see to the loading of the remainder of his troops on the transport ships that would take them to Mexico.

"Herr Bottger, I've run into some problems dealing with Perro Loco here in Mexico," Bergman said.

"Such as?" Bottger asked.

"He states there will be no shared command as we discussed. He says our troops are to fight under the control of his generals."

There was a hesitation before Bottger answered. "All right, we'll play it his way for now. Do what you can under the circumstances, Sergei. The important thing is to take Mexico City before Ben Raines can intervene. Once we're in control of the capital of Mexico, I will deal with this Perro Loco in the usual manner. Then we'll see who's in command."

"Yes, sir. I just hope these idiots know something about how to prosecute a war," Sergei said.

"When I get there next week, if we see that his generals are totally incompetent, we may have to take action sooner than planned. Until then, try to do as much as you can to advance our troops toward Mexico City."

"Yes, sir, I'll try."

At the strategy meeting later that day, General Gonzalez outlined the general plan of attack.

"Our troops will proceed up the Pan American Highway with our heavy equipment, tanks, half-tracks, and personnel carriers. The lighter equipment will be sent up the east coast on the smaller roads, taking the less populated towns and clearing them of the Mexican troops stationed there. Our advance will be covered in the air by several of the Apache and Cobra helicopters provided us by President Osterman of the U.S."

Bergman nodded slowly as he surveyed the topographical map of Mexico on the table.

"And my troops, General Gonzalez?"

"We have fifteen of the Chinook choppers for the transport of your men. They can each carry from thirty-five to forty troops, depending on the weight of their weaponry. I want you and your men to proceed up the western coast, to take and hold the states of Oaxaca, Guerrero, and Michoacan on Mexico City's western flank."

"I see by the map that the country there is very desolate, with many jungles and mountains," Bergman said, giving Bundt a sidelong glance.

Gonzalez nodded. "Yes. Therefore your men will be without heavy equipment cover, no tanks or personnel carriers. But we have some smaller helicopters available to give you what air support and cover you may need, some Defenders and Kiowas."

"And the opposition we'll be facing?" Bergman asked.

"Minimal, I suspect. Since the area is so remote, the Mexican Army is depending primarily on local police and militia to defend it. Much of your fighting will be in small villages and towns rather than in large engagements with the Army."

"If the area is so remote and underpopulated, why bother with it at all?" Bergman asked.

"The Mexican people must be made to realize there is to be a new leadership in the country. Just taking Mexico City will not be enough. We must show a presence throughout the countryside to maintain control after we take the country."

Bergman had to admit the general had a point. It was not going to be enough to merely take over the government. The people themselves must be subjugated and made to understand a new world order was about to begin.

Besides, he reasoned to himself, better to let Loco's troops get chewed up in fighting the Mexican Army. They would undoubtedly suffer tremendous losses, while his troops would make short work of the peasants and locals they were going up against. All in all, he thought, the plan would work to their advantage.

"All right, General," Bergman said, "I'll have my men ready to move out in the morning."

Gonzalez nodded. He knew Bergman probably thought his job was going to be easy. Little did the German know how tough the mountain guerrillas were when it came to defending their homes and villages.

"I'll see that the helicopters are made ready and you are provided with all the supplies and ammunition you'll need for your campaign," Gonzalez said.

"And how will we be resupplied once the fighting begins?"

"The Chinooks can travel back and forth for food and ammunition. They cruise at one hundred thirty-eight knots, and have a range of over two hundred miles fully loaded. We'll set up fuel dumps along the way and there shouldn't be any problem."

"How about your troops along the coast? The roads there won't support heavy trucks."

Gonzalez smiled. "That's why we're going to use ships and boats for supplies along the way. We'll just send them up the coast to rendezvous with the troops as they make their way northward. Supplying the troops on the Pan American Highway won't be any problem, as our trucks can travel along it quite easily."

"You seem to have it all figured out, General," Bergman said, admiration in his voice.

"Thank you, Sergei. I'll give your communications officers the command frequencies we'll be using so we can keep in touch during the battles. If you run into trouble, I can use the Chinooks to send you reinforcements."

Bergman shook his head. "I'm sure that won't be necessary, General. My men are the best in the world at guerrilla warfare. I'm sure a bunch of peasants and policemen won't give us too much trouble."

Gonzalez smiled. *Famous last words,* he thought.

Eighteen

In the Presidential Palace in Mexico City, Presidente Eduardo Pena was discussing their situation with General Jose Guerra, leader of his Army.

"But, *presidente,* General Raines of the SUSA has said his intelligence sources say Perro Loco is about to make another move against us," General Guerra said.

Pena shook his head as he sipped dark red wine from a fluted, crystal glass. "No, I do not believe it. This Perro Loco has given me his word he will not move his troops any further north as long as we do not allow Raines and his Army to come into Mexico."

"And you believe this man?" Guerra asked skeptically.

Pena slowly took a long, thick cigar out of a humidor on his desk, ran it under his nose with an expression of almost ecstasy on his face, then clipped off the ends with a golden cigar cutter. "Of course. After all, we've shown him he cannot possibly prevail against us. Didn't we defeat him soundly the last time he tried?" He smiled around the butt of the cigar as he lit it with a gold lighter.

Guerra shook his head. The *presidente* was living in a dream world. He knew they would never have stopped Loco without the help of the Americans, but the young fool was too proud to admit it, even to himself it seemed.

"But, *presidente,* perhaps it wouldn't hurt to at least let Raines send us some of his equipment and weapons just in case Loco goes back on his word. Our matériel is outdated and all but useless against the more modern equipment at Loco's disposal."

The Mexican president stared at Guerra through clouds of blue smoke that smelled faintly of rum. "How many times do I have to tell you, Jose? Once we let the colossus to the north get a foot in our country, they will want to take us over just as surely as this Perro Loco *hombre.*" Pena shook his head and turned his back on Guerra to stare out his window at the peasants in the courtyard below, selling wares to the few tourists that still came to their country.

Guerra clamped his jaw shut, lest he say something he would regret. His president was a political animal who knew next to nothing about the realities of modern warfare. He would be the ruin of the country.

"Yes, *mi presidente,*" he said, dipping his head in obedience as he left the office.

He had a bad feeling about the upcoming weeks. He felt sure Perro Loco was not going to be satisfied with occupying only southern Mexico, and would soon be moving northward toward Mexico City. He returned to his office and began to make plans for that eventuality. He needed to ascertain who he could count on if push came to shove and he had to attempt to take over the government to save the country. He began to make a list of men he would approach over the next few days to discuss that very possibility. He would have to be very careful, for if the *presidente* found out he was contemplating a coup, it would mean a firing squad.

Buddy Raines was on the phone with Ben Raines. "Ben, I'm a little worried about Harley and his team," Buddy said, his voice scratchy and tinny from the scrambler.

"Why?" Ben asked.

"Jersey said she'd check in every day or two and give me a status report, but I haven't heard from her for sometime now."

"Do you have any evidence of trouble?"

"Not directly, but we saw a number of C-130's taking off and heading northward over the ocean yesterday. I think whoever is in charge of the mercs has moved the timetable up and is preparing to strike earlier than we had heard."

"Well, they can't be planning to move twenty thousand men by airplane. Have you seen any ships in the area that might be used as transports?"

"No, but they'd probably dock right on the island itself and not come through Santos."

Ben thought Buddy was right to call him. It wasn't like Jersey not to keep in touch with her backup. "If Harley and his team had to make a run for it, do you know which way they'd come?"

Buddy hesitated while he consulted a map. "Yeah, once they crossed the strait between the island and the mainland, there's only one road they could come up. There's a river a couple of miles inland that would keep them near the coast."

"Why don't you send a team of scouts along that route, just in case they're on the run and need your help. If they had to leave in a hurry, they might not have had time to pick up their radio."

"Good idea, Ben."

"And, Buddy, keep me informed, will you? I'll double-check with Mike Post and see if our satellites have picked up any unusual shipping activity in the area."

"Roger. Buddy out."

After he hung up the phone, Buddy went to the wardroom, where most of his team were having coffee and a light snack.

"Captain Stryker," Buddy said to the leader of the SEAL squad on the boat with them.

"Yes, sir," Stryker said, and got quickly to his feet.

"I'd like you to take a squad of men down the coast and see what's going on there."

Stryker raised his eyebrows. "You think Harley's team is in trouble?"

Buddy shrugged. "Don't know, but they've been out of touch for a couple of days. Wouldn't hurt to scout around down there near the passage to the island and see if there's any unusual activity."

Stryker nodded. "Good. My men have been sitting on their butts too long. They need a little action to keep the rust off."

Buddy held up his hand. "Not too much action, Matt. I wouldn't want to tip our hand unless Harley's team needs help."

"Sir," Stryker said with a hurt tone in his voice. "You know SEALs never go looking for trouble."

Buddy laughed. "No, but trouble always seems to find you guys sooner or later."

"Buddy," Corrie said as she stood up from the table where she and Beth had been having coffee.

"Yes, Corrie?"

"Beth and I'd like to go along with Captain Stryker on this mission."

Stryker shook his head when Buddy turned to look at him for his approval.

"I don't think so, General Raines," he said, a doubtful expression on his face. "We're liable to run into some heavy action out there in the jungle."

Beth jumped to her feet. "That's nothing compared to the action you're gonna see here, Captain, if you don't let us accompany you!" she snarled, her face flushed red. "These people are part of our team, and I'm damned if I'll sit on the sidelines while you go traipsing after them."

Stryker shook his head, a grin forming on his lips. "Well, if you feel that strongly about it . . ."

"Damned right we do," Corrie added.

Stryker shrugged. "Then it's okay with me, as long as you think you can keep up."

Corrie glanced at Beth and smiled. "Just watch us, Captain."

* * *

Harley broke out of the jungle and stumbled onto clean, white sand at the edge of the island. He stood for a moment, breathing in the salty sea breeze and staring at the next step to freedom, which was a mere mile or so away. The water in the strait didn't look too rough, and bent in swells rather than true waves. Luckily there were no storms in the area to make the crossing more difficult.

He searched the beach of the Ilha de Sao Sebastiao until he found two small wooden boats pulled up on the sand past the high-water mark. They were almost eight feet in length, and had oarlocks with wooden oars in them. Neither had water in the bottom, a good sign they were seaworthy.

He gave a low whistle, and his team appeared out of the jungle that was just yards from the beach. They slogged through sand that clung to their boots, making them pick their feet up in a quirky high-step as they ran toward him.

"Here's two boats. They ought to get us across the strait," he said, shoving one down toward the gentle waves lapping at the sand in the darkness.

While Hammer and Harley pushed the two boats into the water, Anna took a roll of rope from her backpack and tied the gunwale of one boat to the stern of the other.

Once the boats were floating on the waves, Coop and Jersey stumbled down the beach, their arms around each other for support, and climbed into the second boat, collapsing from the exertion of walking. Jersey was coughing almost continuously, while Coop, not quite as sick, was breathing heavily, his breath wheezing in his chest and sweat pouring from his body as his eyes looked at the others, almost as if he didn't quite recognize them in the darkness.

Anna shook her head when she noticed the flushed redness of their faces and their quick, heavy breathing. "They're both burning up with fever. The aspirin's not holding them."

Hammer dipped his hand in the water. "This water's pretty cold. Let's pour some over them. It'll help lower their temperature while we paddle across."

He took off his cap, filled it with cool saltwater, and poured it over Jersey and Coop's recumbent forms lying in the bottom of the boat.

Coop sat up, sputtering and shivering from the cold water. "Goddamn! What are you trying to do? Drown us?"

"Keep your voice down, Coop," Anna said in a low, soothing tone. "It's for your own good. We need to get your temperatures down before you fry your brains."

Coop wrapped his arms around his chest and shivered almost uncontrollably. "Okay, okay, but hurry and get us across, will you?" He glanced at Jersey lying next to him, concerned that the frigid water had caused little reaction from her. "She won't last much longer."

Hammer and Harley each took an oar and began to paddle out into the ocean, with Anna sitting between them, the rope to Coop's and Jersey's boat in her hands.

It took the two big men almost an hour to paddle the mile across the strait since the current was sideways and they had to struggle to keep the boats on course for the opposite shore. They were sweating profusely when they arrived at the other side, in spite of the coolness of the evening air.

Once on the beach, after Coop had helped Jersey climb from their boat and they'd lain propped up against a driftwood log near the jungle's edge, Harley pushed both crafts out into the ocean and let the current pull them out of sight into the darkness.

"No need leaving any traces of where we came ashore," he said.

He used a small hand flashlight to check his compass, then pointed southward into the jungle and led the team off, threading his way through the dense undergrowth as fast as he could.

"It's a damn shame we didn't have time to pick up our radio," he murmured to Anna, who was walking behind him.

"Yeah, we could've radioed Buddy to have someone meet us here and help us back to the ship."

* * *

It took them almost an hour to find the one trail heading south through the jungle. It was a wide, double-rutted path that showed signs of heavy use by both vehicles and animals. The jungle grew right down to the ruts on either side, and grew almost together overhead, giving the illusion of traveling through a long, dark tunnel in the greenery.

Hammer put his hand on Harley's shoulder. "You think it's wise to use this trail?" he asked. "That helicopter is bound to have let some men off to set up an ambush."

Harley shook his head. "Can't be helped," he said. "There's no way Jersey and Coop could make it if we stayed in the brush. This is our only chance to get them back to the ship before they die."

Hammer unslung his SPAS and jacked a shell into the chamber. "Let me take point a few hundred yards ahead," he said. "That way, when we hit the ambush, you'll have a chance."

Harley stared at his friend. "That won't give you much leeway, pal," he said.

Hammer grinned. "I won't need much. These clowns don't know enough to set up an ambush without me being able to see it first."

Harley nodded, hoping Hammer was right. Otherwise, he'd be the first to get it when the mercs opened fire.

Hammer took off at a slow lope up the trail, his eyes coursing back and forth, looking for signs of enemy presence in the bushes and dirt of the trail.

Just before he got to a bend in the path, Hammer spotted a crumpled-up cigarette package beside the trail. He squatted and picked it up. It was a German brand. His lips curled in a half smile. "Stupid bastards," he murmured to himself. He raised his nose and sniffed softly. He could smell mold, mildew, animal musk, and, yes, the faint smell of hot tobacco up ahead.

He crept back down the trail toward Harley and the others, holding up his hand in the signal to be quiet as he approached. He winced, hearing Jersey's cough from fifty yards away in the quiet of the jungle night, and knew that the mercs would have heard it too and would be ready for them.

"They're up ahead, about two hundred yards," Hammer said in a low voice to Harley.

"Any idea how many?"

Hammer shook his head. "No. I couldn't see 'em, but I sure as hell smelled 'em."

"What's the layout?"

"The road makes a bend to the right at about a hundred and fifty yards. My guess is they've straddled the trail just beyond the bend and are waiting for us to walk right up to 'em."

"You see any signs of mines or booby traps?"

"No, but that doesn't mean anything. The dirt is so soft along there, they could've planted almost anything."

As Jersey doubled over in another coughing fit, Hammer glanced at her. "I heard her from up there, so my guess is they did too. They gotta know we're close, Harley."

"That means we don't have much time to plan anything. If we don't show up soon, they're gonna come looking."

"You think we can flank 'em, come at 'em from the sides?" Hammer asked.

Harley shook his head. "Not in this jungle. They'd hear us coming before we got close enough to attack."

"That means we gotta draw them out of their hiding places to us."

Harley smiled. "You got it. They think we're trapped between them and the squad that was following us. How about we start a little commotion back here and make them think the other squad's caught up with us?"

"Sounds good to me," Hammer said.

Harley looked around at his team. "Okay, guys, here's how we do it. . . ."

Ronald Watanabe stuck his head out from the tree he was hiding behind and stared down the trail. The darkness was unrelieved even by starlight.

"Where the hell are they?" he whispered in a hoarse voice to Lieutenant Johnson a few feet away.

"I dunno, Ron," Johnson answered. "I heard 'em not ten minutes ago. They should'a been here by now."

Watanabe was nervous and scared. He remembered how they'd been snookered by this group before, and he could smell his fear-sweat over the dank, musty smell of the jungle.

"Shit! They're up to something, Larry," he said.

"You don't think they're trying to get around behind us, do you?" Johnson asked.

Suddenly, from up the trail they heard an explosion of small-arms fire and two grenades going off, sending bright, yellow reflections of fire coursing through the darkness. In the distance they heard a high-pitched scream of terror, followed by more explosions of machine-gun fire.

"Goddamn!" Watanabe hollered. "LaFite and Blandis must've caught 'em from behind."

Lieutenant Johnson burst from his cover, his M-16 held out before him. "Shit, Ronny, let's go! We don't want Jean to get all the credit for killin' those bastards."

"Come on, men!" Watanabe shouted. "They're trapped up ahead. Let's go get 'em!"

The fifteen men with Watanabe and Johnson boiled out of the jungle like ants from a disturbed nest, and began to run down the path, eyes alight with blood lust for the upcoming kill.

Running at the front of the pack, Watanabe thought he saw something out of the corner of his eye and slowed, just as a fragmentation grenade came floating out of the darkness and bounced once on the trail in front of him.

He had time to say, "Oh shit!" and to realize he'd once again been fooled, before the grenade exploded in a fireball of molten metal and flames, taking both his legs off at the knees and killing him and Johnson and five men behind them in the wink of an eye.

Two huge figures stepped from the jungle behind the group, SPAS shotguns held at waist level, the figures' teeth visible in the darkness as they grinned and opened fire.

The booming shotguns cut men down like a scythe going through grass, and were joined by the higher-pitched chatter of an Uzi as Anna stepped out onto the trail and raked her automatic weapon back and forth as if she were watering a yard.

The remaining ten men didn't get a shot off as they were blown off their feet and danced under an onslaught of bullets thick as a swarm of killer bees flitting among them.

The air was redolent with the acrid odor of cordite, blood, and human waste as seventeen men were killed in less time than it takes to tell it.

After it was over, Anna trotted back down the trail to find Jersey and Coop where they were sitting, backs against trees, as they fired into the air to distract the ambushers.

Anna shined her flashlight at them in the prearranged signal it was all over.

Coop and Jersey dropped their weapons and leaned back, exhausted by the efforts the ruse had taken on their weakened bodies.

Anna stood as close to them as she dared. "Come on, guys. It's clear sailing ahead now."

Coop glanced at Jersey, and knew she wasn't able to go on. He took a deep breath and climbed laboriously to his feet, then reached down, grabbed her arm, and heaved her up over his shoulder in a fireman's carry.

He turned toward Anna, who couldn't believe he'd found the strength to lift Jersey to his shoulder like that.

"Let's go, girl," he said, attempting his usual grin. "We got a date with a doctor."

Nineteen

Sergei Bergman picked up the phone after being told it was from his commander.

"Yes, Herr Bottger?"

"I have bad news, Sergei. I have been unable to raise either team we sent into the jungle after the spies."

Bergman sighed. He was not surprised after the way the spies had easily handled his best men at the training camp. "I see," he said simply.

"That means you must press the attack as fast as you can. We *must* take Mexico City before any word of . . . our secret weapon leaks out."

"I am sending the first teams out by helicopter today, Herr Bottger," Bergman said. "I will instruct them that speed is of the essence."

"Good. I should be there to join you within the week with the remainder of our forces and equipment. Have you had any further trouble with Perro Loco's men?"

"No. Now that they've given me our assignment, they seem content to let me maneuver our troops in any manner I see fit."

"Excellent. I'll see you in a few days, Sergei."

"Good-bye, Herr Bottger."

General Enrique Gonzalez shook his second in command's hand. Lieutenant Colonel Pedro Vega was to be the field commander for the forces being sent against the Mexicans.

"Colonel Vega, I wish you the best of luck," Gonzalez said.

Vega nodded, eager to be off to prove himself in battle. He'd been in a rear echelon during the previous battles, in charge of supplies, and now hungered for the taste of battle. "Thank you, General. I will do my best to bring honor to you and Perro Loco."

He whirled on his heels and left the office to climb into the brand-new HumVee with his colonel's colors on tiny flags on the fenders. He took the microphone off the hook under the dash and said into it, "Head out! Forward to Mexico City!"

The column of light tanks, half-tracks, and armored personnel carriers cranked up their diesel engines and began to roll out of the Navy base toward the Pan American Highway a few miles distant.

The invasion of Mexico was once again afoot.

At the same time, Bergman saluted Herman Bundt, who was to lead Bottger's forces on the western front. "Good luck, Herman," he said.

"Thank you, Sergei," Bundt answered. Then he climbed up into the lead Chinook and made a circular motion with his hand over his head to indicate the pilot should take off.

The Chinook, followed by fifteen others fully loaded with troops and equipment, all lifted off. There were four Bell OH-58 Kiowas accompanying them, flying point to protect against any aircraft the Mexicans might send up against them. It would be an uneven match, for the only choppers the Mexican government had were ancient Hueys of Vietnam vintage. The brand-new Kiowas could fly at 120 knots, and were armed with 20mm Miniguns as well as antitank missiles. They would make short work of any Huey that dared to challenge them.

Bundt was taking this first load of a little over six hundred men directly to the port cities of Salina Cruz and Luchitan in Oaxaca near the Gulf of Tehuantepec. Loco had specified those cities should be taken first, for then the Mexican Navy wouldn't be able to use their ports to stage a surprise attack on his flank.

An additional benefit, if the ships in the port could be captured, would be to use them to supply Bundt's troops by sea as they moved up the coast, a much simpler exercise than relying solely on aircraft for resupply.

In the jungle, Harley Reno and his men brought their guns up to port arms as several bright lights silhouetted them on the trail.

"Yo, Harley," Captain Stryker called.

Harley relaxed the grip on his SPAS and turned his head. "It's all right, people, it's friendlies."

Stryker and the SEALs, along with Beth and Corrie, ran up to them on the trail. When they got there, Stryker looked around at the dead men lying everywhere on the trail and in the fringes of the jungle.

"We heard sounds of a firefight and thought you might need some help," he said, "but I can see now you did just fine by yourselves."

"Yes, sir," Harley said. "But we've got a couple of sick troops and we may need some help getting them back to the ship."

Stryker leaned over and glanced past Harley to look at Coop, near the rear of the group, still carrying Jersey on his shoulder.

"Jesus," Stryker said, awe in his voice. "He looks half dead."

"At least half, sir," Harley said. "They've contracted some sort of sickness from a BW they discovered at the camp. We need to get them back as soon as possible so the docs can go to work on them."

Stryker whirled around to his men. "Jones, Baxter, get to work on some of those trees and fix up a travois. Now!"

As his men went to work preparing a sled out of jungle trees, he looked back at Harley. "I suppose it's contagious?"

"Very," Harley said, "and it works fast. It's only been twenty-four hours since Jersey was exposed, and she's very sick."

"Airborne?"

"Probably, though we don't know for sure."

Stryker pulled off his shirt, then his T-shirt. He put his outside shirt back on, and poured water on his T-shirt from his canteen. He wrapped the wet cloth around his nose and mouth. "This should do to keep us from contracting the bug."

Everyone did the same with their shirts, and soon Jersey and Coop were lying side by side on the travois and Stryker's men were taking turns dragging them back toward the ship.

Beth and Corrie and Anna walked alongside the travois, giving words of encouragement to Coop. Jersey was still unconscious, coughing in her sleep.

As they walked, Stryker got on the microphone of his communications gear and radioed the ship.

"General Raines, we got a couple of people exposed to an unknown BW here. They're pretty sick, so I need you to have the medic on the ship get in touch with one of your doctors who's an expert in this and have him tell us what to do when we get back."

"Roger, Captain Stryker," Buddy said. "We'll have everything ready by the time you return."

Dr. Larry Buck spoke with Mike Peavy, the medic on the ship. "Symptoms seem to be primarily respiratory?" he asked.

"Yes, sir, that's what I'm told. Evidently it acted pretty fast. Less than twenty-four hours after exposure, both patients are very sick."

"Okay, here's what I want you to do. Limit exposure of the patients to only one or two caregivers. The rest of the crew is to stay well away. Full isolation precautions; gloves, masks, and showers before and after contact."

"Yes, sir."

"As soon as you have them isolated, draw four vials of blood, two red-top tubes, two purple tubes, and refrigerate them immediately. Start cultures on all media of mucus and throat swabs. Got it?"

"Yes, sir."

"As soon as you've collected the specimens, start IVs and give amoxicillin alternating with whatever aminoglycocide you have on board, at full doses."

"Yes, sir," Peavy said, writing down Dr. Buck's orders as fast as he could.

"Then, once that's done, I want you to call me back with a detailed description of their signs and symptoms, especially any rashes or skin markings."

"Will do, sir."

"And, Peavy,"

"Yes, sir?"

"Be careful. Whatever this bug is, it's designed to spread fast. You might want to use your extra antibiotics to give doses to everyone on board, yourself included."

"Okay, Doc. I'll get on it as soon as they get here."

"And Ben Raines wants Harley Reno to be available for debriefing after you talk to me."

"I'll tell him, sir."

After Dr. Buck finished talking to Peavy about the symptoms Coop and Jersey were having, Harley got on the phone with Ben Raines.

"How's it look, Harley?" Ben asked.

"I don't know, General. They're both pretty sick, especially Jersey. She's barely coherent most of the time."

"Damn! And the docs have no idea what it is?"

"Uh-uh."

"How about the leader of the mercs? Any clues to his identity?"

"I've been wanting to talk to you about that, Skipper. I got to thinking back to the time we spent in Africa a few years ago."

"Oh?"

"Yeah. The leaders of the mercs's training camp are all Germans, a Bergman and a Bundt. Then we come upon a BW they're obviously working on to use against us. That bring anybody to mind?"

Ben snapped his fingers. "You think it might be Bottger again?"

"It's a thought. It'd be an awfully big coincidence to have a bunch of Krauts running the place and working on BW and not be connected to Bottger somehow."

"But we thought Bottger was killed in that helicopter crash after we took his headquarters," Ben said.

"What if he wasn't?" Harley asked. "Or, if it's not Bottger himself, maybe it's another one of the crazies he had working under him or with him. All of those New World Order guys had screws loose if you ask me."

"Good thinking, Harley. I'll have Mike Post get to work on it to see if there's any record of Bottger or one of his known associates surfacing in South America in the past five years."

"Skipper . . ."

"Yeah, Harley?"

"I just want you to know, Jersey and Coop infected themselves on purpose in order to bring us a specimen of the bug those bastards are working on. It was the bravest thing I've ever seen."

"I know, Harley. They're very special people, and we're going to pull out all the stops to make sure they come out of this okay."

"Right, General. Harley out."

Harley hung up the phone, and walked down the corridor to the door to the cabin that had been made into an isolation room for Jersey and Coop. He stood there, staring through the window at their bodies lying on the beds.

Jersey's skin was covered with sores and scabs, and was flushed red from the temperature Peavy was having trouble controlling. As he watched, she reared up in bed, coughing and gagging and choking until he couldn't watch anymore.

He slowly turned and walked back down the corridor, wondering if he would've had the courage to do what they'd done.

One of the SEALs who was working as Peavy's assistant while he took care of Coop and Jersey appeared at the end of the corridor, syringe and needle in hand.

"Mr. Reno, sir, time for your next injection of antibiotics."

"Again?" Harley asked.

"Yes, sir. Dr. Buck says we're all to get these every six hours until we get back to base."

Harley shook his head as he rolled up his sleeve and followed the sailor to the sick bay.

"Hell, I'd almost rather be shot than take all these injections."

The medic glanced up at him as he filled the syringe with colorless fluid from a vial. "Being shot is easy, sir. The question is, would you rather be like Coop and Jersey or get the shots?"

Harley sat down and clamped his jaw shut. "Well, when you put it that way . . ."

After the medic stuck him, Harley asked, "Peavy say there's been any change in Coop or Jersey?"

The young man glanced up, a sad look in his eyes. "Not yet. They're both still running fevers, but the oxygen seems to be helping Jersey breathe a little easier at least."

"Any idea what it is yet?"

The medic shrugged. "Dr. Buck says it sounds like maybe anthrax."

"Anthrax? But we've all been inoculated against that already."

"Doc says this bug is special. Evidently, they've altered it so that the old vaccines don't work."

"Great," Harley said. "That means even more shots when they get it figured out."

The medic glanced up, a worried look on his face. "You mean, *if* they get it figured out."

Twenty

Lieutenant Juan Villareal, called Juanito because of his height of barely over five feet tall, walked around the perimeter of the fortifications surrounding the town of Cardenas, just fifty miles north of Villahermosa.

He'd received a call from General Jose Guerra himself, warning him to be on the lookout for movement from the rebel forces stationed at the Navy base at Pariso. The general had told him he and his outpost were very important, as they would be the first to see the rebels if they decided to attack northward.

Juanito took pains to explain this to the soldiers manning the gun placements, that they should be very alert and that El Jefe himself had his eyes on them.

Cardenas was a rather small village, typical of southern Mexico, with no real importance other than its location just north of the rebels' encampment. The citizens were for the most part poor dirt farmers who barely grew enough food to feed themselves, with none left over to send to market. A few of the men made the one-hundred-mile round-trip to hire on as fishermen on the coast, but that pay was low and it meant spending weeks away from their families doing extremely hard work on deep-sea shrimpers and long-line fishing boats.

The Pan American Highway ran smack through the middle of the town. Hence its importance as an early warning device for the generals in Mexico City, for there was no other way the rebels could travel northward if they decided to press their war against Mexico.

Juanito clapped a young soldier on the back as he stood next to the fifty-caliber machine gun in his sandbagged outpost on the edge of town. The soldier put down the field glasses he'd been staring through and smiled at Juanito, who was a very popular commanding officer.

"Hola, Juanito," the boy said.

Juanito took a pack of American cigarettes out of his breast pocket and offered one to the boy.

"Hola, Carlos," he said. "Cigarette?"

"Ah, *americano,* eh?" Carlos said, reaching for the pack. It was a real treat when anyone had American cigarettes, as they were much better than the Mexican ones, which tasted like so much bullshit when they burned, if you could keep them going at all.

"Sí," Juanito answered, pulling one out for himself and lighting both with a kitchen match. "The generalissimo knows how important we are to the safety of Mexico, so he arranges for these to be flown in on the weekly supply plane."

Carlos glanced around at the adobe huts that made up most of the village. "Why is this flyspeck of a town so important?" he asked.

"We are the closest to the rebels," Juanito answered, though trying to explain this to a young boy with no education and a very limited intellect would be impossible, he thought.

"But I thought the war was over," Carlos said, a puzzled look on his face. "Didn't the rebel leader himself, Perro Loco, promise El Presidente he would not move farther north?"

"And since when did you begin to believe the promises of politicians, or military leaders for that matter?" Juanito said with a laugh as he took a deep drag of his cigarette and blew smoke from his nostrils.

As Carlos started to answer, Juanito noticed a large dust cloud on the horizon to the south.

"Carlos, give me those glasses," he said, taking the binoculars from around the soldier's neck and putting them to his eyes.

He choked on the smoke curling up into his face from the cigarette in the corner of his mouth when he saw a line of tanks and half-tracks coming up the Pan American Highway, with hundreds of soldiers walking along the side of the road next to the vehicles.

"Holy Mary, Mother of Christ!" Juanito whispered. "They're coming!"

Carlos took a last drag of his cigarette and threw it in the dirt, grinding it out with his boot heel. He turned and crouched behind his fifty-caliber machine gun, jacking the loading lever back to pull a shell into the firing chamber.

"Don't fire too soon," Juanito ordered. "Wait until they are within range. I've got to go radio Mexico City and tell them Loco's on the move."

Carlos nodded, sweat breaking out on his brow under his helmet. He knew he was going to die in the upcoming battle, and he hoped he would remain brave and not bring disgrace on his family.

Juanito didn't stop running until he reached the small room above a cantina he used as his office. He slapped his radio operator's feet off his desk and yelled, "The rebels are coming! Get me Mexico City on the radio."

After a moment of fiddling with dials and frequencies, the man handed the handset to Juanito.

"This is Lieutenant Juan Villareal. I must speak with General Guerra immediately!"

A tinny voice came out of the speaker. "The general is having his breakfast and cannot be disturbed," the voice said.

Juanito rolled his eyes heavenward and gritted his teeth. Here he was about to die to protect a man who couldn't be called from his table.

He took several deep breaths to calm himself, and spoke in a reasonable tone. "Then, when the general is finished with his eggs and bacon, would you inform him the rebels are on the move and are about to attack Cardenas?"

"And just where is Cardenas?" the voice asked, as if discussing the weather.

"The general will know, if you ever give him my goddamned message!" Juanito shouted before he slammed the handset back onto the radio.

He ran to a corner closet, put on his helmet and side arm, and picked up an ancient M-1 carbine dating from World War II. He walked rapidly toward the door. Just before exiting, he turned to the radio operator. "Try and notify as many of the neighboring outposts as you have time for. They must do everything they can to get ready for the onslaught."

The radio operator's eyes widened. "Can we hold them off, Juanito?"

Juanito grinned sourly. "Can a pig fly?"

Juanito made the rounds of his men, pulling some from the sandbagged outposts and putting them on roofs around the village. There was no way they could stop the rebels, but he damn sure intended to make it expensive for them to take the town.

Carlos waited until the rebel tanks and half-tracks came within five hundred yards before he opened up with the fifty-caliber.

He gritted his teeth and pulled the trigger. The big gun exploded and began to chatter and buck in his hands as it spewed forth hundreds of bullets per minute at the rebels.

Several of the soldiers walking alongside the tanks fell in their tracks, and the others scrambled to the sides of the road and fell facedown in the small ditches that ran there.

Hundreds of nine-millimeter bullets ripped into the sandbags around Carlos's emplacement, but he kept his head down and continued to fire until the barrel of the fifty-caliber was so hot it was smoking.

Carlos shifted the barrel to the tank and peppered it with fire, but the bullets ricocheted harmlessly off the armor plate of the tank.

The turret slowly swiveled until Carlos was looking down the black hole of the long barrel of the tank's cannon.

He paused in his firing long enough to cross himself and whisper a prayer to the Virgin Mary. Then he squatted and pulled again on the trigger, sending a steady stream of bullets into the tank.

He saw a puff of smoke and flame shoot out of the tank's barrel, and had time only to blink before the shell hit his outpost, exploding on impact and blowing sandbags, machine gun, and Carlos into a million pieces.

The other outposts opened fire, and men around the tanks and half-tracks burrowed even deeper into the caliche and sand around the Pan American Highway, waiting for the tanks and half-tracks to soften the village up for them.

Henry Gomez jerked on the tube of the TOW rocket in his hands, extending and arming the handheld antitank rocket. It was one of the few modern weapons that had been sent to Cardenas, and he intended to make it count in the battle raging around him. TOW stood for Target On Wire, and the shell, when fired, was guided by a fine wire attached to the launcher. All the man firing it had to do was keep the sights on the target and it would hit it up to fifteen hundred yards.

Henry leaned over the parapet of the roof he was on in time to see the tank blow Carlos into dust. His lips pressed into a fine line—Carlos was from the same village as Henry and they'd played together as children before joining the Army together to see the country.

He put the TOW rocket launcher to his shoulder and sighted on the tank. Taking a deep breath and holding it, he depressed the trigger.

A giant *whoosh* and the rocket was on its way, the wire attached to it visible as a gleaming line in the sun.

When a bullet tore into Henry's left side, just above his

waist, he jerked to the side, sending the rocket off course momentarily.

With almost superhuman effort, he straightened back up and resighted the tank. The rocket curved back and struck the tank just below the turret.

For a second, nothing happened, and Henry thought perhaps the rocket was a dud. Then the tank exploded in a giant fireball, sending a plume of black smoke and flames two hundred yards into the air. Seconds later, the fifty-caliber machine-gun bullets and several of the tank shells inside exploded. It was like the finest fireworks Henry had ever seen. Dozens of the soldiers walking behind the tank were mowed down like a harvester going through a wheat field.

Just as Henry's lips curled in a smile and he whispered, "Gotcha," an M-16 bullet entered his forehead, exploding his brain into mush and killing him instantly.

Juanito, observing this from the upper room of a nearby building, made a fist and said, "Way to go, Henry."

The burning tank was blocking the roadway, and had halted the rebels' advance for a short time.

Carlos stuck his M-1 out the window and began to fire down upon the troops pinned down at the road's edge. He managed to kill two and wound another three before he heard a strange *whoop-whoop* sound in the hot, dry air.

He glanced up in time to see a machine out of hell. It was a coal-black HueyCobra helicopter coming down at the town out of the sun. Juanito recognized it from the classes he'd taken in Officers' Candidate School. For some reason, the fact that it carried eight TOW antitank missiles and two rockets, and sported a 20mm cannon, popped unbidden into his mind.

He jerked his M-1 up at a forty-five-degree angle and began firing at the Cobra as fast as he could pull the trigger. He had little hope of doing any damage. It was like trying to hit a hawk flying overhead with a .22 rifle.

He must have done something, however, for the gunship

changed course slightly, pointed its ugly-looking snout at him, and dived.

He could see the three barrels of the 20mm cannon belching fire and flame as the helicopter roared at him out of the sky at ninety miles an hour.

The windowsill and the walls on either side of Juanito dissolved in a maelstrom of debris and splinters as three hundred 20mm slugs tore across the building. Juanito was thrown backward against a far wall, a row of red flowers blooming on his chest where the slugs had stitched a line across his body.

He groaned, blood bubbling from his lips. His last thought was to wonder if the general had finished his breakfast yet.

Lieutenant Colonel Pedro Vega had his driver pull closer to the outskirts of Cardenas. He'd learned from the previous commander of Perro Loco's troops, who'd been killed in his staff command car by a land mine while riding point, not to stray too close to the front until most of the action was over with. Vega kept his HumVee well to the back of the forward line of his troops.

The action had slowed to an occasional pop as another sniper or hidden defender of Cardenas was found and dispatched by Vega's men. All of the sandbagged outposts and gun emplacements had been destroyed. In fact, most of the inhabitants of Cardenas had been killed along with the soldiers defending the town. The streets were littered with bodies of women, children, old folks, and even cats and dogs. No one had been spared by the invading army.

Vega stepped out of his HumVee and stood next to the scorched sandbags and melted, destroyed fifty-caliber machine gun, still red with Carlos's coagulated blood on it.

Vega walked over and leaned his arm on the bent and twisted metal. "Miguel," he said to his driver. "I am ready."

Miguel Hernandez took the colonel's digital camera from a

bag hanging by a strap around his neck and quickly snapped off a couple of shots.

"Be sure to get the bodies on the street in the background," Vega ordered, adjusting his stance a bit.

Miguel shifted to the side, sighted through the viewfinder, and snapped two more times.

Vega nodded. "Good. Now get on the radio and have the tanks level the town."

"But, Colonel Vega," Miguel protested mildly, "all of the soldiers have been killed or already have run away to the fields to hide."

Vega fixed his driver with a steely stare. "Miguel, do you enjoy the privilege of driving for me?"

"Sí, mi comandante!" Miguel snapped smartly.

"Then please do not argue with my orders. I want this town leveled to the ground as a lesson to the other towns that stand between us and Mexico City. Tonight, after we bivouac for the evening, I will print up hundreds of copies of the pictures and have one of the helicopters fly ahead and drop them on the towns to the north of us."

Miguel nodded, as if he understood what his commanding officer was saying and the advanced reasoning behind it. He did know that every night the colonel downloaded the pictures that had been taken of him in various leadership roles to a laptop computer and printed them out for his scrapbook.

Miguel thought this quite silly, but then he knew little of the thought processes of officers and their need for constant aggrandizement.

Twenty-one

Herman Bundt, who, unlike Colonel Vega, flew in the lead helicopter, leaned forward and stared through the Plexiglas of the front windshield of the big Chinook chopper.

They were only a few miles from the neighboring towns of Luchitan and Salina Cruz that lay on the shores of the Gulf of Tehuantepec.

His eyes, experienced in the art of warfare, noted that though the region was mountainous and jungled inland, it leveled out into a relatively flat area near the shores of the gulf. It was a perfect staging point to test his mercenary troops in their first under-fire battle under his command.

He leaned over and pointed downward to the pilot. "Drop us off right there, where the jungle thins out and becomes a sandy plain on the outskirts of Luchitan."

"Roger," the pilot said, nodding his understanding. He spoke briefly on the ship-to-ship radio to let the other pilots know the plan.

"Have the Kiowas fly low over the town to draw any fire while we unload the troops. That's our most vulnerable time," Bundt ordered.

The pilot nodded, and relayed his orders to the pilots of the Kiowa gunships accompanying them.

The pilot grabbed Bundt's arm and pointed toward the west. Three dark shapes rose like huge buzzards from a tiny airstrip north of the town.

"Skids," the pilot said over the intercom.

"What?" Bundt asked, not familiar with the term.

"Skids. Old Huey helicopters, the kind that flew in Vietnam. They must've picked us up on their radar."

The pilot spoke again into his radio, and Bundt saw the Kiowas that were escorting them peel off into attack formation.

"Those ships must be forty years old," Bundt said. "Our Kiowas will make short work of those antiques."

The pilot turned his head to glance up at Bundt. "Don't be too sure. The skids are big, slow, and clumsy, but they're tough to bring down. 'Bout the only way to down one is to hit the prop or to kill the pilot and copilot."

"How are they armed?" Bundt asked, more out of curiosity than out of any worry about the Kiowas.

"Main weapon is a fifty-caliber machine gun in the side hatchway. The gunner is strapped to the chopper walls so he won't be thrown out when the chopper dives and banks," the pilot answered shortly.

As the Chinooks hovered feet above the ground and the assault troops bailed out of them like ants from a disturbed mound, Bundt couldn't help but stand and watch the air battle taking place in the skies over Luchitan.

The Hueys moved forward in a modified-V formation, with the two lead choppers flying almost sideways so the big fifty-caliber machine guns in their hatches could be brought to bear, while the back chopper at the apex of the V gave them cover on their flanks. Evidently the men flying the big helicopters were experienced in combat, unlike the men Bundt had flying his Kiowas, who were barely out of flight school.

First Lieutenant Gunter Kalb, pilot of the lead Kiowa, saw the lumbering Hueys and almost laughed. "No need to waste one of our missiles on those," he said on the intercom to his copilot. "I'll just rake him with our Minigun and blow him out of the sky."

The copilot, Hans Gruber, laughed into the mike. "Look how slow they are," he said. "It's a wonder they don't fall from the sky like bloated cows."

Kalb jerked up on the collective in his left hand and advanced the throttle, and the Kiowa put its nose down and screamed through the air at the Hueys, who were going so slow they almost seemed to be hovering, as if waiting to be slaughtered.

When he got within range, Kalb depressed the trigger on the 20mm Minigun in the Kiowa's nose, and grinned at the vibration from the gun as it spewed forth death at a thousand rounds a minute.

Kalb felt an almost sexual thrill as he saw the tracers in his ammo stitch a line of holes across the body of the Huey, expecting it to burst into flames and fall from the sky.

His thrill turned to panic as he saw the Huey shudder under the impact but remain otherwise unaffected.

As his ship rapidly closed on the Huey, he jerked back on the collective and tried to turn, but it was too late.

He could almost see the gunner's teeth in the wide-open hatchway of the Huey as he grinned and opened fire with his big fifty.

The gun jumped and shook in the gunner's hands, flame shooting from the barrel along with hundreds of molten lead bullets that had the Kiowa's name written on them.

The Plexiglas windshield of the Kiowa shattered, sending hundreds of razor-sharp shards of plastic into Kalb's and Gruber's faces and eyes.

Kalb let go of the collective and the throttle to cover his ruined face just as the stream of fifty-caliber bullets tore into the Kiowa's fuel tanks.

The chopper exploded in a ball of flame and smoke, sending pieces of the ship and its pilots floating toward earth.

"God damn it!" Bundt screamed on the ground when he saw the ship disintegrate above him. "You stupid bastards," he growled to himself, "use your missiles."

Almost as if the other pilots heard Bundt's plea, they peeled off from their attack and climbed out of range of the other

Hueys's machine guns. They made a wide circle overhead, able to stay out of range due to their crafts's superior airspeed.

Viktor Lassinov, a Russian pilot who'd hired on with the mercenaries under Bruno Bottger, vowed not to make the same mistake his friend, Gunter, had. He lined the lead Huey up on his mast-mounted sight and flipped the switch arming his missiles. When he pressed it, the ship shuddered as the missile was launched, and he could see the smoke of its trail as it arrowed toward the Huey.

The pilot of the Huey, who must have seen the missile streaking toward him, turned the big, clumsy Huey almost on its back in a desperate attempt to dodge the missile, but his ship was just too slow.

Seconds after the missile launch, the Huey disappeared in a ball of smoke and flame, and its wreckage soon joined that of its previous victim on the ground next to the jungle below.

The other two Hueys, seeing they were outgunned, turned tail and raced to the northwest, toward the neighboring town of Salina Cruz on the coast.

When the Kiowas turned to give chase, Bundt grabbed the mike through the window of the Chinook and ordered them back.

"Leave the bastards alone," he cried. "We need you to cover our attack of the town."

The Kiowas dutifully gave up the chase and flew back down over the outskirts of Luchitan, raking the defenders' emplacements with fire from their Miniguns and blowing a couple of ancient tanks up with their missiles.

Bundt wasted no time. He spread his hundreds of troops out to the right and left and ordered them forward, to attack the town.

All in all, Bundt felt his men acquitted themselves rather well. Though this was their first test under his command, most of the mercenaries had seen action many times before, for many different commanders. They fought not out of patriotism or any conviction for one sort of government over another, but out of greed. And Bruno Bottger was paying them very well indeed for their loyalty.

Most of the men carried Kalashnikov AK-47's, or the Chinese equivalents of them, and they poured a murderous fire into the defenders of the town of Luchitan.

A seaside port city, it wasn't built for defense from a land-based attack, most of its buildings being situated near the wharves and waters of the gulf, from which almost all of its citizens earned their meager livings.

Wisely, perhaps, the Mexican government hadn't wasted much equipment or manpower on such a small, unimportant village, so the defenders were mostly men and boys of the village who had little or no battlefield experience.

Nevertheless, they never gave up, but fought to the last man with a ferocity only those defending their homes could show. In the final event, the scouts and rangers of Bundt's force had to go door to door to root out the men who were fighting them. Bundt figured he lost more men to snipers than to the sandbagged outposts at the edge of the village.

By nightfall, all of the male inhabitants of Luchitan were dead or lying severely wounded in the streets. Most of the females were also, but the men had managed to capture quite a few. They shot the old and ugly ones, and saved the young, pretty girls for their nighttime entertainment.

As Bundt sat at a table in the mayor's office, where he'd set up his radio to contact the base at Villahermosa, he could hear the screams and pleas of the women as they were being beaten and raped repeatedly by the mercenaries.

He shook his head. Sometimes he felt this was what most of the men signed up for, rather than the money they were paid. Where else could you get a license to rape and pillage and be above any law other than God's?

Bundt was, on the other hand, a professional soldier, and he despised what was happening now in the town he and his troops had conquered. But he was also a realist, and he knew if he tried to stop what the men were doing, he'd end up with a bullet in the back before the campaign was half over.

No, better to let the animals have their fun as a reward for their fighting. After all, he reasoned to himself, one couldn't win a war fighting with choirboys.

He keyed the radio on the frequency General Enrique Gonzalez had given him.

"General," he said when Gonzalez was on the line.

"Yes, Colonel Bundt."

"Luchitan is ours," Bundt said simply.

"And your losses?" Gonzalez asked.

"One Kiowa, and thirty troops."

"And Salina Cruz?"

"We advance on it tomorrow at first light," Bundt said.

"Good. Our men are having similar success. Perhaps it will not be as difficult as we thought to take Mexico City."

"Good night, General," Bundt said. He didn't bother to tell the man these faraway towns had been practically ceded by the Mexican government, and that the closer they got to the capital, the fiercer the fighting was going to be. *The man ought to know, without me telling him, that the leaders of this country are not going to give up their positions of power, prestige, and wealth without a hell of a fight,* Bundt thought.

Bundt hung up the radio mike and leaned his head on the table. He was desperately tired, and smelled of cordite and gunpowder and blood and excrement. He wondered if he could find the energy to bathe before he ate supper.

He raised his head and saw a bottle of whiskey on the sideboard in the mayor's office. He got up, picked up the bottle, and walked slowly back toward his bunk in the next room.

"The hell with eating," he muttered as he twisted the cap off the bottle and put it to his lips.

Perhaps if he drank enough, it would drown out the sounds of women's screams and the hoarse shouts of men having their way with them.

Twenty-two

"Well," Mike Post said to Ben Raines, "it looks like the stuff has finally hit the fan."

Ben looked up from the papers on his desk. "You mean Perro Loco has started his move northward?"

Mike took the pipe out of his mouth. "Yeah. We have reliable reports his forces leveled the town of Cardenas just north of Villahermosa. Word is they left nothing in the town alive, not even the animals."

"Anything else?"

"Uh-huh. Our German friends have started a similar move on the western coast, taking out Luchitan and beginning an attack on Salinas Cruz on the Gulf of Tehuantepec."

"Any word yet on who their big man is?"

Mike nodded. "Yeah, and you're not gonna like it. Seems some of the natives in Brazil speak of a man with a thick German accent. They have a name for him in Portuguese which translates roughly as 'man with no face.' "

"No face?"

"Sounds like he's got some terrible burn scars that have left him without much expression."

"Burn scars, huh? I guess it could be our old friend Bruno Bottger after all."

"That certainly ties in with our team down there finding out they're working on BW. Bottger was always a fan of better killing through chemistry."

"What's the word on Jersey and Coop?"

"The SEALs are taking the ship out to sea and are going to steam at full throttle toward us. Meanwhile, Doctor Buck is on the way down there in one of our Ospreys."

"But there's no place for an Osprey to land at sea," Ben said.

Mike grinned. "Buck wouldn't take no for an answer. He says he'll parachute into the sea and let the SEALs pick him up. He wants to see the cultures firsthand, and wants to make sure Jersey and Coop are getting the care they need."

Ben laughed. "Can you imagine Doc Chase doing that?" he asked. "There's something to be said about having a young hotshot as our medical officer."

Mike nodded. "And, best of all, Buck's no fool. He's having all the information he's gathered forwarded to Doc Chase at his quarters. He says there's no one else in the world with as much experience with BW as Lamar."

"We're going to need both of them if we're going to manage to get a vaccine in time for it to do any good."

"What about our plans for the U.S.?" Mike asked. "I've also gotten reports from Pat O'Shea and Dan Gray that Osterman's troops are starting to move southward toward our borders."

Ben nodded and glanced at the reports on his desk. "Yeah, but no real battles yet, just some movements suggesting that Osterman plans to try and keep us busy so we won't have time to help Mexico if they ever ask us to."

"What's the Mexican president say?"

"The fool still thinks he can handle Loco by himself. I personally think he'll hold off asking for our help until they're knocking on his door . . . and then it'll be too late to save Mexico City."

"So, we just sit and wait?" Mike asked.

"Oh, no. I've just sent Jackie Malone and a couple of hundred of our best scouts up to our northern border with the U.S. They're going to parachute in and start to play some games with Osterman on her own turf. I imagine she'll be plenty pissed when Jackie starts raising hell up there."

"Sounds like things are starting to get interesting. What are your plans personally?"

"I'm going to manage things from here for right now. When my team gets back, we'll decide where the hottest spot is, and then I'll go down there and see what we can do."

"Don't you think it's about time to heed Doc Chase's recommendation and stay out of the field?" Mike asked.

Ben shook his head. "I'm not that old yet, Mike. And I hate being an armchair quarterback. I've got to be involved in the action to see how things are going."

Mike held up his hands. "Okay . . . okay, don't get your panties in a bunch."

Ben laughed. "Believe me, Mike, I'll know when it's time to hang it up."

Jackie Malone stood in the cargo bay of the big C-130 plane and looked behind her. Her second in command on this mission was a small man named Tiger Tanaka. He stood only five feet four and had a slim body that belied the muscles that rippled under his skin. He was an advanced *sensei* of several martial-arts schools, and was second to none in hand-to-hand combat.

He smiled at her as he put on the helmet that would allow him to breathe during the upcoming HALO drop. HALO stood for High Altitude, Low Opening, and was one of the most dangerous of all parachute drops. They would bail out at twenty thousand feet, encased in a full body suit similar to the ones worn by scuba divers, with self-contained oxygen masks and altitude gauges strapped to their wrists. They wouldn't open their specially designed chutes until they were under five thousand feet, at which time they'd be falling at over 120 miles an hour toward the earth.

HALO flights were designed to drop combatants behind enemy lines, where the hang time in chutes had to be minimized so as to get the men on the ground before the enemy knew they were there.

Tiger gave Jackie a small nod, his grin magnified behind the Plexiglas of his oxygen helmet, indicating the men were ready for the drop.

Two hundred men were crammed into the cargo bay, and on the jump master's signal, they would all walk out the back of the plane and jump off a specially designed ramp that was to be lowered just before the jump.

Jackie tried to smile back, but her face wouldn't cooperate. She'd received a crash course in HALO jumps, but she'd never done one before and the truth was, she was scared shitless. The idea of jumping out into the darkness, into air that was several degrees below freezing, and falling like a stone for what was surely going to seem an eternity, just didn't appeal to her at all.

Jackie was a control freak, and didn't like any situation in which she wasn't in complete control of her destiny. It was going to be hard to put her faith in the small altitude gauge on her wrist. If she was off in opening her chute by even twenty seconds, she'd end up splattered all over the countryside below.

The jump master stood beneath a red light at the end of the cargo bay, an intercom to his ear. When he got the word from the pilot, he flipped a switch turning the light from red to green, and the ramp at the rear of the ship lowered.

He gave Jackie a thumbs-up, and she took a deep breath and stepped out into the darkness.

As she fell, she put her hands at her sides and her feet together and shot downward like an arrow toward the ground below. She counted to herself so as to know when to start looking at her altitude gauge, hoping she wouldn't wait too long.

Finally, she pulled her right arm up against the resistance of the air and glanced at the gauge . . . time to do it!

Grasping the D-ring on her chest, she gave a yank. At first nothing happened, and she had time to think, "Oh, shit! My chute didn't open."

Just as she was reaching for her backup chute cord, she felt as if she'd hit a wall as her chute opened and slowed her from 120 miles an hour down to ten in a couple of seconds. "Damn, it's a good thing I double-tied my boots, or they'd have been jerked off," she thought, her heart hammering with relief as she slowed to what seemed like a crawl after the speed of her initial fall.

After discussion with Otis Warner and General Joe Winter, Ben Raines and Jackie had decided her group should parachute into eastern Iowa, between Cedar Rapids and Davenport. The area was mostly rural, with large expanses of rolling hills, few towns, and no Army bases of any size. Best of all, it was only a few hundred miles from Indianapolis, where Claire Osterman had her headquarters.

Ben and Jackie felt they could sow the seeds of hate and discontent best, as well as be a major embarrassment to Osterman, if they struck close to her main base.

Jackie hit the ground, and immediately curled into a ball and rolled, as the jump instructor had told her to. She ended up in a large field of some sort of maize, with plants growing to four feet in height. She rolled up her chute and kept her eye on the sky above her, as one of the main dangers with this many troops dropping was that one would land on your head if you didn't keep an eye out.

Slipping out of her jump suit and helmet, she immediately keyed a signal device on her shirt that would lead the others to her, so they could rendezvous in the dark.

As usual, Tiger Tanaka was the first to reach her. He had a Mini-Uzi on a strap around his neck, and held it at port arms as he turned in a small circle, making sure no one was around to give them any trouble.

Within an hour the entire force had congregated in the middle of the field.

"Injury report," Jackie said to Tiger.

"We lost six men, three whose chutes malfunctioned, two who didn't open soon enough, and one who landed on a fence post," Tiger said in a calm voice.

"Damn!" Jackie said with feeling.

"That is a very acceptable ratio for a HALO drop, Miss Jackie," Tiger said.

She glanced at him. "Try telling that to the poor bastards who hit the ground at over a hundred miles an hour," she said. Jackie hated nothing more than losing any of her troops.

She knelt in the field and pulled out her map and compass. After studying them for a couple of minutes, she stood up. "All right, men, we head out south by southwest. We're only a couple of miles from Cedar Rapids. I expect us to be in control of the town by daylight."

Jackie sent squads out in a circular ring around the town. The first objective was to cut the town off from the outside world.

All telephone lines coming into the city were cut, and transformers were blown off their poles so that merely splicing the wires back together wouldn't resume service.

Next, the cellular microwave transmitting towers were dynamited, destroying the usefulness of any cell phones that might still be in use in the town.

After all communications, other than shortwave or CB radio, were halted, Jackie led a squad to take over the town's authority figures. Separate squads were sent to each police station as well as the mayor's and city council's offices.

Most of the police, when faced with commandos carrying Uzis and/or M-16's, gave up quietly. A couple who tried to resist were shot, but only one had to be killed.

By 0800, the town was in Jackie's hands. Roadblocks were set up on all roads leading into or out of the town, with her troops dressed as local policemen. The story used to turn away travelers was that there was a plague of unknown origin in the town and it had been placed in quarantine for the time being.

Interrogation squads began their work, ferreting out citizens who were sympathetic to the SUSA's aim to prevent another war with the U.S. These men and women were issued guns and allowed to resume some of the governmental functions of the city.

Jackie's plan was to delay face-to-face confrontation with the Army of the U.S. as long as she could. She wanted to take as many small towns and villages as possible before Osterman and her cronies knew they were under siege.

Once Cedar Rapids was secure, she left a token force to hold the town while she and the rest of her troops moved on to Davenport, a hundred miles closer to Indianapolis and Claire Osterman's home grounds.

The guerrilla war had begun.

Twenty-three

After Captain Matt Stryker and his men picked Dr. Larry Buck out of the ocean in a Zodiac, along with a large waterproof bag containing his equipment, they took him to the ship.

Thirty minutes later, dressed in a state-of-the-art Racal suit to prevent contamination, he was examining Jersey and Coop in the cabin used as a medical ward.

He had Jersey sit up in bed, her back propped up against pillows, and raised her gown. He put a stethoscope to her chest, just under her left breast.

"Breathe in and out slowly," he said, his voice muffled inside the self-contained helmet of the orange Racal suit.

Jersey looked much better after her course of antibiotics, but she was still having fever and chills and still coughing frequently.

After listening for a few moments, Buck nodded and stepped back from the bed. "Your lungs are sounding better, Jersey. Some of the pneumonia is clearing."

"They don't feel much better," she complained. "I still feel like an elephant is sitting on my chest."

He nodded. "That's typical of respiratory anthrax, but if Captain Stryker's medic hadn't pumped you full of antibiotics, you'd be dead by now."

From the next bed, Coop, who'd turned his head when Jersey's chest was bared, spoke up. "I always said Jerse was too damned tough for any bug to kill."

Coop, who hadn't been as far along in the sickness when the antibiotics were started, was looking almost well.

Buck examined him by listening to his lungs and poking around on his stomach to see if the swelling in his liver had gone down, and pronounced him cured of the infection.

"Jersey, however, is going to have to stay in quarantine for a few more days."

Coop bounded out of bed and began to put his clothes on. "Looks like you're going to lose your roommate, Jerse," he said with a grin.

She turned her pale face toward him and tried to smile. "I never thought I'd say this, Coop, but I'm gonna miss you."

He stepped to her bedside and leaned down to plant a gentle kiss on her cheek. "I'm gonna miss you too." He stood up and smiled. "But I'm sure as hell not going to miss those blasted needles the medic has been sticking in me every hour."

Buck smiled and shook his head. "No, I don't believe you are going to miss those, Coop. Now that you're cured, your blood is full of antibodies to the bacteria. We're going to need to get lots of it to try and use it to make a vaccine against this new strain of anthrax."

Jersey gave a short laugh. "Poor Coop. Out of the frying pan and into the fire."

"You mean I'm gonna have to be stuck some more?" he cried, a look of horror on his face.

"Lots more, I'm afraid," Buck.

Coop held out his arms, showing the doctor the myriad black and blue spots where needles had penetrated. "I don't think I have any veins left in my arms to get blood out of, Doc," he said.

Buck shrugged and winked at Jersey so Coop couldn't see. "Well, if that's the case, we can always draw it from your femoral vein."

"My femoral vein? Where in the hell is that?" Coop asked, a look of disbelief on his face.

Buck pointed at his groin. "Right there, next to your pubic bone."

Coop covered himself with both hands. "Oh, no, you don't. I'm sure you can still find a small vein or two in my arms," he said, nodding his head.

"I hope so," Buck said, " 'cause a femoral stick is very painful."

"Shit," Coop said, putting his hand on his forehead. "I think I feel a relapse comin' on, Doc. Maybe my antibodies aren't quite ready yet."

Buck laughed and said, "Get the hell out of here, Coop. I need to talk to Jersey for a while. Tell the cook to fix you a couple of steaks. We need to build your blood up for the upcoming tests."

"Yeah, I already feel like I'm a quart low," Coop said dejectedly as he walked out of the room.

Jersey looked at Buck as he sat on the edge of her bed. "Any progress with the cultures so far?" she asked.

He nodded. "It looks like the scientists took a regular strain of anthrax and played with it until they got the mutation they wanted. Normal respiratory anthrax is only caught by inhaling spores, and isn't capable of being passed person to person. This strain, however, in addition to being much more virulent, can evidently be caught from anyone who is infected."

"That's right," Jersey said. "I was the only one who was in actual contact with the liquid sample I took from the lab. Coop caught the bug from me."

"That's what I feared," Buck said, a serious look on his face.

"But why didn't our previous vaccine work against this strain?" she asked.

"I think, actually, it did to a small degree," Buck said. "Otherwise you would never have made it as long as you did without treatment."

"How long will it take the new vaccine to do its job?"

"In most cases, we need to vaccinate troops at least two

weeks before they're exposed, or the new vaccine won't have time to build up the antibodies necessary for full protection."

"But what if the mercs use it before we're ready?"

"What I plan to do is to give all of our troops shots of gamma globulin now, to kick their immune systems into high gear while we're making the new vaccine. That may buy us a little time until the vaccine takes effect. And it should cut the response time down to one week instead of two."

"I'm afraid that's still gonna be cutting it close," Jersey said. "The mercs were all ready to move out last week."

Buck nodded. "Yeah. We just heard from Ben on the radio that the attacks have already begun in Mexico."

Jersey held out her arms. "Then take all the blood you need, Larry. We need to get that vaccine ready as soon as possible."

"I'm already working on it, Jersey." He walked toward the door to her cabin. "With any luck, we'll have the first vials of vaccine coming out in less than a week, thanks to yours and Coop's blood."

General Bradley Stevens, Jr., walked into Claire's office and threw a sheaf of papers onto her desk.

"What are those?" she asked.

"Reports from our radar installations. There was an unidentified plane flying over our airspace last night."

"How high?"

"It never got below twenty thousand feet."

"You think it was a bomber?"

He shook his head. "No. If it had planned to drop bombs, it would have dropped to ten thousand feet or less for a night drop."

She leaned back in her chair, her eyes narrowed. "Parachute troops?"

He shrugged. "I just don't know. If they were going to parachute troops in, I'd think there would have been many more planes. And I don't see how they'd be able to drop troops from that altitude."

"Where did the flight originate?" she asked, knowing somehow Ben Raines had some dirty trick or another up his sleeve.

"Looks like it came from Louisiana, curved over the panhandle of Texas, then straight up toward Iowa."

"Iowa? What the hell would they want with Iowa? You think maybe the SUSA's short of corn or grain?" she asked with a sarcastic smile on her face.

"No, but Iowa's one of the few places where we don't have a strong military presence. It also happens to be the state with a populace more sympathetic to Raines and his brand of government than most of our other ones are."

"Well, General," she said, leaning forward to put her elbows on her desk, "if Raines wants Iowa, he's welcome to it. As far as I can see, the state is practically worthless."

"Except it produces almost a third of our foodstuffs, Madame President. And I don't know if the people are going to put up with much more rationing."

She slammed her hand down on the desk. "The people will do what I damn well tell them to do, and don't you forget that for a moment, General Stevens."

He clamped his jaw shut. He'd forgotten how resistant Claire was to anything she didn't agree with. It was her worst failing as an administrator. She continually surrounded herself with yes-men who didn't dare to tell her the truth, unless it was favorable to her beliefs. She reminded him of Adolf Hitler in a lot of ways, and, he reminded himself, Hitler had managed to lose a war that he should have won.

"What would you like me to do about these reports?" he asked.

She thought for a moment, then said, "Send a platoon of troops from the nearest base we have over there to check it out. Make sure they carry some radios that can contact us with what they find. If Ben Raines is trying something sneaky, I want to know about it."

"Yes, ma'am," Stevens said, saluting and leaving the room before he got himself in further trouble by speaking his mind. That was one of the worst sins you could commit in Claire's presence, speaking the truth.

When he got to his office, he called his aide and said, "Send a squad of troops to Iowa, the Cedar Rapids area. Check 'em out a helicopter and tell 'em to report any suspicious sightings or happenings in the area."

After he gave the order, he went back to his battle plans. Claire had ordered him to step up the activity on the southern border with the SUSA, and he needed to make sure it was done right.

Twenty-four

Lieutenant Tommy Bell sat in the rear compartment of the Huey helicopter with the rest of the eight men that had been sent to check out a radar sighting over Cedar Rapids, Iowa.

He was plenty pissed off. The rest of his battalion was moving south to confront Ben Raines's Rebel forces, and here he was playing nursemaid to a squad of men doing police duties.

Damn, he thought, *I'll never get promoted unless I get to see some action.* Both of his brothers, neither of which had graduated from Officers' Candidate School with grades as high as his, were a full rank ahead of him. Due mainly to their luck in being in the right place at the right time and seeing heavy action in the last war.

As the Huey circled lower and lower over Cedar Rapids, Bell leaned out the hatchway and took a close look at the town. Nothing seemed amiss. People were moving about on the street; traffic, what little there was of it due to stringent gasoline rationing, seemed to be moving normally; and except for the roadblocks on the highway leading into town, all was as it should be for a sleepy little farming town.

Bell grabbed the intercom mike and said, "Put her down in the town square, there near the police station."

As the big, ungainly chopper settled to the ground on its skids, Bell jumped from the hatch, his M-16 cradled in his arms, and jogged across the grass-covered square toward the main police station. He intended to ask the officer in charge if anything strange had been reported the night before and to get him to explain the purpose of the roadblocks.

Jim McAfee and Joey Rodriguez, his corporals, followed him toward the station after telling the rest of the men to stand easy in the chopper.

The three soldiers entered the police station, their rifles at the ready in case of trouble.

The ready room of the station was empty, except for a short Asian man sitting behind the main desk with a sign on it that said DESK SERGEANT.

"Can I help you gentlemen?" he asked, evidently not taking much notice of their rifles.

"Who's in charge here?" Bell asked, looking around the room suspiciously. There wasn't much action, but then it was early in the day and a town this small probably didn't have a whole lot of crime anyway.

The desk sergeant wrinkled his forehead. "Why, that'd be the chief of police, Jackie Malone," he answered.

"Would you get him down here?" Bell asked.

"Sure," the man answered, "only it's a her, not a him."

"What?" Bell asked.

"The chief is a lady," the desk sergeant answered with a smile as he walked to a nearby door that had CHIEF OF POLICE written on it.

He knocked on the door, opened it, and stuck his head inside. "There are a couple of gentlemen to see you, ma'am."

After a minute or so, a slim, attractive woman wearing a blue uniform walked into the room from the office.

She and the desk sergeant stood in front of Bell and his corporals. "What can I do for you?" she asked.

"We're here to see if anything out of the ordinary was reported last night. We had a radar sighting over in Indianapolis of an unidentified plane flying over this area."

Before she could answer, Jim McAfee cocked his M-16 and lowered the barrel to point at the two police officers.

"There's something fishy here, Tommy," he said, glaring at the two people in front of him.

Bell glanced at Jim, thinking his corporal had gone crazy. "What's the matter with you, Jim?"

McAfee pointed with his rifle. "Looky there. Their name badges are all wrong."

Bell turned around to look. The name badge on the Asian man's pocket said Myron Applegate, while that on the female's chest read John Malcolm.

"Son of a . . ." Bell started to say as he began to raise his rifle.

Tiger Tanaka exploded into action, his right leg moving almost faster than the eye could see, swinging up and around, clipping Jim McAfee on the chin and dropping him like a stone. Continuing his spin, Tiger whirled around and with a spinning back-kick, caught John Rodriguez in the stomach, doubling him over and to his knees.

Before Bell's rifle moved six inches, Jackie Malone stepped in and swung a straight right jab into his chin, putting out his lights and knocking him to the floor.

After handcuffs were applied all around, Jackie motioned with her head toward the chopper outside, still sitting on the square with its rotors turning.

"Get them in here," she said. "We can use the Huey."

Tiger glanced at the name Bell on Tommy's left breast pocket, then walked nonchalantly out the door toward the chopper.

When he was almost to it, he made a cutting motion across his neck to the pilot and waited until the engine had been shut down.

He walked under the slowing blades without ducking—at his height he had no need to—and called to the men. "Lieutenant Bell says for you men to come into the station and get some donuts and coffee. He's gonna be a while."

The men grinned and piled out of the Huey, a couple pausing to light cigarettes.

"Follow me and I'll take you to your lieutenant," Tiger said, suppressing a smile at the gullibility of the soldiers, who clearly were expecting no trouble.

He stepped to the side as they entered the station, and picked up Bell's M-16, which he'd left there.

Jackie Malone was standing behind the desk sergeant's desk, smiling sweetly at the men as they gathered before her. None had their weapons at the ready.

She pulled an Uzi from behind the desk and casually pointed it at the soldiers. "I'm terribly sorry, gentlemen, but I'm afraid I'm going to need your helicopter."

Two of the men at the rear made a motion to raise their rifles, until Tiger, who was behind them, cocked his M-16 with a loud metallic click.

"Stand down, soldiers," he said in a gruff voice, pointing the rifle at them.

They all dropped their weapons and raised their hands.

"If you men would be so kind as to strip down to your skivvies, I'm going to need your uniforms too," Jackie said with a smile.

After the men were stripped down to undershorts and T-shirts, Tiger put them all in the drunk tank, along with Bell, McAfee, and Rodriguez.

He walked back to the office Jackie was using. "Not a bad morning's work," he said.

She agreed. "Now, we can use those uniforms and that chopper to make a little trip to the Air National Guard base down the road. I'll bet they still have a couple of choppers or airplanes we can use."

"I can't wait," Tiger said with a savage grin.

The Huey, piloted by one of Jackie Malone's men and containing fifteen men, most of whom were dressed in Tommy Bell's squad's uniforms, came in low out of the sun toward the landing field at the George W. Bush Air National Guard

Base in Peoria, Illinois, a little over a hundred miles northwest of Indianapolis.

The radio crackled to life. "Unidentified helicopter, this is the air traffic control tower at Bush Air National Guard Base. Please identify yourself," the scratchy voice commanded.

George Grant, pilot of the chopper, keyed his microphone. "Search and rescue squad from Indianapolis under the command of Lieutenant Thomas Bell," he said. "One of our men has been badly injured and we need to land for immediate medical attention."

"We're at minimal status currently," the voice answered. "Most of our troops have been sent south. Can't you make it to Indianapolis?"

"Negative," Grant said, putting some urgency in his voice. "Our man is bleeding badly and we need to stabilize him before traveling further."

"Come in on Landing Field Z-22," the tower said. "We'll have our medic standing by."

Grant grinned over his shoulder at Jackie Malone, who was standing in the doorway behind him. She returned the smile and gave him a thumbs-up sign.

Tanaka, who was lying on a stretcher in the cargo hold with ketchup and bandages on his uniform, laid his head back and assumed an agonized expression.

"Take it easy, Tiger," Jackie said. "You're not trying for an Oscar here."

He nodded as he slipped a .45 automatic under the bandages on his chest, and feigned unconsciousness as the chopper settled to the tarmac near a large hangar.

As Jackie and the other men jumped to the ground, an ambulance screeched to a stop next to the Huey and a young man who looked to be no older than eighteen rushed to the hatchway.

He motioned to two of Jackie's men, and they picked the stretcher up and put it in the back of the ambulance.

Just before the medic climbed in, Jackie asked, "The tower said you were at minimal staffing. What's going on?"

The medic glanced at her lieutenant's bars, then replied, "Most of the troops and aircraft have been sent down to Oklahoma to fight the Rebs. There ain't but a few of us left here."

"Exactly how many?" Jackie asked casually.

Sensing something was wrong, the medic jumped into the back of the ambulance, only to be met with Tiger's .45 pointing at his face.

"The lady asked how many," Tiger said, a menacing scowl on his face.

The medic hung his head. " 'Bout six, I guess."

"Okay, that's better," Jackie said. "Now, where is your commanding officer's office?"

Lieutenant Colonel Hadley Crow was sitting behind his desk when Jackie and two of her men walked in without knocking.

Crow jumped to his feet. He was unarmed. "What's the meaning of this?" he barked, as if he were still in command of the situation.

Jackie gave a casual shrug. "You've just been invaded, Colonel. We are taking over your base."

"But . . . but . . . that's impossible!" Crow sputtered, looking around as if he needed someone to explain further.

"No, it's not," Jackie said patiently. "Now, if you don't want your men slaughtered unnecessarily, you'll get on the phone and have them assemble here in your office."

"But what reason can I give them?" he asked.

"Tell them it's a surprise inspection."

"They'll never believe that."

"You'd better make them believe it, Colonel, or you'll have the deaths of your entire command on your conscience," Jackie said in a voice that showed she wasn't kidding.

The colonel slumped back into his chair and reached for the phone.

Within twenty minutes, he had seven airmen standing at attention in the hangar below his office. Jackie accompanied him to stand before them.

"You men are all under house arrest," she said as her troops stepped out from hiding and surrounded the men. "If you'll go with the colonel here, I'm sure we can find room for all of you."

After the colonel and his men were led off, Tiger and Jackie walked around the hangar, inspecting the planes that were there.

"Jesus," Tiger said, "here's an A-10 Warthog, one of the best of the old ground-attack/strike fighters."

"Yeah, and over there's an F-111 Aardvark," Jackie said, "one of the first fighter-bombers that could make low-level precision bombing attacks by day or night."

Tiger glanced at her, grinning. "You know, with these and the Huey, we could give President Osterman a real sleepless night."

Jackie nodded. "You've got a point there, Tiger. Let's go get on the horn to Ben and see what he thinks of the idea."

Twenty-five

Claire Osterman was furious. She grabbed an ashtray on her desk and flung it against a far wall, narrowly missing General Bradley Stevens, Jr., who ducked and then, realizing how silly it made him look, stood back at attention.

"What the hell do you mean you haven't heard from the squad you sent out yesterday?" she screamed, making even Herb Knoff, who was more or less used to her tantrums, wince.

"As I said before, Madame President, we haven't been able to raise Lieutenant Bell or the pilot on any of our frequencies since they flew over Cedar Rapids, Iowa, yesterday."

"And just why not, General? Do you think they vanished into thin air?"

"No, ma'am. It could be anything from a radio malfunction to a simple plane crash. They were flying in a fifty-year-old Huey helicopter and it may have developed engine trouble . . . or something."

"I don't believe that for a moment, and I have a sneaking suspicion you don't either, General," Claire said, calming down somewhat.

Stevens shook his head. "No, ma'am. If they had a radio malfunction, they would have landed and checked in on a land-line, and if the chopper had crashed, we would have had a report of it by now from the civilian authorities."

"So, like me you think Ben Raines had something to do with this disappearance of one of my helicopters?" she asked, glancing at Herb to make sure he was paying attention.

"Either that, or possibly a group of our own rebels, supporters of Otis Warner or General Winter," Stevens said, choosing his words very carefully so as not to trigger another outburst from Claire.

"Son of a bitch!" she hollered again, slamming her hand down on her desk so hard the phone jumped in the air. "First those bastards try and kill me and take over the country. Then they set traitors on my soldiers and kill *them.*" She looked at the ceiling as if speaking directly to God himself. "Will I never be quit of those assholes?" she asked rhetorically.

"What would you like me to do, Madame President? Send another squad to check on the first?" Stevens asked diffidently.

She glared at him. "You're the fucking general, General, do whatever you think best."

He nodded and turned to leave.

"But," Claire continued before he could reach the door, "if it were me, I'd be very careful about sending more men and expensive equipment to try and find men who are already undoubtedly dead. Otherwise, you may end up sending yet another squad to check on the checkers." She paused, a deadly look on her face. "Do you get my drift, General?"

"Yes, ma'am, I understand."

"After all," she said with a shrug, "even if rebel forces have captured the helicopter, how much damage can a fifty-year-old machine do to us?"

Stevens was afraid to tell her just how awesome a fighting machine a Huey with a fifty-caliber machine gun mounted in the hatchway could be, even if it was fifty years old. If she hadn't seen films of the Vietnam War or Desert Storm, who was he to risk his stars by reminding her?

Ben Raines threw back his head and laughed out loud. "Jesus, Jackie, I sent you up there to do a little guerrilla warfare and maybe recruit some rebels. I didn't expect you to invade the U.S. and capture their bases one by one."

"Like they say, General Ben, never send a woman to do a man's job. She may just surprise you with the results."

"You can say that again," Ben said, still laughing. "Now just what do you have in mind to do next? Charge Indianapolis and make Sugar Babe Osterman surrender?"

"Something like that," Jackie purred.

"What?" Ben asked, sitting up straight in his chair. "Now, Jackie," he reasoned, "don't do anything foolish."

"Too late, Ben, I've already joined the Army."

Ben chuckled. Jackie was one of his best commanding generals. In spite of her good looks and youthful appearance, she was known as Ironsides by her troops. When given an objective, no matter how tough or impossible it seemed, she drove her men, and herself, unmercifully until the goal was accomplished. There was not one of her troops who wouldn't throw himself on a grenade to save her life.

"Seriously, what are your plans?" Ben asked.

"Well, I thought you might give that bitch Osterman a call and demand she draw her troops back from the border."

"And just why would she do that?" Ben asked, intrigued at the way Jackie's mind worked.

"Because you might remind her that if she crosses us again, there is no place on earth safe for her to hide in, and if we coordinate it just right, at that exact moment my troops and I can hit her base with a few bombs and rockets."

"You'll never hit her," Ben said. "From what our intel says, she's dug in deep underground in fortified bunkers."

"That's not the point, Ben, darlin'," Jackie continued. "I'm not trying to kill her, just to show her she can run but she can't hide. Can you imagine the paranoia she's gonna feel when you tell her you can get her and seconds later my attack bombers hit her base? I guarantee it'll scare the shit out of her to be so vulnerable in her own home base."

Ben hesitated a moment while he thought it over. "That's a great idea, Jackie, but do you think you can pull it off with minimal casualties? I'd love to put a scare into Sugar Babe, but not if it means risking your life to do it."

"Sure, it'll be a piece of cake. From takeoff to strike, our time is fifteen minutes. She won't have time to scramble an egg, much less her defense fighters. I figure we can make two or three quick passes, then get the hell out of there before they know what's hit them."

"And then?"

"We sweep around under their radar and land back here at the National Guard base. They'll think we just disappeared in thin air."

Ben nodded, though Jackie couldn't see the gesture. "Good. Let's do it."

Claire Osterman's head was thrown back against the pillow and she had her hands in Herb Knoff's hair. "Come on, baby, come on," she urged as she bucked beneath him.

She almost screamed in frustration when the phone on her bedside table rang.

"Oh, goddamnit!" she growled, the mood broken. She pushed him off her, ignoring the sweaty, pleading look on his face.

"This had better be damned important," she yelled into the phone, breathing heavily and glancing at the clock. It was five minutes until midnight.

Her secretary said, "I hate to interrupt you, Madame President. . . ."

"Not as much as *I* hate it, Gladys," she growled. "What is it?"

"I have a man on the phone who says he is General Ben Raines."

"Ben Raines?" Claire asked incredulously.

"Yes, ma'am. Shall I tell him to call back at a more appropriate hour?"

"Of course not, you fool! Put him through."

"Yes, ma'am."

There was a series of clicking, buzzing noises, and then the voice of the man Claire hated above all others was on the line, speaking as if he were a long-lost friend.

"Hello, Sugar Babe," he said.

"Don't call me that, you bastard! What do you want?" she asked heatedly.

"I thought I might prevail upon you to move your troops back from our borders and prevent you from making another terrible mistake."

"My troops are just undergoing training exercises on our own territory, Ben," she said, trying to calm herself.

"Yeah, sure, Sugar Babe. But I would like you to try and remember what happened the last couple of times you tried to cause trouble between our countries. You got your ass kicked but good," he added.

"Listen, you arrogant son of a bitch," she yelled into the phone. "It's you that's going to get his ass kicked this time, and that's a promise."

"Modern warfare is such a bitch, Claire," he said reasonably, as if he hadn't heard her. "In the old days, leaders could sit behind their desks thousands of miles from the front and send young men and women into combat with nary a risk to their own life and limb."

"So what?" she asked, puzzled at what he was trying to tell her.

"Well, those days are gone forever. Now, if a leader decides to cause a war, that leader must be shown that there is no safe place for those who cause the needless death of others."

"What are you saying, Ben?" she asked, sitting up straight in bed and shoving the covers aside. "Are you trying to threaten me?"

"Not trying, sweetie, I'm promising you that if you continue with this ill-advised course of action, it will be you who pays the ultimate price, not just your troops."

"Listen, you son of a bitch, I'm not in the least afraid of you or what you think you can do," she shouted.

"You should be, Claire, you should be very afraid. Look out your window, if you think I'm blowing smoke," Ben said, and then he hung up, the click loud in Claire's ear.

She slammed the phone down, shaking from anger. She looked at Herb, lying next to her, a puzzled look on his face, trying to understand what had just been said.

She lay back on her pillows and stretched her hand out to rub the hair on his chest. "Now, where were we, darling?"

As Herb grinned and rolled over to snuggle up against her, the entire room shook from an explosion that must have been directly overhead.

Plaster fell from the ceiling and sprinkled down on the bed as if it were snowing inside the room, while another deep booming vibrated the bed, knocking her phone off the bedside table and breaking the lamp.

"Shit!" she hollered, and scrambled from the bed, grabbing a nightgown from the chair and running to her door.

General Bradley Stevens, whose room was just down the hall of the underground bunker, appeared in the hallway, his hair tousled as if he'd just woken up.

"What the hell . . ." he said, looking around him in disbelief as pieces of the walls disintegrated and began to tumble to the floor.

"Get on the phone and find out what the hell is happening!" Claire screamed at him, forgetting her nightgown was unfastened and her breasts exposed.

Stevens glanced at her, then quickly turned away as he hurried down the hall to the guard's desk at the end of the corridor.

He grabbed the phone and dialed a series of numbers, having to yell into the phone to make himself heard over the *rat-a-tat* of heavy machine-gun fire coming from above.

After a second, he yelled at her, "Get back in your room and lock your door . . . we're under attack!"

He threw the phone down and ran up the stairs to the first

floor, and burst out the fortified steel door onto the grass outside the building.

He ducked as what looked like a Warthog dived directly at him, spraying the ground with 30mm cannon fire, which danced a trail of death four feet to his left and shattered the walls next to him. Though the walls were made of three feet of reinforced concrete over stainless steel, the armor-piercing shells tipped with depleted uranium went though them like grain through a goose.

Stevens dove to the ground and covered his head with his hands. He peeked out from under his arms to look at the nearest hangar, where several men were trying to get fighter planes launched.

He was just in time to see an F-111 Aardvark follow the Warthog in a steep dive at over six hundred miles an hour. As the Aardvark pulled up, twin rockets loosed themselves from its wings and arrowed down at the fighter planes, still on the ground.

The missiles exploded, blowing both planes and a dozen men into tiny bits, and sent a fireball three hundred feet into the air.

Stevens rolled to the side and caught sight of an ancient Huey helicopter hovering near a distant hangar, pouring fifty-caliber rounds into the motor pool vehicles. A HumVee, with the general's flag on its fenders, exploded and jumped into the air as if it'd been kicked. The fireball from the HumVee incinerated six men nearby and set three other vehicles on fire.

Stevens laid his head on his arms, wishing Claire Osterman could witness the damage a fifty-year-old machine could do.

Two minutes later, the attackers were gone, as if they'd never existed, leaving behind them a base in utter ruins. Buildings were shattered and caved in, planes and wreckage were burning, sirens wailing, men screaming and groaning in pain, and all was mass confusion.

Stevens jumped to his feet and began to run across the tarmac, yelling at soldiers to get some planes airborne to chase the bastards who'd done this to his base.

It took another fifteen minutes to scramble anything, as burning wreckage had to be moved and fires put out before other planes could be fueled.

By the time they were in the air, Stevens was in the control tower, bending over a radarscope, yelling at the airman there to find out where the attackers had gone.

The young man glanced up, fear in his face. "I don't know, sir. They came in under the radar and left the same way. Nothing ever showed up on my scope at all."

"That's impossible!" Stevens screamed, already wondering how he was ever going to explain this to Osterman.

"What do I tell the pursuit planes, General?" the tower controlman asked, holding a mike in his hand.

"Tell 'em they'd better damned well find something to shoot at or not to bother coming back!" he yelled, making the man cringe back as if he were about to be hit.

He bent over his mike. "Tower to Eagle One, Two, and Three, quarter the skies and search for bogeys. Repeat, search for bogeys until you find something," he repeated, looking over his shoulder at Stevens.

Twenty-six

Bruno Bottger stood on the prow of the first of three large transport ships as they sailed into the harbor at Pariso. In the ships with him were twenty thousand battle-hardened mercenaries along with various and sundry equipment they would need on the campaign to take first Mexico City, then to invade and eventually conquer the SUSA and Ben Raines's Rebel forces.

Perro Loco, Paco Valdez, and Jim Strunk were on the dock to welcome him.

"Look at him, riding the front of the ship like some conquering hero," Valdez sneered to Loco. "I think he is one we're going to have to watch very carefully, *comandante,*" he said.

"I agree, sir," Strunk added. "He is used to commanding, and I do not believe he will take kindly to playing second fiddle to anyone."

Loco dismissed their warnings with a wave of his hand. "Do not worry. I am not underestimating the difficulty of sharing a command with such a person." He grinned as the gangplank of Bottger's ship was lowered to the dock. "As the old saying goes, 'when you grab a tiger by the tail, it is most important not to let go, lest you be eaten.' "

"So, you plan to 'share' command with this German bigot?" Valdez asked.

"I think it would be wise to let him think so," Loco said. "I will do as General Eisenhower did in the Second World War with the British General Montgomery, who was at least as big an egomaniac as this Bottger is reputed to be. I will give him command of his troops on the western borders of Mexico, at least until we reach and take Mexico City." He shrugged. "After that, it may well be time to see if an unfortunate accident cannot be arranged for Herr Bottger."

Strunk grinned, his fingers caressing the hilt of his commando knife in its scabbard on his belt. "I can hardly wait, *comandante.*"

Bottger strolled up the dock, looking around as if he owned the world, followed closely by his second in command, Sergei Bergman, who was talking earnestly in his ear.

At the end of the pier, Loco approached him.

Bottger gave a quick nod of his head and stuck out his hand. "It is a pleasure to finally meet you face-to-face, Señor Loco."

"Likewise, Herr Bottger," Loco said, smiling widely and taking the hand.

Loco had to fight the urge to stare at the mass of scar tissue that covered Bottger's face and head. It was as if the man were wearing a rubber mask that hardly moved as he spoke, the tissue slick and shiny in the Mexican sun.

Bottger, who was used to such a reaction, briefly fingered the scars. "I see you have noticed the gift Ben Raines gave me on our last encounter. As you might well imagine, I have much to repay him for."

Loco cleared his throat and forced his eyes away from the horror that was Bottger's face. "Come, Herr Bottger. I have a meal ready for us at my headquarters, and have prepared a suite of rooms that you may use to freshen up from your sea voyage."

"Thank you. That would be appreciated."

Later, in the dining room of the officers' quarters Loco used as his command center, they feasted on the finest Mexican cuisine. Loco had searched for and found several cases of German wine that he'd heard Bottger preferred.

Bottger kept the talk general and light until the meal was finished and they'd repaired to Loco's office for brandy and cigars.

As Bottger inhaled deeply of the Cohiba Especiale and sipped the Napoleon brandy, his eyes never left Loco's.

"Tell me, Loco, how do you envision the separation of duties of our collaboration to proceed?"

Loco smiled and leaned forward in his leather armchair. "I think the most efficient way for us to divide the duties is for you to command your mercenaries and for me to command my troops. That way there is no overlap of responsibilities."

"And the deployment of the soldiers will be under whose orders?"

Loco leaned back, waving his cigar in the air to dispel some of the smoke that was rapidly filling the air in the room with a blue cloud.

"Since I have some experience with the situation here in Mexico, I would hope that you would not mind some suggestions from me and my staff as to the most efficient way to maximize the troops under your command." He hesitated. "In other words, we will discuss the situations as they change day to day, and come to an agreement about the disposition of the various men and matériel under our joint command."

Bottger leaned his head back and gave a hearty laugh. "A very diplomatic way to put it, Loco," he said, grinning.

Loco returned the smile. "Of course, with both of us being very experienced in conducting warfare, I would hope that we will agree on what needs to be done the majority of the time."

Bottger nodded. "I can see that this will be an entertaining experience, having someone of your caliber to exchange ideas with." He glanced at Sergei Bergman. "My aide, Sergei, tells me you've already given him the authority to run his campaign along the western border, in the mountainous region along the coast."

"That's correct. Since his troops were much more experienced in guerrilla-type warfare, I thought they would do best in the less populated areas, while my more conventional troops could best serve by moving up the center of the country where most of the Mexican Army is concentrated."

Bottger took another drag of his cigar. "Very wise, Loco. I would have done the same thing in your place."

Loco raised his brandy snifter. "Then we are in agreement on how to proceed?"

Bottger mimicked his toast. "Certainly, Loco. After all, we both want the same thing, do we not? The complete and utter destruction of Ben Raines and his accursed SUSA."

The ship carrying Harley Reno's team pulled into the harbor at New Orleans. The members boarded a waiting Osprey and were flown to Base Camp One, where Ben Raines was waiting to meet them.

Jersey and Coop were taken to the state-of-the-art medical lab facilities by Dr. Buck, while Harley and Hammer and the others met with Ben in his office.

"Then I take it Jersey and Coop are completely out of danger?" Ben asked.

"Yes, sir," Harley replied. "Dr. Buck says they're both gonna have to take it easy for a while, especially Jersey, but that they shouldn't have any permanent disability from the infection."

"Good," Ben said. "Dr. Buck informs me this bug is a mutated form of the type used by Bruno Bottger several years ago here and in Africa."

"That's what he believes."

Ben shook his head. "Then I guess there's little doubt that it's Bottger who's behind the mercs in South America."

Harley nodded. "It certainly fits with the evidence."

"It seems Claire Osterman has made a bargain with not one, but two devils, Perro Loco and Bruno Bottger."

"They're gonna be a tough team to beat, especially if they establish a strong foothold in Mexico City," Hammer said.

"I don't see any way to prevent that," Ben said, "short of our precipitating an international incident by invading Mexico ourselves."

"Then the Mexican president is still refusing to accept our help?" Harley asked.

"Yes. The idiot thinks his troops can hold off both Loco's army and Bottger's mercenaries."

"He's a fool then," Hammer said.

"Yeah, it looks like the Americans in the U.S. aren't the only ones to elect an imbecile for a leader."

"If you can call Mexican elections the voice of the people, as corrupt as they are," Anna said.

"Well, that's neither here nor there. We've got problems of our own. Osterman's troops are pushing us along all of our northern borders, so we're going to have plenty to do just to keep the wolves from our own doors without worrying too much about saving Mexico's bacon."

"What can we do?" Harley asked.

"I've divided our battalions up among the various states of the SUSA; Texas, Louisiana, Kentucky, Missouri, Arkansas, Mississippi, Alabama, Georgia, Virginia, and North and South Carolina. In addition, I've sent Jackie Malone with a squad of the best of our scouts to parachute in and harass Osterman at every opportunity in her own backyard."

Harley glanced at Hammer and smiled. They'd both served under Jackie in the past, and had the utmost respect for her abilities to cause problems for those she opposed. "I'll bet Osterman is shitting bricks," Harley said.

Ben laughed. "I suppose so. Jackie took over an Air National Guard base in Peoria and attacked Sugar Babe's home base last night, inflicting fairly severe damage."

"You go, girl," Beth whispered, a wide grin on her face.

"I've already heard that Osterman had the gall to complain

about an unwarranted attack by our forces to the United Nations this morning."

"She's got *some* balls," Harley said, reluctant admiration in his voice.

"And then some," Ben agreed. "Jean-François Chapelle, Secretary General of the U.N., called Cecil Jeffreys and asked him what was going on."

"What'd Cec tell him?" Anna asked.

"Cec said he had no idea who had attacked Osterman, but that it might have been dissidents in her own Army, since the planes involved were hers."

"Did Chapelle buy that cock-and-bull story?" Hammer asked.

"Not for a minute, but he couldn't do much since Claire had no proof we were involved. And when Cec asked him to look into the provocative troop movements of Osterman's, he said he'd take it under advisement."

"So, as usual, the U.N. is useless as teats on a boar hog?" Harley asked.

"Right," Ben answered. "They won't get involved unless some Third World country goes crying to them, which isn't going to happen any time soon. The U.N. looks upon this as just another squabble to stay out of, letting us settle it between ourselves."

"You know, Ben, they might act differently if we tell them about this plague Bottger is going to try and unleash on the world. If it gets out of hand, it may affect many more nations that just ours," Anna said.

"That's a thought," Ben said. "I'll pass it along to Cec and let him run with it, though I doubt it'll do any good. The U.N. is so used to burying its head in the sand, I don't think anything will convince them to take a stand, until it's all over."

"And what about us?" Harley asked.

"I want you to rest up for a few days, get a little R and R, and be ready to ship out next week."

"Where to?" Hammer asked.

"I thought a little trip down Mexico way might be good for you, since you're already acclimated to the climate by your stay in South America."

"Mexico? But I thought the president didn't want us down there," Harley said.

"He doesn't, but what he doesn't know won't hurt him, will it?" Ben said with a grin.

Twenty-seven

Comandante Perro Loco was sitting at his breakfast table, remembering the beginnings of the war for Mexico, when Ben Raines had interfered and dashed his hopes for a quick, decisive victory just a few months ago, as he studied old field reports from his spies and commanders north of the Mexican border.

Field Marshal Bruno Bottger walked in, followed by his second in command, Sergei Bergman.

"Good morning, *comandante,*" Bottger said, evidently in a better mood this morning after a full night's sleep.

"Buenos dias, Field Marshal," Loco replied, straightening the papers on the table next to his plate of scrambled eggs covered with hot sauce.

Bottger and Bergman took their seats and gave orders to the Mexican waiter to bring them whatever the *comandante* was having, along with a pot of coffee.

Then Bottger spied the papers in front of Loco. "What are you reading, Loco? Field reports?" he asked.

Loco shook his head. "No, I am just reviewing what information I have about Ben Raines and his form of government. I believe, like Cicero of the Roman Republic, to win at war, one must first know one's enemies as well as one's allies."

Bottger smiled, nodding. "What have you found out about Raines?"

"I have just been reading from transcripts given to one of my spies by a newspaper reporter from New York." He passed the paper across the table to Bottger, who began to read it. The report by Robert Barnes, war correspondent for the United Press, read as follows:

> "As North America began to slowly pull itself out of the greatest economic and social collapse in world history, Ben Raines found himself to be the most hated man in all of America. That really didn't come as any surprise to Ben, for right after the collapse, Ben had gathered together a small group called the Rebels—a mixture of political/militia/survivalist-oriented men and women—and told them, 'We're going to rebuild. Against all odds, we're going to carve out our own nation. And we're going to be hated for our success.'
>
> "As it turned out, hate was not nearly a strong enough word. Ben and his Rebels first went to the Northwest and settled what would be forever known as the Tri-States, with the Tri-States form of government. The philosophy was based on personal responsibility and common sense. It soon became a hated form of government for those living outside the Tri-States, for liberals and other left-wingers don't want to be responsible for anything they do and they don't appear to possess any common sense.
>
> " 'Of course, that isn't entirely true,' Ben once said in one of his rarely granted interviews with the press. 'But that's the way it seems to those of us who believe that government should stay out of the lives of its citizens as much as possible.'
>
> "In the Tri-States, if you got careless and stuck yourself in the face with the business end of a screwdriver, you didn't sue the manufacturer of the screwdriver for damages . . . you learned to be more careful in handling tools.
>
> "Common sense.
>
> "Ben Raines realized that not everyone could, or would, live under a system of law that leaned heavily on common sense and personal responsibility. From the outset he es-

timated, correctly, as it turned out, that no more than two or three out of every ten Americans could live under a Tri-States form of government. People who came to live in the old Tri-States did not expect something for nothing . . . and that was wise on their part, for they damn sure weren't going to get something for nothing.

"In the Tri-States, everybody who was able worked at something. No able-bodied person sat on their ass and expected free handouts from the taxpayers . . . that just wasn't going to happen. You might not like the job that would be found for you, and it would be found very quickly, but you worked it, or you got out.

"Criminals discovered almost immediately that in the Tri-States, they had very few rights. All the rights belonged to the law-abiding citizens. If a criminal got hurt during the commission of a crime, he or she could not sue for damages. If they got killed, their family could not sue for damages. And in the Tri-States, a lot of criminals got killed during the first years. The Tri-States was not a friendly place for criminals . . . and it didn't take criminals long to discover that. The residents of the Tri-States didn't have a problem with drugs; the penalty for selling hard drugs was death; when caught, and after a very brief trial, the criminals had a choice, hanging or firing squad. Consequently, very soon drug dealing in the Tri-States dropped off to zero.

"Life was so good in the Tri-States, the central government, once it got back on its feet after only a few years, couldn't stand it and moved against the Tri-Staters. It was a terrible battle, but in the end the old Tri-States, located in the Northwest, was destroyed.

"But Ben Raines and his dream lived, and Ben gathered together the survivors of the government assault, and declared war on the government . . . a dirty, nasty, hit-and-destroy-and-run type of guerrilla warfare.

"Eventually, the entire United States collapsed inward

and Ben and his Rebels, now hundreds and hundreds strong, were able to move into the South and set up a new government. This time it was called the SUSA: the Southern United States of America.

"It was a struggle for a few years, and one time the SUSA was overrun by rabble from outside its borders. But the Rebels beat the attackers back and rebuilt their nation, larger and stronger and more self-sufficient than ever before.

"The Rebels are now the largest and most powerful and feared fighting force in the free world, so much so that the Secretary General of the newly reorganized United Nations met with Ben Raines and made a bargain with him: You deal with a few trouble spots around the world, especially with Bruno Bottger and his band of Nazis, and we'll recognize the SUSA as a free and sovereign nation.

"The two men shook hands, sealing the deal, and Ben took his Rebels and sailed off to Africa."

As Bottger put the paper down, Loco said, "The report ended just as Raines was heading off to fight you, Field Marshal, in Africa, some years ago."

Bottger pursed his lips, a wry expression on his face. He glanced at Bergman, who was scowling.

"We remember the time very well, *comandante,*" Bottger said in a low voice, as if he didn't appreciate being reminded of his defeat at the hands of Raines.

Loco pushed a journal-type document across the table. "This is a journal, written by one of Raines's team that accompanied him throughout that campaign," Loco said. "It too gives fresh insight into the way Raines's mind works, and speaks directly toward his motivation in trying to save the world from men such as he believes we are."

Bottger thumbed through the journal, reading as he sipped his coffee.

"Ben poured a fresh hot mug of coffee from the thermos and shook his head and sighed, remembering all too vividly the bad days in America, before the collapse, before the terrible germ war that wiped out every government around the globe, even before the nationwide taxpayer revolt that cost hundreds of Americans their lives as hardworking and hard-pressed-by-the-government citizens protested the amount of money extorted from them every year by the government . . . and in many cases, at least in the minds of many, the money carelessly pissed away by Congress.

"Ben sat in his tent and sipped his coffee, recalling the smooth and highly effective actions of the insidious gun-grab folks at work, until they finally got their way and all handguns (except those in the hands of selected citizens—the suck-ass types) were seized by federal agents and carefully handpicked and trained members of the military.

"Ben recalled even before then, when morally the nation was sliding down into the gutter.

" 'Morally we were bankrupt,' Ben muttered, after taking another sip of coffee. 'Many Americans were happy and content to be playing among the turds and the puke in the sewers.'

"And Ben knew the nation was definitely morally bankrupt in the years before the Great War and the collapse. There was filth and perversion every day on the television and in the movies. The same garbage, and in many cases, much worse, could be found in cyberspace, on the information highway called the Internet.

"Liberals and many members of the press screamed that it was freedom of speech and to interfere would be a violation of the Bill of Rights.

"But Ben had grave doubts about that.

"A few years before the entire world fell apart there had been a rash of schoolyard killings: kids killing kids for no apparent reason. The hysterical gun-grabbers howled that it was the availability of guns that caused the kids to kill. But Ben and millions of others who applied common sense to everyday living know that was pure horseshit: nothing but mealymouthed, out-of-touch-with-reality liberals making excuses for deviant and otherwise totally unacceptable behavior.

"Ben stirred restlessly in his camp chair as old memories came flooding back with startling clarity, vivid images of him, years back, sitting in the den of his home trying to watch television, but instead seething with anger at the TV news commentators and movie and TV personalities (all of them so left-leaning and liberal it pained them to have to give a right-hand turn signal), excusing the behavior of dope dealers, violent criminals, gang members, and degenerates . . . and especially saying the Bible was passé.

"Ben had listened to those types espouse their views that the Bible didn't really have to be followed . . . not down to the letter. If a certain passage of Scriptures didn't please the reader, well, just ignore it and go on to another passage that better suited the reader's lifestyle.

"Ben had always wondered, often, as he recalled, what the Almighty thought about that.

"Ben was not an overly religious man, but he certainly believed in God and he did read the Bible: He carried a Bible with him in the wagon and read it often, taking a great deal of comfort in the words.

"He recalled a radio interview he'd done with a talk show host one time, just a few months before the Great War and the collapse. The interviewer was one of those who believed that only the police and the military should own guns, and no civilian should be allowed to carry a concealed weapon . . . except for certain selected individuals, that is; but he would never say who those selected people might be. But Ben knew: people who gave lots of money to the whiny, I-want-to-run-your-life and the give-me-something-for-nothing parties. The interviewer placed the blame for many of society's ills solely on guns . . . but never, ever on the person holding the gun.

"Ben had finally lost his temper with the left-winger and the interview turned decidedly nasty. The ratings for that show were the highest ever known.

"Ben smiled as he recalled that long-ago TV show. That had been a fun interview! He had succeeded in making the left-wing liberal prick angry and the man had lost his cool. Ben had been good at doing that.

"Ben's smile faded. Now the city where the station had been located no longer existed, except in the ashes of memory. Those wonderful people the interviewer had so staunchly defended had turned the streets into a battleground, as punk gangs fought for control . . . until the Rebels came along and killed them."

Bottger sneered as he put the journal down. "This is bullshit, written by a woman obviously infatuated with General Raines. No one in a position of power is that naive, that altruistic," Bottger said.

Loco shrugged. "I would not be too sure, Field Marshal. I, for one, believe Ben Raines is just as he's reported to be, a fanatic about self-reliance and loyalty. Just read what the journal says about his relationship with the president of the SUSA."

Bottger picked the journal back up and read:

"Cecil Jeffreys was the president of the SUSA, the first black man elected to such a high office in America . . . and it took the separation of the nation and the men and women of the South to accomplish it.

"Cecil and Ben had been friends for many years. Cecil had left the grueling life in the field to enter politics after a heart attack nearly killed him during a campaign."

Loco pointed at the transcript of the expedition written by Robert Barnes, war correspondent, Associated Press, and the journal written by an unnamed member of his team. "Ben Raines is part madman," Loco said, "as you can see by his antiquated beliefs in the importance of the individual, and I believe that makes him a far more formidable adversary than we have believed. I think part of his success against both of us has been that fact, that we've underestimated him, thought him to be more like us, when in fact he is just the opposite."

Bottger put down the lengthy article. "Ben Raines and his men are very tough," he said, "and they are apparently completely unafraid of us and our armies, a fact we must take into consideration. We can only hope that Raines's battles with the forces of the USA will weaken him and divide his attention from us long enough for us to prevail here in Mexico."

"It is a gamble worth taking, Field Marshal," Loco said, leaning across the table to make his point. "After all, for a chance to control all of the American continent, what difference would it make if we lose a few thousand men? Fighting men and equipment are expendable and easily replaceable. Central and South America are full of men who are willing to risk their lives for the promise of money."

Bottger grinned and raised his cup of coffee. "For which we both should be eternally grateful."

Twenty-eight

Captain Dimitri Zubov was deeply concerned. Worried was a better word for the way he felt. In all his years as a hired mercenary since leaving the former Soviet Union, he'd never encountered anything quite like this. His men were spread out across muggy, jungle-thick hills in a Mexican state known as Oxaca.

They'd been dropped off at the port town of Salina Cruz by freighter and told to move northward and kill everyone and destroy any villages they came upon. They'd been promised that the Mexican Army was weak and poorly represented in this state and that they'd face little opposition except from poorly armed Indians and half-breeds.

However, a seek-and-destroy mission in this terrain was about as tough as it could get. Captain Zubov lead a force of ex-Blackshirts, the special assassination troops trained in guerrilla warfare by the elite USA Subversive Corps. Blackshirts, as they were called, were only sent into a war zone for highly specialized assignments. Most of these men had left the U.S. when Claire Osterman had been forced from power last year, and had joined up with mercenary forces. Zubov commanded one of these units, made up of mercenaries from around the world.

General Herman Bundt had directed him to search for a Mexican Army unit made up of special troops reported to be in these hills. And yet no sign of them had turned up anywhere . . . not so much as a single footprint. A bombing run by the helicopters assigned to his unit had used their antitank missiles to wipe out most of the citizenry of this region, leaving only a few farm animals and wild creatures roaming the mountainous jungle region.

He spoke to his sergeant, Sergi Rikov, another highly skilled Soviet guerrilla fighter, whispering to him in the fog of an early spring morning in southern Mexico.

"Nothing. We were given bad information by General Bundt about these Mexican troops. They are not here. Otherwise, we would have found something. . . ."

"Why would anyone fight to hold this useless territory?" Sergeant Rikov asked. "What strategic value could it possibly have?"

"Who knows? I'm beginning to wonder about the competence of leadership under this man whom we never see. No one seems to know what they are doing."

Zubov glanced up at cloudy skies. A silence blanketed the valley below them. "No airplanes. No rockets. Not a shot has been fired."

"It may be too quiet," Rikov warned. "Remember what Leonid said about silence when we went through our training in Mongolia. Silence can be a deadly thing . . . a warning. I have never been in a place as quiet as this. It is far too quiet to suit me."

"Nor have I seen a place so quiet," Zubov agreed, sweeping the pine-studded valley with field glasses.

"If these Mexican troops intend to challenge us over this place, they would surely send up aircraft in order to have our position," said Rikov. "Even the quietest surveillance airplane flying at high altitude makes some noise." He glanced at his superior lying next to him. "Or perhaps the presence of our attack helicopters scared them off."

"They may not be able to get a fix on us," Zubov said. "We don't know how well equipped this General Guerra and his armies are. We have ten rocket launchers, and only thirty men for them to find. If these Mexican soldiers are here, we will certainly have them overpowered by weaponry . . . and skilled guerrilla fighters."

"At the very least, we have *good* men," Rikov said with a glance behind him. "Our Soviet and Yugoslav assault teams are the best in the world. I have absolutely no doubt about it. All we have to do is find the enemy."

Zubov let out a sigh. "What good will it do us, or this cause championed by General Bundt and Field Marshal Bottger, if they have sent us to the wrong place? There are times, like now, when I question the value of their intelligence reports on enemy activities."

"General Bundt sounded so sure. A unit of the Mexicans' crack assault troops was coming south by way of this old road, to launch an attack on Salina Cruz to try and take back the port so we couldn't use it for reinforcements. No one had any doubts, according to the general."

"I have my doubts now," Zubov said. "This is nothing but jungle and empty villages, a few wandering cows and some pigs beyond that hilltop. There are no enemy soldiers here. We have wasted our time in difficult terrain based on inaccurate information. No one, not even a civilian, is here now."

"We were ordered to wait."

Zubov scowled. "Yes. To wait for the enemy. But as you can see, there is no enemy, unless we intend to wage war against pigs and cows."

"According to General Bundt, we will be paid no matter what we find."

"I'm beginning to wonder," Zubov added, turning the focus knob on his field glasses. "I hear rumors that Bottger and Perro Loco are going broke . . . that they have very little money left after the disastrous defeat last year at the hands of Ben Raines's Rebels. Most of their attempts to take Africa and Mexico failed miserably, which only makes me wonder more about their leadership. And now I hear they are broke."

"I have heard the same thing," Rikov said. "If this is indeed true, we will be forced to take our money from them at gunpoint."

"I was told the Central Americans have not been paid in silver or gold. They were given paper currency that is worthless. None of the stores in any of the towns in the USA will take this paper money."

"Until Field Marshal Bottger breaks a promise to us, we have no choice but to follow his orders. If anything he has told us is not true, including the amount and type of money we will be paid, then I will kill him personally."

Rikov suddenly looked away. "I heard a noise, Captain."

Zubov jerked around. "What kind of noise?" he whispered when all seemed quiet at the front, to the north of their present position.

"A cry . . . like the crying of a small child, but very soft and far away."

"Who the hell would be crying in this wilderness? There are no children here. We haven't seen anyone since we crossed that ridge miles behind us."

"It may be nothing," Rikov said, although he continued to keep an eye on a hilltop roughly half a mile away. "I could have imagined it, I suppose."

Zubov went back to his field glasses, sweeping the jungle again. "Nothing," he hissed, clenching his teeth. "But I have the distinct feeling that something is wrong."

"Look!" Rikov exclaimed, pointing to a grassy slope to the north. "It is Yarimere! What is he doing out in the open like that?"

Zubov turned his binoculars on the slope. Yarimere Hecht, an old friend from Russia, was staggering down the hill, stumbling and almost falling. And now Zubov heard the crying sounds too, for they were distinct in the silence surrounding them.

"What the hell is wrong with him?" Rikov wanted to know, focusing his field glasses on a man in a black shirt and black beret stumbling toward them, dark stains on his clothes and an agonized expression on his face.

Zubov sighed, reaching for his AK-47 automatic rifle. "He is badly wounded, comrade. Someone has shot him several times in the chest and belly."

Rikov tensed, reaching down for his own automatic rifle. "Then they *are* here," he whispered.

The sudden staccato of automatic-weapons fire thundered from the jungle hills south of them. Yarimere Hecht went down in a heap as if he'd been struck over the head by a heavy hammer, blood squirting from a number of wounds across his back and sides, his head coming apart in a spray of blood and bone and tufts of his long black hair.

"Son of a bitch!" Zubov hissed, looking for the source of the bullets. "How the hell did they get behind us?"

"It is not possible," Sergeant Rikov said as more and more gunfire erupted from trees to the south and west of their position.

The endless blasts of large-bore guns echoed across the Oxacan jungle. Men in black vests and berets tumbled out of pine thickets, shooting at unseen targets to their rear before they were gunned down.

"They have us cornered," Zubov exclaimed. "We have no choice but to head north, and that is all very thick jungle country."

"To hell with this," Rikov shouted as the gunshots came closer, lead slugs whistling through the air above their heads now.

He came to a crouch and took off at a run, keeping low to make as small a target as possible.

Captain Zubov had cupped his hands around his mouth to warn his sergeant against such a retreat, when he felt the earth shudder beneath him.

Sergeant Rikov stepped on a land mine less than thirty yards downslope. He was blown skyward, arms windmilling, his AK-47 flying into the air only fractions of a second before his legs were severed from his body. Pulpy bits of bone and flesh swirled away from his torso, and as he met his appointment with death, he let out a bloodcurdling scream.

Zubov did not watch his sergeant land in pieces around a deep crater where the land mine had been planted. All he could think of now was making it out of this place with his skin intact.

Men were screaming across vine-choked ridges behind him, and he had proof the land south of his position had been mined . . . his trusted sergeant's body decorated the dark green grass running into the valley below him.

"How the hell did they slip up behind us without any of my men knowing about it?" he wondered aloud, inching backward until he was protected from flying bullets by a ledge of rock jutting from the hill.

It was not possible, and yet the shrill cries of wounded and dying men made it all too clear his squad was in deep trouble in the pines.

Zubov saw two of his men break from a stand of trees at a dead run, spraying automatic-weapons fire in their wake as they ran toward safety.

A mortar thudded somewhere on a hillock west of the valley, and then an earsplitting explosion blew his Blackshirt squad men away, leaving nothing but flying dirt and vines and clods of grass where they had been only moments before the blast.

To hell with this, he thought, bending low to make a run to the east where no guns riddled the slopes. He dashed across the low side of the ridge with his AK-47 cocked, ready to unleash its deadly load should any target present itself before he reached the apparent safety of a jungle grove nestled in a swale between two hills.

Too late, he caught a glimpse of a shadowy figure in the trees, and the glint of early morning sunlight off the barrel of a rifle.

Zubov threw himself flat in the grass, bringing his rifle to bear on the shape.

The pounding of rapid fire filled his ears, and he felt a stinging sensation spread across the top of his head and his right shoulder.

The sky above him began to spin, and he lost his bearings for a moment.

"What the hell . . . is happening?" he stuttered, feeling a wet substance flow out of his mouth when he spoke.

He looked down at the grass below his chin. A crimson stain spread between his elbows, and pain raced through his skull unlike any pain he'd ever known.

I am shot, he thought dully as he felt himself spinning in widening circles. Tiny pinpoints of light flashed before his eyes as the world around him darkened.

How did they get behind us? he wondered again, until a deep wracking cough filled his mouth with blood.

His eyes batted shut, and the pain was gone.

Captain Raul Perez stepped from cover and stood over the bodies of the mercenaries as his men came out of the jungle to join him. They all wore the red berets of the Mexican Special Forces units that Harley Reno and Hammer Hammerick had trained the year before when Perro Loco first attacked Mexico.

Sergeant Julio Yara stepped to Perez's side. "I see our training last year was not in vain, Captain," he said with a grin.

Perez looked around at his men, who'd suffered no loses in their ambush of the mercenaries. "Yes, the tactics the *americanos* taught us worked extremely well."

Sergeant Yara turned to the other men. "Pick up all the weapons and ammunition you can and strip the bodies for the buzzards. We shall leave a message the mercenaries will not soon forget."

Twenty-nine

Bruno Bottger was furious when Bergman told him of Bundt's report of the mercenary unit slaughtered in the mountainous region of Oxaca.

"Why are we wasting valuable troops and equipment trying to occupy land that is so remote?" he asked scornfully.

Bergman shrugged. "We did not feel the Mexican Army was such a threat, Field Marshal. Evidently, they have learned some lessons from fighting with the Americans last year."

"From now on, we will concentrate on taking Mexico City, not worthless mountains and jungles that have no strategic significance," he ordered. He looked at General Bundt. "Herman, you will use the port cities we've already captured as staging points for reinforcements to build up a force that is to be used only in our final attack against Mexico City. Once we have the seat of government in our hands, the Mexican Army will have no choice but to surrender."

"Yes, sir, Field Marshal," Bundt said, his face flaming with embarrassment at his failure.

Bottger consulted a detailed topographic map of Mexico. "I want you to leapfrog our troops to take Acapulco and then Las Truchas next. From there we can ship in helicopters and gunships as well as men for the final assault on Mexico City."

"Yes, sir, it will be done," Bundt said.

"I do not want any more reports of failure, Herman, or you will soon be fighting as a private, do you understand me?"

"Yes, sir," he said, saluting smartly and hurrying from the room.

After the general left, Sergei looked at his boss. "Why the haste to take Mexico City, sir?"

Bottger sighed. "My bank accounts are depleted, Sergei. We need to get to the gold stored in the capital city as soon as possible, before our mercenaries find out we have nothing left with which to pay them."

Bergman nodded. "I understand."

"And, Sergei, have the scientists get the plague missiles and bombs ready. As soon as we've secured Mexico City, I want to launch BW attacks against Ben Raines and his troops. We cannot afford a repeat of Africa."

"Yes, sir."

Perro Loco's men were doing better. The roads toward Mexico City that ran through the middle of the country were well maintained and hadn't been mined extensively, so his heavy equipment and tanks were making short work of the Mexican Army's defenses. In fact, his men had progressed almost to the city of Puebla, less than a hundred miles south of Mexico City, well within the range of his helicopter gunships. He was almost ready to give the order for an all-out siege of the capital city.

Ben Raines was going over the intel reports with Mike Post when Dr. Larry Buck knocked on his door and entered, a smile on his face.

"Hello, Doc," Ben said, looking up from the maps spread on his desk. "You look like the cat that swallowed the canary."

"Better than that, Ben. We've finally managed to get the formula for a vaccine against the bug Bottger is planning to use. I've ordered full production, so we should be ready to begin inoculations within twenty-four hours."

Ben nodded, returning the doc's smile. "Good, 'cause it looks like Mexico City will fall within the week. After that, Bottger is sure to begin deployment of his BW as soon as he can."

"There is something strange going on, though," Mike Post said.

"What's that, Mike?" Ben asked.

"My spies in the U.S. say there is no program of inoculation going on there among Osterman's troops. What do you make of that?"

Ben glanced at Buck. "Is there any way they could already be immune, Larry?"

"No way, Ben. This bug is completely new and different from anything I've seen before. If Osterman's not already immunizing her troops, then they're going to be as vulnerable as ours would have been."

Ben scratched at a two-day growth of beard on his face. He'd been too busy lately to shave, and the new growth itched terribly.

After a minute, he looked up. "That must mean Bottger is planning to double-cross Osterman. I'll bet he figures the plague will devastate both our countries, leaving the entire North American continent ripe for picking."

"But, that'd mean millions of deaths," Buck said, a look of horror on his face. "No one can be that callous toward human life."

"Don't count on it, Larry," Ben said. "If there's a spark of humanity in Bruno Bottger, I haven't seen any sign of it yet."

"Ben, I don't know if I can in good conscience withhold this vaccine from Osterman. Even if we are at war, those are still Americans living there. Can you stand by and see millions of innocent people die just to defeat a crazy woman?"

"No, Larry, of course not. I never regret killing men in battle who are trying to kill me, but I've never countenanced killing civilians along with the military, not even to win a war I didn't start. Of course, we'll share the formula with Osterman, but we'll not give her the actual vaccine until all of our men have had a chance at it first."

"What do you want me to do?"

"Gather up all your papers on the illness Jersey and Coop suffered after exposure to the bug, as well as your culture reports and basic information on both the bug and your vaccine. I'll contact Sugar Babe tomorrow, after we've begun to vaccinate our troops."

"I'll have the information on your desk first thing in the morning," Buck said.

Thirty

Less than an hour after Ben had faxed the information on the BW of Bruno Bottger to Claire Osterman's office, his phone rang.

He picked it up and said, "Hello, Claire."

"What is this shit, Raines? What have you got up your sleeve now?" she asked in a harsh voice.

"I thought the information was pretty self-evident," he replied in a reasonable tone of voice. "Are you seriously having trouble believing a man like Bruno Bottger would be planning to double-cross you?"

"How did you know—" she began.

Ben interrupted her. "How did I know you are in cahoots with Bruno Bottger?" he finished for her.

"I don't know where you got the idea Bottger is still alive, or that I'm in cahoots with him, as you say," she said lamely.

"Oh, come on, Claire. Who else would have the technical know-how to take the same bug Bottger used against the world a couple of years ago and cause a mutation that would make it even more deadly?"

When he was met with silence on the other end of the phone, Ben continued. "And as far as knowing about your deal with the devil, we've known about that from the very beginning, Claire," Ben said, stretching the truth to make her even more unsure of his sources.

"Well, anyway," she continued in a stronger tone of voice,

"why should I trust any information you give me after you sent your assassins to try and kill me?"

"Claire, if I wanted you dead, you'd already be decomposing."

"Bullshit, Raines. You know attempted assassination of a country's leaders is expressly forbidden by the Geneva Convention rules of war."

Ben threw back his head and laughed. "Claire, I'm surprised you even know the Geneva Convention rules, since you've broken every single one of them since you've been president of the U.S., especially the ones concerning the use of chemical and biological weapons."

She paused, then: "Nevertheless, answer my question. Why should I trust you now?"

"Because you know it fits with Bottger's character, or lack thereof," Ben said patiently.

"If he's got this weapon ready, why hasn't he used it already?" she asked, her tone becoming more businesslike.

"Probably because he needs you to keep me busy until he can gain control of Mexico by taking Mexico City. Once he's established there and the Mexican Army is out of the picture, I think he'll launch a full-scale attack on the SUSA with his plague bacteria."

Another hesitation while she pondered the reasonableness of Ben's idea.

"And, Claire," Ben continued, "if you're thinking that might be good for you, think again. If the plague gets a hold here in the SUSA, even on a minor scale, remember what happened last time he and you played with biological weapons. Plagues know no boundaries. The sickness will surely cross the border like a wildfire out of control, and burn you as badly as us."

"Not if he shares the vaccine with us," Claire said, an uncertain note in her voice.

"Has he made any effort to even inform you of his plans, much less share his vaccine with you?" Ben asked.

"There's still time," Claire said, "if what you're saying is the truth."

"Now who's bullshitting whom, Claire?" Ben asked. "My medical experts tell me the vaccine will take from one to two weeks to become effective after inoculation. If that's true, and Bottger is only days away from taking Mexico City, then you haven't got a lot of time to prepare, have you?"

"Shit!" she said, evidently realizing she'd been set up as surely as night follows day.

"Claire, in spite of our . . . philosophical differences, our countries share a common history and a common blood bond. We are all, in a sense, Americans. For that reason, and for that reason alone, I don't wish to see your citizens die by the millions."

"What do you suggest?" she said slowly, as if thinking over his words.

"I'd like to make a deal."

"What kind of deal?" she asked, more suspicious now.

"Call it a quid pro quo," Ben said, "a tit-for-tat sort of deal."

"Oh, so your humanity has a price?" she said scornfully.

Ben chuckled again. "In the words of the immortal writer Robert A. Heinlein, Claire, there ain't no such thing as a free lunch."

"So, what's this 'lunch,' as you call it, going to cost me?"

"Simply pull your troops back from our borders and stand them down."

"That's it?" she asked.

"That's it, Claire," he answered. "It's a war you know you can't win anyway, so you have nothing to lose by doing the deal."

"And if we do this?"

"I'll ship you detailed instructions on the manufacture of a vaccine effective against the anthrax plague, as well as a supply to get you started with your vaccinations until you can make your own."

"And that's all?" she asked.

"Oh, and one more thing," Ben said.

"I knew it," Claire said.

"You've got to allow inspectors from the United Nations to monitor your troop withdrawal."

"What?"

"It's not that I don't trust you, Claire, but you've got to admit, you're not known for keeping your word."

"You're a son of a bitch, Raines! You know that?"

"Son of a bitch or no, Claire, you know I always keep my word, especially when it means the saving of millions of lives," Ben said.

After a few seconds, Claire answered, "All right, Raines, I'll do it."

"Good. You've made the right choice, Claire. I'll arrange with President Jeffreys to have Jean-François Chapelle get some inspectors on their way to your country immediately."

"What about the vaccine?" Claire asked. "If what you say is true, time is of the essence."

"I will take you at your word and send it right away," Ben said. Then, in a harsher voice, he added, "And, Claire, if you double-cross me after I send it, I make you a solemn promise. I will bomb you and your country into the Dark Ages."

The only answer Ben got was a loud click as Claire slammed her phone down.

He called Mike Post and told him of his deal with Claire.

"Do you think you can trust her?" Mike asked.

"You never know with Claire, so here's what I want you to do. Have communications get in touch with Jackie Malone and her crew of guerrillas, and have them cease all aggressive tactics, but to stay there undercover, just in case Claire doesn't come through on her end of the bargain."

Mike chuckled. "Jackie's not going to like sitting around with her hands in her pockets," he said.

Ben smiled. "I know, but tell her it's the best we can do

right now. If I know Claire Osterman, Jackie will get another chance at her before all this is over."

Claire slammed the phone down, muttering, "That arrogant prick! Just who does he think he is?"

Herb Knoff, who'd been sitting across the room listening to half the conversation, raised his eyebrows quizzically.

Claire glanced at him. "Get General Stevens and Harlan Millard in here right now!"

After her advisors had been assembled, Claire got right to the point. "Ben Raines called. He said he's got proof Bottger is planning a double-cross."

"What?" General Stevens said. "But how? His troops are thousands of miles from here, and on the other side of the SUSA from us. How in the hell can he hurt us?"

"The son of a bitch has got a new BW. A mutation of the plague he tried in Africa some years back."

"But, Claire," Millard said diffidently. "We knew that when we agreed to use him, and we've all been inoculated against his BWs."

"Not this one, according to Raines," she said, striding back and forth in front of her desk.

"Can we trust Raines?" Herb Knoff asked.

"Ben Raines is a lot of things," Claire said, "a son of a bitch not the least, but he's not a liar. If he says something, you can take it to the bank, even if you don't much like him."

"What about this so-called proof?" Stevens asked.

She pointed to the pile of papers and culture reports Ben had faxed her. "It's all in there. I want you to get it to our medical people immediately."

"What does Raines suggest we do about it, and what does he want?" Stevens asked.

"For us to pull back our troops from the borders with the SUSA. And for that, he'll give us the formula for the vaccine and some samples until we can get our own made."

"But if we pull back, that'll give Raines room to invade us," Stevens said.

Harlan Millard glanced at the general. "Raines would never invade, not unless we attacked first," he said. "It would go against everything the man stands for."

"What do you mean?" Stevens asked, unbelieving.

"The main tenet of Raines's entire philosophy is that man is accountable only to himself, and responsible for his own actions. The SUSA itself is built upon that fact, so they would never, ever try and force people to live under their rules. Hell, even when he's defeated us in the past, he's always allowed the prisoners he's taken to return here if they wanted to, and he's never taken any additional land from his original borders. He is, at heart, an isolationist."

"Harlan's right, Brad," Claire said. "The only thing we lose by pulling back is the advantage we're giving Perro Loco and Bruno Bottger by dividing Raines's troops and his attention."

"But . . ." Stevens began as Claire held up her hand.

"No, General, listen to me. Loco and Bottger are on the very steps of Mexico City, so even if Raines wanted to, he couldn't stop them from taking the country. Therefore, our ruse has served its purpose and we now have two powers right on the SUSA's back door. Once Loco and Bottger fight it out over who's going to control Mexico, we'll be able at some point to deal with the victor and can, if we then wish, resume our hostilities with Raines and the SUSA. But until we have protection against this BW of Bottger's, we need to play it cool."

"So, what happens after we get the vaccine?" Millard asked.

Claire smiled evilly. "For one thing, we'll only give the vaccine to those people loyal to my command, and to the most productive citizens. If Bottger does end up using the BW, it will give us a way to cut some of the deadwood out of our system, like all the bastards on welfare who refuse to work to help the country."

Millard's face blanched. "Claire, I can't believe you are just going to sit by while thousands, perhaps millions of your citizens die a horrible death."

"Believe it, Harlan. Face facts. This country's almost broke. We can no longer afford to support the idle, those who won't help themselves. There just isn't enough to go around."

"I won't be a party to this genocide!" Millard said heatedly.

Claire gave him a cool look. "All right, Harlan. If you feel so strongly about it, you can give your vaccine to one of the needy you're so concerned about."

Harlan sat back down, his face ashen.

Claire grinned. "I didn't think so."

Stevens cleared his throat. "By the way, Claire, are you going to contact Perro Loco and tell him of Bottger's possible double cross?"

She considered this as she walked around to sit behind her desk.

Finally, after a few moments, she shook her head. "I don't think so, Brad."

"Why not?" Herb asked. "After all, if Bottger does use this plague bacteria, Loco's troops won't be immune any more than we or the SUSA would be. He and his men will be totally wiped out when the sickness spreads."

"You're assuming Loco knows nothing of this, Herb. How do we know that?" Claire asked. "What if Loco and Bottger are in this together, and have made some arrangement behind my back to divide up the North American continent after we're all dead or dying?

"If I approach Loco, and he is in on the plan, it will tip Bottger off that we're on to him. No, I think it best to get the vaccine from Raines and sit back and see what happens."

Thirty-one

About the time Herman Bundt's mercenary forces in Las Truchas, a coastal town 250 miles west of Mexico City, were being resupplied and reinforced with additional troops by freighter, and Perro Loco's forces were pounding the Mexican Army's defenses into rubble to the south, El Presidente Eduardo Pena told the leader of his Army, General Jose Guerra, to contact Ben Raines and see if the SUSA might after all be able to send some troops to help protect Mexico City and his government.

Guerra felt like pulling the Colt .45 automatic pistol from his holster and shooting his leader between the eyes, but that would leave only himself to take the blame for losing Mexico to these rebels. Instead, he took a deep breath and tried to explain the facts of life to the imbecile leading his country.

"But, El Presidente," Guerra said, as patiently as he could, "the German mercenary troops are at Las Truchas to our west, and Perro Loco's army has just taken Puebla to the south and Veracruz to the east. It is much too late for anyone short of God to do anything to save Mexico City."

The president leaned over his desk and picked up the phone. "Get me Ben Raines immediately," he ordered, staring at Guerra as if he didn't know what he was talking about.

"We will see, General," Pena said while waiting to be connected to the leader of the SUSA's Army. "Mexico is much too important for Raines to let it fall into the hands of Loco and his ally, President Osterman. You will see, he will move heaven and earth to save us."

The phone buzzed and Pena switched on the speaker. "General Raines, this is Presidente Eduardo Pena of Mexico."

"Hello, Presidente Pena. How are you?" Raines asked, his voice casual, as if he received calls from heads of state all the time.

"At the present, General Raines, I am not so well. The rebel forces are knocking at the doorstep of Mexico City, and I am now ready to accept the help you so generously offered last week."

There was an audible sigh over the speaker. "I am sorry you waited so long, *presidente,*" Raines said. "But our intel says the rebels are less than an hour away from taking your city. There is nothing I can do for you now. If you had taken my offer in a timely manner, perhaps we could have avoided this terrible outcome."

"But . . . but you must! I command it!" the president shouted.

"Sorry, Eduardo, better luck next time," Raines said, his voice heavy with irony as he hung up the phone.

As Pena glanced across the room at Guerra, the sound of helicopters came through the palace windows, followed by the raucous roar of machine-guns strafing his troops in the square below.

Pena stepped toward the window, then ducked as a couple of Kiowa helicopters buzzed the building, missing it by only yards as they flew past.

"Damn it, Guerra, do something!" Pena ordered, pointing his hand at his general, sweat forming on his brow and darkening his splendid uniform under the armpits and across the back.

Guerra smiled sadly. "As Raines said, it is much too late." He started for the door, then called back over his shoulder, "You've killed us, you fool."

A tremendous explosion sounded just outside the window,

and the wall of the presidential suite fell in, showering both men with stucco and plaster as they dove to the floor, bullets stitching a path yards from them.

"General Guerra," Pena called from his position on the floor under his desk. "What am I to do?"

Guerra looked up as he dusted plaster of paris and wooden splinters off his uniform coat. "I suspect you'll die very shortly, *presidente,* unless you're very lucky."

Mexican Army jeeps, of World War II vintage, pulled up in front of the palace. All of them had twenty-caliber machine guns on posts behind the drivers, and Guerra's troops tried in vain to shoot down the swooping, diving killing machines that were the Kiowas attacking them. Two squads of infantry spread out in a line in front of the palace door, taking shelter behind the balustrade and firing over the walls at Perro Loco's troops, who were swarming up the manicured lawn of the palace grounds like ants from a disturbed bed.

Two of the jeeps in the courtyard exploded, jumping into the air under the impact of the antitank rockets the Kiowas carried. The drivers and machine-gunners' bodies were torn apart and scattered over the white-hot cement of the yard like broken rag dolls as mangled parts of the jeeps rained down upon them.

Guerra ran from the building, shooting into the air with his .45, and jumped into the third jeep, shouting at the driver to take off.

"What about El Presidente?" the man asked as he pressed the starter button and pumped the accelerator pedal furiously.

"Fuck the president! *Go!*" Guerra screamed, snapping off shots from his pistol until the slide locked open signaling the magazine was empty.

The driver spun the wheels and took off, just as the cement where they'd been erupted under the onslaught of 20mm Minigun fire and a helicopter roared by overhead, banking heavily into the midday sun.

Taking the corner on two wheels, the driver of the jeep

carrying General Guerra managed to get under the cover of the fifty-foot-tall stately palms ringing the drive to the palace courtyard, bullets from Perro Loco's troops pinging the metal fenders of the jeep, but miraculously missing the occupants.

Once it was away from the building, the choppers seemed to ignore the jeep, and concentrated on the soldiers still trying to protect the palace. They dove and swooped, pumping thousands of rounds of machine-gun fire into the porch, ripping soldiers to pieces and cratering the front of the building with hundreds of pockmarks in the stuccoed walls.

As Guerra's jeep turned a final corner down the main boulevard, he glanced back to see several Chinook helicopters land in the palace courtyard and disgorge hundreds of mercenaries, who swarmed the palace like ants at a picnic, killing the last of the remaining defenders, even though many of them had their hands in the air trying to surrender.

In the distance, tanks and half-tracks containing more of Perro Loco's troops could be seen churning up the concrete of the main streets leading toward the palace, facing only token resistance from the Mexican Army, which by now was in full retreat.

The German mercenaries were congregating on the other side of the palace, some on foot and others riding in HumVees and half-track personnel carriers. All were waving their rifles and machine-guns in the air and shouting in victory.

"Where to now, General?" the driver asked, his eyes wide with fright as he negotiated the narrow roads leading away from the palace and out of town.

"Drive north, Jose," Guerra said. "If we can make the Navy base at Tampico, perhaps there is still a chance for me to convince Raines to help us. Meanwhile," he said, as he picked up the microphone from the radio under the jeep's dashboard, "I'll have what's left of the Army pull back to the north of the city, and we'll arrange to rendezvous near the Army base at Durango with as many troops as can get there."

"Do you think there's still a chance Mexico can be saved?" Jose asked.

Guerra glanced at him, wondering whether he should tell him the truth or give him false hope.

"There is always a chance, Jose. As they say in America, the opera's not over until the fat lady sings."

Jose, clearly not familiar either with the saying or with opera, wrinkled his forehead but continued staring straight ahead, and didn't ask any more stupid questions.

By suppertime, most of the dead and wounded soldiers had been carted away, to be placed in mass graves dug by bulldozers. The wounded were thrown in the pits along with those already dead. Both Bottger and Loco said they had neither the time nor the inclination to care for wounded men who'd fought against them.

The soldiers of both Loco's and Bottger's armies were sent out into the city to make sure there were no surviving soldiers to act as snipers or commit sabotage. The soldiers relieved the stress of their latest battle by raping and pillaging the city, killing almost as many innocent citizens as they had soldiers in the battle.

Meanwhile, Bruno Bottger and Perro Loco, along with their lieutenants—Jim Strunk, Paco Valdez, Rudolf Hessner, Herman Bundt, and Sergei Bergman—gathered in the presidential dining room to be served a dinner that had already been prepared for El Presidente Pena.

Eduardo Pena's cries could be heard through the open window. When he'd tried to give himself up to the invading soldiers, they'd taken him out into the courtyard, stripped his elaborate uniform off, and hung his naked body upside down by his feet.

Both Bottger and Loco had smiled their approval of his status when they marched side by side into the Presidential Palace just before sundown.

While they ate dinner, Bottger and Loco discussed how they each planned to proceed next.

"I see no reason to change our tactics, since they have been so successful so far," Loco said, spearing a piece of prime beef on his fork and transferring it to his mouth.

Bottger, who'd elected to eat beef enchiladas smothered in salsa and cheese, wiped his mouth and took a deep drink of his wine before replying.

"I agree, Loco," he said amicably. "I will have my troops move up the western coast toward the coastal city of Mazatlan and then, once we've established a beachhead there, inland toward Durango. From either of those two locations, we will be within air-strike range of the southern border of the SUSA."

"Excellent, Field Marshal," Loco said. "And I will position my army on the eastern border up the coast toward Tampico and eventually to Monterrey. That way we can form a pincer movement against Texas and the lower borders of the SUSA that will make Raines divide his troops to resist us."

Bottger nodded. "And if President Osterman fulfills her side of our bargain, Herr Raines will be kept very busy indeed defending his pitiful country."

Loco picked up his brandy glass and clinked it against Bottger's wineglass in a toast to their mutual success.

Later, in his personal quarters, Bottger addressed Bergman and Bundt. "I think as soon as we've taken Mazatlan, we can start our bombardment with the anthrax plague."

"Do you think our helicopters and airplanes will be able to deliver the bombs against the SUSA," Sergei Bergman asked as Rudolf Hessner prepared the field marshal's bed. "After all, I've heard the SUSA has excellent air-defense measures."

Bottger shrugged. "Whether or not the planes survive the attack is immaterial. The bombs will be on board, and the scientists have designed them so that even if the aircraft are shot down, the bacteria will still spread. Within a matter of two weeks, the SUSA will be devastated by the effects of mass sickness and death. If we're lucky, the soldiers of Ben Raines will begin to die like flies."

"What about the soldiers of Perro Loco, Field Marshal?" Herman Bundt asked. "Won't they also begin to be affected by the plague?"

Bottger smiled as he rubbed into his scarred face a special cream that the doctors had prepared to keep the skin soft. "Of course, Herman, that is the idea. Soon, the only army not wiped out by anthrax will be under my command. A situation I have dreamed of for the past ten years."

In Loco's quarters, Loco was also discussing details of the upcoming campaign with Paco Valdez and Jim Strunk.

"I thought once we took Mexico City, you were going to let me kill that Kraut bastard," Jim Strunk said.

Loco held up his hand. "Don't be too anxious, Jim. There will be plenty of time and opportunities to dispatch our friend after he has outlived his usefulness to us. Once we are within striking distance of the SUSA, I will give the order and the field marshal will suffer a fatal dose of food poisoning, leaving me in command of his troops."

"What about his associates?" Valdez asked.

Loco shrugged. "Once their leader is dead, they can either go along with the program or they can die. What do you think they will decide to do?"

"And his troops?" Strunk asked.

"They are mercenaries," Loco said, stretching and yawning as he prepared for bed. "They will fight for whoever has the money to pay them to fight."

"He's right, Jim," Valdez said. "Mercenaries' only loyalty is to their paycheck."

"I hope you are right, Loco," Strunk said. "Because I'm getting awfully tired of that strutting peacock of a German."

"Be patient, Jim, your time will come soon enough," Loco said.

Thirty-two

While Dr. Buck sent teams of medics to all of the various battalions scattered around the SUSA to make sure all of the troops received the new anti-BW vaccine, Ben gathered his team in his office.

Harley Reno, Hammer Hammerick, Coop and Jersey, fully recovered now, and Anna, Beth, and Corrie all waited to see what Ben had in mind for them in the upcoming battle with Bottger and Loco's troops.

"Get your gear packed, guys, we're heading south," Ben said without preamble.

"By we, you mean you're going with us, sir?" Harley asked.

"Yes. I've just gotten off the phone with General Guerra from Mexico. He and several battalions of Mexican Army troops have retreated after the fall of Mexico City to Durango and the Navy base at Tampico."

"And just why are we going down there?" Coop asked, playing the spoiler as usual.

"He's asked for our help in positioning and training his troops to slow or stop the advance of the rebels' armies," Ben said. "And I've agreed to send him our best people at staging guerrilla warfare."

"And if I may ask, sir, why are you coming with us?" Harley said, a questioning look on his face. "Aren't you needed here to coordinate the defenses against Osterman's troops?"

"I've reached an agreement with President Osterman, and she's going to call off her Army in exchange for our providing her with the new vaccine against anthrax," Ben said, aware that his team knew nothing of his talk with the president of the USA the night before. "Therefore, since I'm doing nothing but sitting on my butt here in this office, I've decided I need some time in the field before I go terminally stale."

"An agreement with Sugar Babe?" Coop asked, screwing up his face. "Do you think you can trust her to keep her part of the bargain?"

"Not usually, but in this case I've got the U.N. monitoring her troop withdrawals. If she reneges on the deal, we'll have plenty of warning."

"So, once again, we're going to Mexico to baby-sit the Army and pull their fat out of the fire?" Jersey said with disgust.

"Not only their fat, Jerse," Ben said, "but ours as well. Dr. Buck tells me he needs a couple of weeks before the vaccine takes effect. If we let Loco and Bottger steamroll over the Mexican Army, they'll be able to get within range to send their BW to our borders before our troops are fully protected."

"So, we don't have to kick their butts single-handed?" Harley asked. "We just have to slow them down a bit?"

"That's about the size of it," Ben said. "We also need to buy some time while Striginov gets the 505 Bat moved further down into western Mexico and McGowen gets the 502 situated and dug in in the eastern half of the country."

Mike Post knocked on the door and entered Ben's office. "Ben, I've got the latest intel info for you on Loco's and Bottger's movements."

"Go ahead, Mike."

"Bottger's mercenaries are headed up the west coast toward Mazatlan, while the troops under Loco are moving rapidly toward Tampico on the east coast."

Ben spread his hands. "There you go, guys. We don't have a minute to waste. Get ready and we'll move out in an Osprey at 1400 hours."

* * *

As the Osprey descended from fifteen thousand feet through heavy cloud cover in its final descent toward Durango, Mexico, Ben and the team started to get their gear ready for a quick exit of the plane.

Suddenly, the pilot banked hard to the left and pulled the nose up until the plane was dangerously near stall speed.

"Mayday! Mayday!" the pilot yelled over the intercom. "We're under heavy attack by three Kiowa gunship helicopters."

"Shit!" Harley Reno said, dropping his duffel bag and ripping a cargo-hold door open as he tried to keep from being thrown from his feet.

He reached into the closet-sized space and began to dig out parachutes stored there. As he grabbed them, he pitched them over his shoulder to Hammer. "Everybody get one of these on," he yelled over the roar of the Osprey's twin engines as the pilot jigged and swerved to avoid the fire of the Miniguns that could be heard even over the engine noise.

Ben's team quickly slipped the chutes on, and pulled their Uzis over their heads to let them hang by straps across their chests in case they had to bail out.

The Osprey shuddered under the impact of hundreds of 20mm shells as one of the Kiowas dived on the plane as it made a sweeping turn to the left. The right engine burst into flame and the plane nosed down. After the pilot feathered the engine so the prop wouldn't be as much of a drag, he clicked on the intercom.

"General Raines, there's no way I can climb high enough to avoid the choppers with only one engine. You guys better bail, and bail fast!"

Harley pulled the emergency release handle on the rear door, and the pilot added, "We're about fifty miles north and west of Durango. Looks like some heavy jungle down there, so you should have plenty of cover after you land." He didn't add, "If you don't impale yourself on a tree coming down."

Harley let the door fly off its hinges, torn away by the slipstream wind, and pumped his fist in the air. "Come on, get the lead out!" he shouted over the noise.

One by one, with Ben going last before Harley, the team dived out into the early evening dusk and tumbled toward the jungle below.

Their last sight of the Osprey was of it angling down, trailing smoke from its engine, two of the Kiowas following and continuing to strafe it with Minigun fire.

As they floated on the air currents, pulling on parachute strings to try to stay together in a close formation, the third Kiowa banked steeply and arrowed at them, its Miniguns winking in the darkness as it tried to shoot them out of the sky.

All of the team jerked their Uzis around and began to fire back at the helicopter, catching it off guard as it drew nearer and nearer. It got close enough for them to see the Plexiglas in front of the pilot spiderweb under the impact of hundreds of 9mm bullets from the machine-guns, and then it turned turtle, smoke pouring from its turbines as it fell to the earth below, a giant fireball erupting and lighting up the night as it impacted in dense foliage.

Luckily, no one in the team was seriously hurt upon landing, though Anna suffered a severely sprained ankle, which Jersey had to tape up from the first-aid kit in her pack.

Ben gathered his team around him and consulted his compass. "Looks like we need to head south by southeast if the pilot had our bearing correct."

"Shit, just what I was looking forward to," Coop complained, "another fifty-mile march through snake-infested jungle."

"Look on the bright side," Hammer said with a grin. "At least they're not sending somebody to pick us up from a plane crash with a sponge."

After the Osprey exploded and fell burning to the ground, the pilot of the lead Kiowa radioed Sergei Bergman in Mexico City.

"Sir, we've just attacked and shot down an American Osprey heading toward Durango."

"Excellent, Jurgen," Sergei said.

"One thing, sir. Six or seven men ejected from the plane before it went down, and the pilot was on the radio to his base, saying General Raines was in the group and calling for air support."

"What is your location, Jurgen?" Sergei asked, sounding excited at the chance to get Ben Raines.

"Approximately forty-three miles north-northwest of Durango."

"Can you intercept Raines and his men?" Sergei asked.

"No, sir. We burned up most of our fuel in the attack on the Osprey. We'll be lucky to get back to base as it is."

"Come on home then. I'll send another team," Sergei said, signing off.

He put the radio down and rang Bruno Bottger on his private line in his quarters.

"Sir, one of our Kiowas just shot a plane carrying Ben Raines out of the air."

"Is the son of a bitch dead?"

"No, sir. He and several of his men managed to bail out of the plane. But I've got his exact location."

"Send a team after him immediately. This is too good a chance to pass up, Sergei."

"Yes, sir."

Thirty-three

Former Navy SEAL Sergeant Gerald Jones listened to the air whisper through his black parachute as he guided it down with the aid of hand stirrups toward a starlit opening in the jungle. Eleven highly skilled assault troops came from the inky skies above him as their cargo plane, a C-130, swept back to the north at low altitude, staying off Mexican radar as much as it could, flying just above the jungle treetops at dangerously low levels after the chutists made their jump from higher altitudes.

Jones hit the ground, rolling, gathering his chute cords as soon as he came to his feet. All around him, men in black shirts with blackface greasepaint hit the meadow, tumbling, making as little noise as possible despite heavy packs, automatic rifles, and explosives.

"Down safe, so far," he heard Corporal Bill Woods say in a whisper, collecting his parachute only a few yards from where Jones landed.

"Yeah. So far, so good. Get the men in those trees at the edge of this clearing. Make sure everybody's got his chute, so there's no telltale sign of our landing. Any son of a bitch drops so much as a cigarette butt an' I'm gonna kill him myself. Pass the word around. The Mexicans may have patrols out looking for Raines too. We can't let 'em find a goddamn thing."

"Right, Sergeant." Woods hurried off into the night to get the assault team together.

Jones gathered his black chute, dragging it from the meadow to a tangle of palm trees. They were on a special assignment for Field Marshal Bruno Bottger, to find where Ben Raines and his men had landed when they bailed out of a plane, and to kill him and everyone with him. The orders were to take no prisoners, but Bottger wanted Raines's head to prove he was dead.

No one seemed quite sure where General Raines was, despite the best intelligence General Bottger's men could gather. They knew he'd bailed out forty-three miles north-northwest of Durango, but that was four hours ago. He could be almost anywhere in this stretch of jungle by now.

Jones had only heard about Raines . . . he'd never seen him in the flesh. But if all went as planned, he would get his first glimpse of Raines as a dead man, a bullet-riddled corpse, or a pile of pulpy flesh and bone if an RPG got him first. Jones's team carried enough firepower—RPGs, rocket launchers, and other explosives—to blow Raines out of a bunker dug halfway down in the Mexican soil. While other assault groups in the past had failed to get Raines, Jones harbored no doubts he could accomplish his objective, and he'd said so to General Bottger and his second in command, Sergei Bergman himself, even though he harbored a lingering dislike for the German leader. Bottger was the kind of madman anyone could hate, a real lunatic. But the pay was good with his advancing armies.

Jones's men were veterans of other wars, regional conflicts. Older, seasoned, experienced, they would not make the same mistakes made by the younger mercenaries Bruno Bottger seemed to prefer. The hotshot Russians had been particularly stupid in the south, allowing a Mexican band of Special Forces troops to close a circle around them, blowing them to bits in less than ten minutes when the mercs under Captain Zubov walked into a deadly trap.

A figure came dashing toward Jones. As a reflex, the sergeant swung the muzzle of his AK-47 up, ready to blow the man away unless he identified himself with a code word.

"The men are in position, Sergeant," Corporal Lloyd Davis said, out of breath. "We're waiting for orders."

"You forgot the goddamn code word, Davis!"

"Parrot! Parrot!"

"Raines and his group must be over that way. Fan out in a line, Davis. Pass the word down the line, and this time, remember the goddamn code word!"

"Parrot, Sergeant."

"A mistake like that can get you killed, Davis. Don't make it again."

"Should I leave two men back as a rear guard, Sergeant Jones?"

"Of course, you damn fool. How many times have we been through this drill? Send McKinney and Smith back. They know what to do."

"But, Sergeant," Davis stammered, "Bill McKinney can't see a damn thing in the dark."

Jones turned back to Davis with his jaw clenched. "Corporal McKinney can *smell* an enemy at a hundred yards. *Never* question my orders again. I picked Bill McKinney myself, because he doesn't make dumb mistakes . . . like forgetting the goddamn password on a mission."

"Yes, Sergeant. Sorry. I'll pass the word down the line right away."

Jones forced himself to relax. Davis was right. Mckinney's eyesight was failing some. But a soldier with experience didn't need to see like an eagle to know who to kill, or when. Davis was too young, too green, to understand. Davis had been his last choice for the Blackshirt mission, when no more experienced men were available.

Corporal Woods came back with his automatic rifle slung from his shoulder on a leather strap. "The men are ready to advance, Sergeant."

"Move out. But tell them to be careful. Raines has six or seven men with him, according to our intelligence reports. We probably won't be able to see much of them because of this thick jungle. Look for any lights, and listen for the sound of machetes clearing a path through the jungle. They make just enough noise that, on a quiet night like this, we should be able to hear them if they're moving. And tell everyone to be on the lookout for an ambush. Raines is no dummy, and he'll know we're coming for him."

"How can we avoid an ambush in the dark, Sergeant?"

"You can't, you idiot, but have the men spread out so if they open fire on us, we won't be all bunched up together. Now get moving. We don't know exactly how many of them to expect or how well armed they are, except they were evidently able to bring down a Kiowa with whatever weapons they were carrying. They may even have some land mines with them, so watch where you step, and for God's sake be quiet."

"I'll get the word down the line, Sergeant. But land mines are gonna be a problem. We don't have any sweepers, to keep our backpacks as light as we could. Maybe we should have brought at least one."

"We have no choice but to gamble, Corporal. If somebody steps on a mine, then all hell's gonna break loose. We will have lost the element of surprise."

"What about dogs, Sergeant? You think they might have dogs?"

Sergeant Jones looked at him as if he were crazy. "Dogs? You think they parachuted out of a burning aircraft with dogs in their hands, you idiot?" he whispered in a harsh voice to Corporal Woods.

"Uh, no, I guess not," Corporal Woods answered, a chagrined look on his face as he swung off at a trot to deliver Jones's instructions.

The night in these Mexican jungles was as black as any Gerald Jones had ever seen. Not a breath of air moved among the trees. A man could be heard sneezing or farting at five hundred yards, an advantage for his men, and a disadvantage if one of them made a mistake.

Jones waved a silent signal across the grassy meadow. In

the blackness of shadows below the forest canopy, darker shapes began to move toward the crest of a wooded hillside, hard to see in the night, harder to hear because these men were well trained in the art of night combat. Jones would allow no greenhorns on his handpicked assault force. Davis had been a necessary exception.

A ripping explosion sent Lloyd Davis into the air like a wounded buzzard, flapping his useless arms like broken wings, his AK-47 erupting in a spray of gunfire.

Men began to shout, in spite of Jones's order to keep quiet. Someone shouted, "They got Davis, blew him to hell! Shoot the bastards!"

The chatter of an AK-47 filled the night. Another machine gun chattered in the distance, an Uzi by the sound of it, Jones thought to himself as he ducked under a low-hanging bush. Then a man began screaming, "I'm hit, goddamnit, I'm hit! Shoot the son of a bitch!"

Gerald Jones knew things had suddenly gone wrong. Davis had stepped on a mine, and now everyone in Raines's group must know they were under attack.

Squatting down, Jones cocked an RPG and sent the grenade flying high above the roof of the jungle.

The charge detonated fifty feet in the air, blasting trees and undergrowth with shrapnel. Corporal Woods's shrill scream echoed across the forest as he sank to his knees, clutching his face with both hands in the brief flash of exploding gunpowder.

"I'm hit! Help me, Sergeant!"

"Screw you, Woods," Jones muttered. "A paid soldier has to learn how to help himself, you idiot."

He watched the jungle for signs of movement. Other than the fleeting shadows of his own men racing through the woods, he found nothing to shoot at.

The element of surprise was lost, all because Lloyd Davis was so dumb as to step on a land mine. A voice inside Gerald

Jones's head had whispered that he shouldn't take a man like Davis along on a mission this sensitive. However, good men were getting harder and harder to find lately, and his choices were nil on such short notice.

Jones's first priority was to assassinate Ben Raines, at any cost. But how was he to find Raines in the dark like this, with men shooting and dying all around him?

He crept away from the thick palm trunk where he'd been watching the failing assault on Raines and his crew, inching forward, hoping for a shot at Raines. He only knew him by an old photograph General Bundt had shown him, taken years ago when the SUSA was formed.

Staying low, listening to the hammering of automatic gunfire on all sides, he moved toward where he figured Raines and his men must be with all the stealth he could muster. If Gerald Jones could manage one thing well after his years as a Navy SEAL, it was stealth before he made a kill.

He paused at the edge of a clearing less than a hundred yards from the palm trunk, listening, watching, craning his neck to see what was happening to his assault troops. His men were being slaughtered, from the sound of it . . . not that he gave a shit about anyone other than himself. One lesson he had learned over years of fighting was the value of his own life. It didn't matter a damn who else died. Staying alive was priority one.

A voice behind him spoke. "You looking for somebody in particular?"

Jones froze—he did not recognize the man who spoke to him now—but it could be Private Watts, a Southerner from Alabama who'd stayed back with McKinney.

He risked a glance over his shoulder. "Is that you, Watts?" he asked.

"I've been called names. Smith is one of my favorites, but I stopped using it a long time ago."

A cold chill ran down Jones's spine. The man talking to

him wasn't Private Watts or any other soldier in his company of Blackshirts.

"Nice shirt you're wearing," the voice said, coming from a dark stand of trees only a few feet behind him. "Not one of my favorite colors, black, but it's a nice shirt."

Jones tensed, ready to make his move with his AK-47. "Who are you?" he asked to distract the stranger.

"Ben. Ben Raines. I'm sure I'm the one you've been sent here to kill."

Jones closed his eyelids briefly. How the hell had Raines gotten behind him? "There must be some mistake. We came here to fight the Mexicans."

"No mistake," the voice said. "Unless you count letting me get behind you. That was a helluva mistake."

"Would you shoot a man in the back?"

"I'd shoot a sorry son of a bitch like you in the balls if the light was better. I suppose I'll have to take the only target you've given me. But just for the hell of it, I'm gonna give you a chance to turn around before I pull the trigger."

Gerald felt he had no choice. Either he would be shot down from the rear, or he could take a chance at having better aim than Ben Raines.

He wheeled, sweeping his AK-47 barrel toward the trees as his finger tightened on the trigger.

Jones was lifted off his feet by a hail of lead tearing through his body. As he fell over on his back, just before he lost consciousness, he wondered what Ben Raines really looked like.

Ben walked rapidly away from the dead body that was cooling in the humid jungle air. He knew the flash of his Uzi would've been seen by Jones's men, and he needed to get some distance between him and the site.

Within twenty minutes, the last shot was fired and the jungle was filled with silence.

Moments later, a warbling whistle trilled over the jungle

night, and Harley Reno walked into a clearing, holding a flashlight aloft.

As Raines's team gathered to the light, Harley said, "I got the last one a couple of minutes ago. We're okay now."

Ben stepped forward. "We won't be okay until we get to the Mexican Army base at Durango. When they don't hear back from the patrol they sent to kill us, they'll probably send out choppers at first light. We need to be gone by then."

He glanced at Anna. "You going to be able to make double time from now on?" he asked.

She nodded, though the swelling of her ankle could be seen even through Jersey's tape.

"Yes, sir."

Ben consulted his compass again, then glanced at the night sky, studying the star formations there. "Okay, we'll head off in that general direction as fast as we can," he said, pointing to the southwest. "At first light, we'll slow down and make sure we stay under cover in case the choppers fly by."

"I'll take point," Harley said, starting off with his SPAS shotgun cradled in his arms.

"I'll bring up the rear," Hammer said, taking the second most dangerous position in the column.

"Let's go, people," Ben said, glancing around at the bodies sprawled all around them. "We've wasted enough time here."

Thirty-four

When Ben had heard from General Guerra that he needed the SUSA's help at Durango and Tampico, Ben had instructed Striginov and McGowen to get their bats headed south as fast as they could.

Both men called upon HEMTTs (pronounced Hemits) to do the heavy work of transporting the heavy equipment the men would need. HEMTTs, or Heavy Equipment Mobility Tractor Trucks, were first used for cargo, recovery, and carrying tanks filled with water or fuel in the Desert Storm war in Kuwait in the '90s. They were essentially large tractor-trailers, fitted with four huge wheels on each side that were necessary for traveling through desert and sandy areas.

The HEMTTs tooled through the desert as if they were on superhighways, accompanied by the heavy M-1 Abrams tanks, which could travel forty to fifty miles an hour and could laser-target six objectives at the same time; the smaller but no less effective Sheridan tanks, which were modified low-profile tanks fitted with the older optical sights; and the Bradley Attack Vehicles, or BAVs. All of these carried both 120mm cannons and fifty-caliber machine guns as their main armament. Also running alongside were the Vulcans, very small tanklike vehicles that carried a crew of two along with three-man scout teams they could transport quickly behind enemy lines, covering them with their own 120mm cannons.

The troop movements were led by the aircraft the bats used as air cover: Cobras, which had no night-fighting ability but were deadly hunters in good weather, and Apaches, the super-expensive, all-weather attack helicopters that were state of the art in killing efficiency. The venerable A-10 Warthogs, planes that had been known in combat to have a tail and half a wing shot away and still return home safely, were used both as troop transports and tank hunters. They flew vanguard, and swept the area ahead of the troops for any enemy soldiers that might hinder the movements of the thousands of men Ben was sending into Mexico to help General Guerra slow down the advance of Loco's and Bottger's armies.

Harley Reno stepped out of the jungle a hundred yards from the guard post of the Durango Army base and held up his hands.

The guard, who looked to be no more that sixteen years old, leveled an old M-16 and snapped off a couple of shots in his direction.

Harley dove to the ground and considered blowing the kid's head off, then thought better of it. That wouldn't be a diplomatic way to enter the post.

"Hold your fire!" he shouted.

"Who . . . who goes there?" the soldier asked in Spanish.

Harley answered the same way, explaining he was with General Raines from the SUSA and they were there to see General Guerra.

After some confusion, the boy shouted for them to come on in to the camp.

Ben stepped out of the jungle, smiling at Harley, who was still lying on the ground.

Harley glanced up and grinned. "I'm applying for hazardous-duty pay if we're gonna be working with these dopes."

Coop strolled by, smiling. "I guess you just look like the suspicious type, Harley, not a clean-faced, all-American type like me," he said.

"I didn't hear you volunteer to take point, Mr. All-American," Harley growled, jumping to his feet.

"My momma didn't raise no fools, Harley," Coop replied.

"No, just assholes," Jersey called from the back, but she smiled as she said it.

Coop gave her an injured look. "That hurts, Jersey, and after all we shared."

"You can share my bugs anytime, Coop, especially the fatal ones," she shot back as they neared the guard post.

The young soldier, after a fearful look at Harley, who towered over him by at least a foot, saluted Ben and said, "The general said for me to take you to him at once, sir."

Harley gently pushed the barrel of the young boy's M-16 up toward the ceiling. "We'll follow you, soldier," he said. "Wouldn't want you behind me with that thing."

General Guerra rushed from behind his desk to shake Ben's hand, nodding his greeting to the other members of the team.

"General Raines, I am very happy to see you, sir."

"Happy to be here, General. As it turns out, we have a common goal . . . to keep Loco and Bottger out of Durango and Tampico as long as we can."

"That is my hope as well," Guerra said. "Please, gentlemen and ladies, have a seat and I will have my aide bring you some refreshments." He looked over the bedraggled group. "You look as if you could use them."

"A couple of nights and a day in your jungles will do that to you, General," Ben said.

"Please, call me Jose and I will call you Ben."

Ben shrugged. "All right."

After Guerra gave the orders for them to be brought food and wine, he sat behind his desk, ready to get down to business.

"What are your plans, Ben?" he asked.

"Of course, I'd like you to remain in command of all the

Mexican troops, Jose, but I'll have to insist on giving the orders concerning the disposition and conduct of my men."

"Certainly, Ben, that is to be expected."

"Good, I'm glad we agree," Ben said. "Now, what is your latest intel on Loco's and Bottger's movements?"

Guerra whirled his desk chair around and pulled a large-scale map of Mexico down from a roller on the wall. "Here we are at Durango, Ben," he said, pointing to the map. "Bottger's mercenaries have taken Puerto Vallarta, Guadalajara, and are now attacking Valparaiso, about ninety miles to our south."

"How about Loco?"

"They are massed at Ciudad de Valles twenty-five miles south of Tampico, and are now staging attacks against the Navy base there with helicopters and some older-model jet airplanes."

"No foot soldiers?"

"Not as of yet. The terrain there is very . . . how you say, wild. My officers think it will take them another two days for the troops to get in position to attack them."

"Why aren't they just airlifting them in with Chinooks?" Harley asked.

Guerra smiled. "The base at Tampico is not without its own defenses. While our helicopters are of the older, Huey vintage, my pilots are fearless and have inflicted heavy damages to the more modern helicopters of Perro Loco's army. I feel he is afraid the Hueys would shoot the slower Chinooks down, so he is waiting until most of the Hueys are neutralized, as they soon will be, by the vastly superior Kiowas."

Ben nodded. "That gives Ike McGowen a couple of days to get some reinforcements to your base. If you will get me a radio, I'll get on the horn and tell him to put it in high gear. We've got some helicopters with the 502 that will make the Kiowas look like kids' toys."

"Oh?" Guerra asked.

"Yeah," Harley said, grinning. "The Apaches will eat the Kiowas for lunch, if they've got the *cojones* to face 'em."

Guerra grinned. "I've heard of the Apache helicopter, but I admit, I've never seen one."

"The Apache is the most sophisticated and most expensive attack helicopter ever built," Ben said. "It's equipped with night vision and target acquisition and designation systems to enable it to fly and fight in all weathers, day or night. It's armed with Hellfire missiles that can lock onto and destroy any known tank, and for softer targets it's also equipped with 2.75-inch rockets and an extremely accurate thirty-millimeter Chain Gun."

Harley grinned. "And it flies at one hundred fifty-five knots and has a range of three hundred miles. It kicked butt in the Gulf War and in Africa against Bottger a few years ago."

"Ike's also got a couple of Aardvarks," Ben said, "and their range is over nine hundred miles. Maybe he could send a couple of them to keep Loco's troops busy until he gets in range for the Apaches."

"That is excellent news, Ben," Guerra said. "Perhaps Tampico can be saved after all."

Lieutenant Tommy Bartholomew took off in his Aardvark from an improvised airstrip that'd been bulldozed in the desert by the big Catapillar Cat-9's the night before. He'd barely had time after his night landing to get six hours' sleep and eat a quick breakfast before Ike McGowen had told him of Ben's request for a little harassment of Loco's troops at Ciudad de Valles.

The General Dynamics F-111 Aardvark was the first supersonic fighter-bomber with the ability to make low-level precision bombing attacks by day or night, in any kind of weather. Known as the Aardvark because of its droop-nose silhouette, the swept-wing F-111 entered service over Vietnam in 1968. In 1986, F-111's based in England struck at Colonel Qaddafi's

Libya, and in 1991 the F-111 was one of the anti-Saddam Hussein coalition's most important aircraft. Now, almost fifty years since its first combat flight, the F-111 was still a mighty killing machine, and Bartholomew loved it as most men loved their wives.

Carrying almost eleven tons of bombs, it took almost three thousand feet to get airborne, but once in the air, the fighter flew at almost eight hundred knots southward toward Loco's troop concentrations in the City of the Valleys.

Assured by McGowen that there were few if any civilians in the occupied city, Tommy dove out of the sun at just under the speed of sound, his electronic sights picking out targets of tanks, ammo dumps, fuel storage tanks, and troop bivouac areas.

On his first sweep, catching Loco's men completely unaware, he dropped his bombs so low that he flew through the dark red mushroom clouds of debris and flames that rose upon exploding. Sweeping up in a wide turn, he glanced over his shoulder and saw several helicopters and two smaller jet fighters angling on the runway south of the city to get in position to take off.

Banking so steeply his cheeks bulged and flattened against the G-forces, he whipped around and made another run, this time the craters of his bombs marching inexorably toward the hapless planes still warming up for takeoff. Two of the helicopters managed to get off the ground before Tommy's bombs totally destroyed the runway, three hangars, and most of the control tower of the airport.

His left wing shuddered under the impact of the Kiowa's 20mm Minigun as he swept past the first helicopter. Ignoring the damage and the red warning lights that lit up his instrument panel like a Christmas tree, Tommy keyed the second Kiowa into his fire-control computer and pressed the button on his wing guns.

Every fifth bullet was a tracer, and the red dots of death screamed toward the helicopter, finally mating with it in a fiery explosion that rocked the F-111 as it flew by. Tommy watched the wreckage land in a field of scattering troops, incinerating at least a couple of dozen screaming men.

The control stick shook and shuddered in his hands, and he could see pieces of his left wing peeling off where the 20mm shells had stitched a pattern across.

He made one more pass at high altitude to stay out of range of the remaining Kiowa, and dumped the rest of his bombs indiscriminately over the city, watching most of them disappear under clouds of smoke and dust and flames.

Reluctantly, he pointed the nose of his beloved F-111 north toward Tampico and keyed the mike on his radio.

"Mayday, Mayday," he said calmly, dialing in the frequency of the Navy base at Tampico that he'd been given in his preflight briefing that morning.

"This is Big Bird One-One-One to base at Tampico. I have a Mayday."

"Come in, Big Bird, this is Tampico Navy base," a Spanish-accented voice said in fairly good English.

"I've taken a hit on my left wing and the stabilizer is out. I need clearance for a straight-in approach on Runway B-12," Tommy said, glancing at the map strapped to his right thigh.

"Come ahead, Big Bird. We'll have fire trucks and foaming equipment standing by for your landing."

"Roger, Tampico. Get the beer ready. I've got a mouthful of dust to cut."

"Roger that, Big Bird. Good luck, *amigo,*" the voice said, signing off.

Minutes later, his wings wiggling and shaking more than Elvis's hips ever had, Tommy lowered the nose of the F-111 toward the base at Tampico and lowered his flaps, hoping they would help calm the jittering of his wings on final approach.

His speed slowed, making control of the aircraft more difficult, and sweat began to pour from his forehead and face as he gripped the control stick with both hands, using his feet on the pedals to try to keep the plane in the air for another quarter mile.

"It's gonna be close, old girl. Hang in there for me another couple'a seconds," he whispered through a dry mouth to his plane.

The F-111 hit the ground, bounced once, skidded slightly to the right, then began to slow to manageable speed in the center of the runway.

Tommy leaned his head back, breathed a quick prayer of thanks, and let the air he'd been holding out of his lungs.

Thirty-five

Lieutenant Commander Johnny Held and Lieutenant Josh Fuentes were in the lead Apache flying out of Georgi Striginov's 505 Bat, while Lieutenant Commander Jerry Stringer and Lieutenant Wally Fuller were flying backup in the second Apache.

Their orders were simple: Find the mercenaries operating under the command of Field Marshal Bruno Bottger and destroy as many men and as much equipment as they could. If they managed to down a few helicopters, all the better.

Their last intel was that the mercs were attacking the village of Valapraiso ninety miles to the south of Durango, where General Ben Raines and his team were meeting with the head of the Mexican Armed Forces, General Jose Guerra.

As they flew along the tributaries of the Grande de Santiago, the large river on the West Coast that sent its smaller branches up near Valapraiso, they could see smoke and flashes of light as the mercs systematically destroyed the meager defenses of the small town.

"Whirlybird One to Whirlybird Two," Held said to Stringer over the ship-to-ship radio. "Looks like the bad guys are having *some* fun down there, pickin' on the smaller boys."

"Yeah," Stringer answered. "Let's go kick some sand in their faces and teach them some manners, American style."

"Roger that," Held said. "Drop your socks and grab your cocks, boys, we're goin' downtown!"

The two Apaches separated slightly, put their noses down

for increased speed, and rushed toward the conflagration below. Held could see a couple of small black dots flitting around the outskirts of the town, and knew them to be either Kiowas or Defenders. It was too far to tell which they might be, but it really didn't matter too much, for the Apache outclassed both of them in combat by a large margin.

Deciding to save his 2.75-inch rockets for the big boys, the Chinooks he knew must be in the area, Held fingered the trigger on his 30mm Chain Gun. The Chain Gun was a hellish instrument that could fire 30mm slugs so fast it sounded like a steady whine instead of the usual chatter of a machine-gun.

One of the enemy helicopters, a Kiowa, must have seen them coming, for it turned its back and headed off in full retreat.

"Smart boy," Held said to his copilot, Josh Fuentes, who was busy checking the area for other targets or risks.

The second helicopter, a McDonnell Douglas OH-6 Defender, made the mistake of turning to face the Apache and letting go with a stream of 20mm shells from its Minigun while the Apache was still far out of range.

"That boy's got more balls than brains," Josh said. "The Defender may be good against tanks and ground installations, but it's not worth spit as an attack chopper."

"He's gonna find that out in about twenty seconds," Held said as he locked his target acquisition computer sights on the smaller helicopter and pulled the trigger on the Chain Gun.

The Defender seemed to just disintegrate under the onslaught of the first burst of 30mm shells, breaking into pieces too small to see, then exploding in a fireball of av-gas and ammunition.

Without slowing his descent, Held asked, "Next target?"

Josh keyed his computer and said, "Half-track personnel carrier at three o'clock low, off to the right. It's already keyed into right-pod rocket launcher."

"Roger," Held said, and fingered the trigger to the right-hand-side rocket launcher.

A 2.75-inch rocket shot from under the right turbine engine, and curved in a gentle arc downward toward a large truck with tank threads on its rear part, full of soldiers. As the rocket flared on its way down, Held could see a couple of men try to jump out of the vehicle. They were in midair when the rocket buried its nose in the engine compartment of the truck and exploded, sending crumpled, blackened metal and bits and pieces of soldiers' bodies flying through the air.

"Incoming!" Josh hollered as his computer picked up the trail of a handheld GTA SAM missile that'd been fired at them by one of the soldiers.

Without thinking, acting on reflex since he had only seconds to react, Held pulled up on the collective, jerked the throttle stick to the side, and pumped his feet on the pedals, sending the Apache in a sideways, leaning dive toward the ground. The SAM passed by less than thirty feet from the right turbine, too close to turn toward the heat.

In one continuous move, Held bent the Apache's nose back around and arrowed toward the ground, his finger holding the trigger of the Chain Gun down, strafing the thousands of troops scattering like stampeded cattle before him.

A 30mm bullet makes quite a mess of human flesh, and the soldiers below were smashed and torn asunder by the fusillade of bullets that rained down on them like hail from hell, killing hundreds of men in the first pass.

A few soldiers tried to fire their machine-guns at the Apache, but it was like trying to hit a hawk with a slingshot, and none of the bullets made contact as Held pulled up out of his dive and prepared for another pass.

"Target?" he asked in a calm voice, as if this were just another day at the office.

"There's a pair of Chinooks over to the left," Josh said calmly. "Looks like they're trying to warm up their engines for a fast getaway."

"Dial 'em in and let's get the bastards," Held said.

Josh's fingers flew over the keyboard to his target acquisition computer, and seconds later he said, "Done."

Held lined up the nose of the Apache, and pulled back on the collective to cause it to hover momentarily. Just as he tapped the fire button on the rocket launcher, one of the Chinooks lifted off, the heavy helicopter trying to get airborne and escape its fate.

The first rocket hit the Chinook on the ground, exploding it in a giant fireball, the metal of its fuselage collapsing around the troops that had been trying to clamber on board and killing all in a split second.

The second Chinook was about thirty feet off the ground and just beginning its turn when the 2.75-inch rocket entered its turbine exhaust port, blowing the engine off the machine.

The Chinook spun wildly, out of control, and smashed to the ground, first flattening out like a giant pancake. Then it too exploded, sending flames and smoke a hundred feet into the air.

Stringer and Fuller were equally busy. Stringer had elected to focus his attack on the troops on the outskirts of the town. He aimed the nose of his Apache at several HumVees and smaller jeeps that were using their pole-mounted fifty-caliber machine guns to rake the buildings of Valapraiso with murderous fire.

When their gunners saw the Apache coming at them out of the sun, they swiveled their guns upward and continued to fire, trying desperately to down the approaching aircraft.

It was no use. The Chain Gun mounted under the Apache's nose exploded into action, sending thousands of rounds of 30mm shells at the vehicles.

Two HumVees disintegrated under the impact, exploding and killing all the men within a hundred yards of their location as molten, twisted metal acted like shrapnel from a dozen hand grenades and scythed through them like a cultivator through a field of wheat, mowing them down and killing them instantly.

One of the jeeps took off in a screeching turn, trying to

escape the fire, but the tracers of the Chain Gun followed it, stitching a path up the road until they intersected with the jeep and blew it twenty feet into the air, its rubber tires on fire and sending out thick, black clouds of smoke.

By now, the mercenaries were in full retreat, running in packs and individually as fast as they could away from the town. Some even dove into the rivers that ran near the city limits and tried to hide in the slowly moving waters.

With most of the heavy equipment either abandoned or destroyed, the two Apaches flitted back and forth, firing their Chain Guns at the running men, killing hundreds as they tried to make their escape.

Soon, most of the larger groups of men were either dead or had dispersed, dropping their weapons and hightailing it toward the sparse jungles in the distance, trying to get under cover and away from the Angels of Death flying overhead.

"Whirlybird Two, come in," Held said, pulling his Apache away from the fleeing soldiers and back toward town.

"Whirlybird Two here," Stringer replied. "What do you think, Johnny? We done enough damage for the time being?"

"Roger that, Jerry. You stand guard up here for a while in case that Kiowa decides to come back and fight. I'm gonna land and see if there are any defenders left in the town to fight."

"That Kiowa won't come back, Johnny, not unless he's got shit for brains, but I'll keep an eye out just in case."

Johnny Held landed his Apache, leaving Josh at the controls in case he needed to take off in a hurry, while he walked toward the destroyed buildings of Valapraiso.

Within ten minutes, bedraggled Mexican soldiers and townspeople began to come out of basements and the rubble of collapsed buildings from all across the town.

Held stood with his hands on his hips until a contingent of soldiers, led by a man with sergeant's stripes on his uniform, walked up to him.

The sergeant saluted smartly, even though blood from two wounds on his left arm was dripping onto the ground.

"Sergeant Raul Dominguez, sir," he said.

"You the commanding officer here, Raul?" Johnny said, sticking out his hand to shake.

"Yes, sir, I am now. Both our lieutenants were killed in the attack."

Johnny looked around. Dominguez had perhaps sixty or seventy men left who looked like they were well enough to fight.

"Why don't you get your men to round up the weapons and ammunition, and a couple of those jeeps over there with the fifty-calibers on 'em?" he asked. "My partner and I will stay aloft and cover you until you're back in the town and get your defenses set back up."

"Yes, sir," Dominguez said. Then he turned and barked orders in rapid Spanish to his men, who scattered and began to pick up machine guns, grenades, and ammunition boxes that were lying among the dead and wounded mercenaries.

Dominguez glanced around. "What shall I do with the wounded enemies, sir?" he asked.

"You got enough men to play nursemaid to a bunch of mercenaries that were doin' their best to kill you an hour ago?" Held asked.

"Uh, now that you mention it, sir, I don't."

"Then leave 'em," Held said. "Buzzards gotta eat too."

Dominguez grinned, and Held knew that was the answer he'd wanted, and probably what he would have done no matter what Held had advised. The Mexican Army was not known for its humanitarian instincts in the best of times.

"Yes, sir."

"We'll hang around until we see your men are all safely back in town. Then we gotta split. Gettin' kinda low on go-juice," Held said.

"You think they'll be back, sir?" Dominguez asked, glancing in the direction the soldiers had taken when they ran off.

Held shook his head. "Not today, but they'll get reinforcements and probably hit you again tomorrow or the next day."

"Can we expect more help from you *americanos?"* Dominguez asked.

Held shrugged. "Yeah, our battalion should be well within distance to help out by tomorrow, but you fellows look like you were doin' all right on your own. Now that you got plenty of ammo and time to dig in, I don't think you're gonna have any problems."

Dominguez saluted again, then turned to make sure his men were thorough in picking through the weapons and ammunition scattered around the battlefield.

Thirty-six

It was almost full dark by the time the Kiowa helicopter that had fled the battle at Valapraiso landed outside the Presidential Palace at Mexico City.

The pilot and copilot were brought to the conference room on the third floor, where Bruno Bottger and Perro Loco and their entourages were having a strategy meeting.

Bottger and Loco sat side by side, glaring across the desk at the tired, sweaty men who stood before them, their heads hanging down.

"Give us your report," Bottger ordered harshly.

"We were about to enter the town, Field Marshal, when two Apache helicopters came at us from the north," said the pilot.

"They had the SUSA markings on them, Herr Bottger," the copilot added.

Bottger glanced at Loco, then back at the two men. "And you didn't stay to fight?" he asked, scorn dripping from his tongue.

The pilot shook his head. "No, sir. The Kiowa is no match for one Apache, much less two. The pilot of the Defender tried to fight them, and was blown out of the sky before he could get a shot off."

"It appears the dead man was much braver than you two," Bottger said, his face turning red.

"I thought it more important to save the helicopter, sir," the pilot said, standing up straight. "I am not afraid to die, but to throw my life away when I have no chance would be counterproductive to our efforts to win this war."

Sergei Bergman leaned forward to speak to Bottger. "He is correct, Field Marshal. The Kiowas, and the men with the know-how to pilot them, are too valuable to us to lose unnecessarily."

Bottger took a deep breath and leaned back in his chair. "Perhaps you are right, Sergei."

He glanced back at the two pilots. "Get yourselves cleaned up and get something to eat. We will need you again in the morning."

"Yes, sir," the two men said in unison, and saluted before turning to leave, much relieved they hadn't been shot out of hand.

After they were gone, Bottger referred to a radio report from the field. "It appears the attack on Valapraiso was completely routed by the arrival of the American warships."

Loco nodded. "The same thing happened to my men at Ciudad de Valles. General Enrique Gonzalez states he barely escaped with his life and that most of his men are either dead or wounded. He desires immediate reinforcements and better air cover."

"Looks like Ben Raines's men have arrived a bit sooner than we expected. This is gonna complicate matters."

Sergei Bergman nodded his agreement. "Yes. It means it will be extremely difficult to occupy the remainder of Mexico in the time frame we first planned."

Bottger thumbed through the intel reports in front of him. "It seems a full battalion of troops has been sent to defend Tampico, and a full battalion to defend Durango."

"Our men will play hell trying to defeat battalions equipped as well as those of the Americans are," Paco Valdez said from his seat next to Loco.

Loco nodded. "I do not believe it can be done as long as our forces are divided."

"I agree," Bottger said, his eyes fixed on a map of Mexico.

"I propose we unify our forces and concentrate on Durango. If I send my men straight from Guadalajara toward Durango, skirting the mountains to the west of the city, they can be there in two days' time." He cut his eyes to the other side of the map. "And if you order your men that are south of Tampico to strike directly west, we might be able to catch Durango in a pincer movement between our two forces."

Loco leaned over to look at the map. "I see. Together, we vastly outnumber one battalion. If we strike fast enough by having our men travel all during the night and lay low during the day, we might be able to catch the defenders of Durango off guard."

"We can transport most of the men still here in Mexico City in our C-130's and land them at Sombrerete, fifty miles southeast of Durango. There is an old airfield there that will let the transport planes land. If we time it right, we will then have a three-pronged attack that will hit Durango at the same time."

Bottger and Loco looked at each other and nodded. "Then that is what we shall do," Bottger said. He glanced at Sergei Bergman. "Sergei, you and Mr. Strunk coordinate the troop movements so that the attacks will occur simultaneously."

Bergman and Strunk nodded and began to gather their papers together.

Sergei knocked on Bottger's bedroom door just before midnight.

"Come in," Bottger said.

"Field Marshal," Bergman said as he entered. "The plan is done and the orders have been given. The attacks will occur day after tomorrow at dawn."

"There's one more thing we have to do," Bottger said.

"What's that?"

"Tomorrow evening I want you to send three jets loaded with our plague bombs to the north. One is to let his bombs off over Durango. The other two are to fly as far north as they can get and drop them as close to the SUSA's southern border as they can."

"But, Field Marshal, they will never get all the way to the SUSA. The air defenses are too good."

"I know that, but with two divisions of Americans here, and with several million people inhabiting northern Mexico, it will not take long for the plague to spread to the SUSA. By the time we've finished with Durango, the disease should be well established in both the SUSA and Mexico."

"You are aware the plague will devastate not only the Mexicans and Americans, but Perro Loco's troops as well?"

"Yes, but by then, we will no longer need Señor Loco or his men. Once the plague has rendered both Mexico and the SUSA impotent, it will only be a matter of occupying the countries with our mercenaries and beginning to take them over."

Bergman nodded, smiling. "And soon after the SUSA falls ill, the U.S. will follow."

Bottger grinned. "Exactly."

After darkness fell the next day, Bottger and Bergman rode out to the Mexico City airport. Bottger had told Loco he was going to send a couple of bombers over Durango to see if they could soften the city up by dropping some bombs from a high altitude.

Loco didn't think much of the plan, but since the planes belonged to Bottger, there wasn't much he could do about it. Of course, he knew nothing of the lethal cargo in the bombs the planes carried.

Bottger and Bergman pulled up to the runway in front of the three F-111's. The pilots were standing on the edge of the tarmac awaiting final instructions.

"Gentlemen," Bottger said, standing in front of them. "You have your orders. It is imperative that the bombs be dropped as planned. It is not important that you are precise in your targeting. The bombs are designed to detonate one thousand feet from the ground to insure maximum spread of the bacteria contained in them."

He pointed to one of the men. "Your target is the city of Durango, or as close to it as you can get. The most important thing is to release the bombs if you come under attack, even if you are not over your target."

He glanced at the other two. "You men are to separate and to head at maximum altitude and speed toward the southern border of the SUSA. Once again, at the first sign of interdiction or if you are fired upon by missiles, release the bombs no matter where you are. Understand?"

The men all nodded. They knew there was little chance of them returning from this mission, but Bottger had promised each of them huge sums of money in the event they succeeded, with the money to go to their families if they died in the attempt.

One after another, the jets taxied up to the end of the runway and took off, climbing at a steep angle to get as high as they could as fast as they could.

A Mexican soldier burst into the situation room at the Army base at Durango where Ben Raines and his team were going over the latest intel reports with General Guerra and his staff.

The soldier and General Guerra spoke back and forth in rapid Spanish for a moment, with Guerra's face becoming more and more worried the longer they spoke.

Ben glanced at Harley Reno. "What's going on, Harley?" he asked.

Harley, who was fluent in Spanish, leaned over and whispered, "That man is the radar operator of the base. Evidently, he's picked up three fast-moving blips at high altitude and coming this way from Mexico City. They'll be over us in less than fifteen minutes."

Without waiting for confirmation from Guerra, Ben turned to Corrie, his radio operator. "Get on the horn, fast, to Georgi Striginov," he said, "and tell him we need a couple of F-111's up here pronto."

Corrie, who was never very far from her compact radio set, rushed to the back of the room and began the call immediately. Her low voice could be heard talking urgently to someone, but the words couldn't be made out.

After a couple of minutes, she came back over to Ben. "Georgi's second in command said he'd get right on it, but there was no way they could be here in time to beat the bogeys from Mexico City."

Ben turned to Guerra, who was listening. "Can you scramble anything that'll help us?" he asked.

Guerra shook his head. "The only aircraft we have here right now ready to go are a couple of old Warthogs."

"How fast are the bogeys moving?" Ben asked the radar operator.

Harley quickly translated the question. When the man answered, he looked back at Ben. "A lot faster than the Warthogs can handle."

Ben looked at Guerra. "Scramble the Warthogs, General. Maybe they'll get lucky with one of their guided missiles."

Guerra nodded and picked up the phone on his desk, speaking rapidly into it. Then he looked up. "They'll be airborne in five minutes. If the jets coming this way drop low enough, we might have a chance."

"Better sound the air raid siren and get everyone under cover," Ben said. "If those are F-111's coming this way, they can carry over eleven tons of bombs and still travel twice as fast as a Warthog."

Lieutenant Colonel Jaime Fuentes eased back the stick on his Warthog, and smiled as it lifted up off the runway at the Durango airfield. Jaime, who'd been trained at Fort Hood in

Texas some ten years ago, lived to fly. To him, the war of aggression by Perro Loco was a godsend, relieving him of the boredom of the years of peace when he'd had to beg for air time to keep his skills intact.

He was a gifted flyer who'd finished first in his class, to the surprise of the college grads he'd beaten from the SUSA schools. Jaime had only a high school education, but he'd been born to fly and the complex movements of hands and feet and eyes came like second nature to him.

The Fairchild A-10 Warthog he was flying had few rivals as a close-support aircraft, carrying both guided missiles and a 30mm cannon in its nose. Its one drawback was it was very slow, flying at only 380 knots at sea level. The F-111's it was going up against could fly at over seven hundred knots, and were better armed.

Jaime didn't think of this as he pulled his beloved Warthog up as fast as it could go. He was going into battle, and his adrenaline was pumping and his heart was racing—in short, he was having the time of his life. Like most pilots, he felt he was the best there was, and counted on his skills overcoming the natural superiority of the planes he was going up against.

"Hog One, this is Base, come in," a scratchy voice on his radio sounded.

"Hog One to base," Jaime answered.

"Bogeys are separating," the voice continued. "Only one bogey is headed this way. The other two are going to pass well to the west of us."

"What is the current altitude of the bogey?" Jaime asked as he stared at his shipboard radar screen to see if he could pick out the blip that was to be his target.

"Fourteen thousand feet and dropping. It's coming in for a bombing run, Jaime."

"Roger that," Jaime said, imitating the pilots he'd trained with in Texas, down to the Texas drawl they'd said it with.

He keyed the intercom switch to talk to his copilot and

gunner, sitting directly behind him in the double cockpit. "Julio, put your dancing shoes on, we're fixing to boogie."

"I'm on the dance floor, but I cannot hear the music, *compadre,"* Julio responded, their personal code meaning Julio had all weapons systems ready to go but the target was still out of range.

"Snap off a quick ATA to see if we can get his attention," Jaime ordered, hoping the air-to-air missile would at least get close enough to cause the other pilot to change his course away from the base.

"It's too far," Julio protested.

"I know, but lead him like you do the geese when we go hunting at the lake, Julio. Perhaps the missile's heat seeker will pick him up as he approaches."

"Sí, and perhaps it will miss him, circle, and pick us up instead," Julio said, "but here goes nothing."

The Warthog shuddered slightly as a missile jumped from the right-wing pods and angled off to the left, toward the unknown bogey, which was still on the very edge of the plane's radar screen.

Jaime shifted course slightly to his left.

"What are you doing?" Julio asked.

"Most pilots are right-handed," Jaime explained. "I'm betting when he sees the ATA coming at him, he's going to jig to the right. I'm altering course to cut the distance down and when he jigs, I'm going to be there waiting for him."

"What if you're wrong and he jigs left?" Julio asked.

"Then we're probably dead," Jaime answered calmly, as if he knew that wasn't going to happen.

Sure enough, when the blip of the missile closed on the blip of the F-111, the plane jigged to the right and downward to get away from the ATA missile, just as Jaime figured he would.

Jaime's A-10 was already pointed at the F-111 as it dove, and he thumbed the button on the 30mm cannon and simultaneously fired another ATA, hoping if the other pilot managed to dodge one, the other would get him.

Several blips appeared on the screen as the ATA missile and machine-gun bullets arched toward the F-111.

"He's dropped his bombs," Julio said exuberantly, "well short of the base."

Suddenly, the night sky was lit up by the explosion of several tons of aircraft above and directly in front of the Warthog.

Cursing, Jaime jerked his stick to the side and put the A-10 in a slip-sliding dive, trying to avoid the shrapnel-like wreckage of the F-111.

The windscreen in front of Jaime shattered and his face felt as if it'd been punched by a heavyweight fighter as pieces of the F-111's fuselage punched through the Plexiglas.

Jaime's head snapped back under the impact and he lost consciousness for a few seconds. When he came to, Julio's voice was hollering in his ear over the intercom.

"We're in a spin . . . we're in a spin! Pull up, Jaime, pull up!"

Groggily, with only his instinct to guide him, Jaime's hands and feet began a delicate dance together to regain control of the aircraft before it plunged into the desert sands below.

The Warthog leveled out at less than five hundred feet, Julio's voice saying the Lord's Prayer in Jaime's ears as he finally cleared the blood out of his eyes and banked back toward the base for a landing.

Thirty-seven

There was jubilation in the war room of the Durango Army base when the radar operator reported the F-111 from Mexico City had been shot down well short of the base.

While the other men were celebrating the heroism of Jaime Fuentes, who was in the medical ward having the cuts on his face stitched up, Harley stood next to the radar operator and continued to question him closely about what he'd seen.

Harley's face was glum when he came back to Ben to report. "Something strange about this whole thing, General," he said.

"What's that, Harley?" Ben asked, putting down the glass of wine that Guerra had passed out on the news of the successful interdiction of the attacker.

"The radar man says it looked like the F-111 dropped his bombs before he was blown up."

Ben shrugged. "So what? They evidently fell over land that was sparsely populated."

"That's not what's bothering me, sir," Harley continued. "The radar man says it looked to him like the bombs exploded at one thousand feet instead of falling all the way to the ground."

"Shit!" Ben exclaimed. "There's only one type of bomb designed to detonate in the air like that."

Harley nodded. "Yes, sir. BW bombs."

"That means the other two that're headed toward our southern border are probably filled with the anthrax bug too," Ben said, "and even if we shoot 'em down, the bug is going to be released over northern Mexico or the southern SUSA."

"Yes, sir, my thoughts exactly," Harley said.

Ben leaned back in his chair and ran his hands through his hair. "I guess it's time to tell the general what's going on, and to get Dr. Buck to ship as much of the vaccine as he can spare down here pronto."

"I'll have Corrie get on the radio to Mike Post at headquarters immediately, Ben, while you talk to the general," Harley said.

After Ben had explained how Bottger had most probably released a potent biological weapon over General Guerra's country, they made plans for the quick distribution of the vaccine to all units of the Mexican Army, to be followed as rapidly as possible by the vaccination of as many of the citizens of Mexico as could be gotten to.

"The problem," General Guerra said, a sad look on his face, "is that this part of Mexico is very rural, with the population spread over many thousands of acres. It will be almost impossible to vaccinate everyone before the plague begins to spread."

"You're right, Jose, but that will work in our favor too. The plague is spread person to person, so if the people are very spread out, fewer of them will come in contact with those afflicted by the plague. We just have to get on the radio and TV and newspapers to tell everyone to stay away from congested areas, like towns and markets."

"I will have my information officers get right on it, Ben, and we will pray that the vaccine gets here in time to prevent the loss of most of my Army to sickness."

"Those that do contract the illness can be treated with antibiotics, which I will also have sent along with the vaccine, Jose."

"Muchas gracias, Ben."

At that moment, Harley returned from Corrie's side. She'd been talking with Mike Post in Louisiana at Ben's headquarters.

"Good news, Ben," he said.

"Tell me," Ben said. "I could use some good news right about now."

"Mike says no problem on the vaccine and antibiotics. They'll be on the way here by midnight, and should arrive in time to start inoculations first thing in the morning. He's also sending extra teams of medics to help with the shots, both in the Army and in the countryside."

"That is good news," Ben said, a look of relief on his face.

"There's more. General Striginov's interceptors were able to shoot down both of the other bogeys before they reached our border. One went down near Chihuahua and the other over Monterrey."

"Damn," Ben said, some of the elation leaving his face. "That's good for us but terrible for the Mexicans. There's going to be tremendous loss of life before we can get the vaccine down there."

"I know, but it could have been worse," Harley said, "if they'd made it over Houston or El Paso."

"You're right, Harley. Guess we need to count our blessings."

As they spoke, another man entered the room, a worried look on his face. After Guerra spoke with him, the general approached Ben.

"Our advance scouts report heavy troop movements to the south."

Ben stared at him. "From the east or the west?" he asked.

"Both," Guerra said shortly. "It appears as if Loco has given up on his idea of taking Tampico and has coordinated with Bottger to have both their armies converge on us here at Durango."

"When does it look like they'll arrive?" Ben asked.

"Our scouts figure they'll attack at first light tomorrow, or shortly thereafter."

Ben turned to Corrie. "What's Striginov's ETA here?" he asked.

"He said if he pushes it, he can be here early in the morning with most of his heavy equipment. The ground troops will be a few hours later."

"Get back on the radio and tell him to push it," Ben said. "Looks like we're gonna have some visitors by breakfast time."

Claire Osterman called a meeting of her advisory staff for eight o'clock in the evening. When they arrived, she looked like a cat who'd just swallowed a canary.

Harlan Millard, Major General Bradley Stevens, Jr., his assistant Colonel James King, and Herb Knoff all helped themselves to coffee from a sideboard in her office and took their seats, waiting to see just what Claire had on her mind.

Stevens and King had been very busy for the past week making sure all of her troops were moving back from their stations on the borders with the SUSA, as well as getting medics around to all the battalions to inoculate the troops against Bruno Bottger's dreaded plague bacteria in case it was launched.

Claire took her time, letting the suspense build for a while as she shuffled papers on her desk and fiddled with her coffee, getting it just right with cream and artificial sweetener. Proud of her new build after her incarceration of the year before, she was still on a strict diet and daily workout regimen.

Finally, Stevens could stand it no longer. "Madame President, you called us here for a reason?"

"Yes, Brad," she said sweetly. "I have here a collection of reports from my spies in Perro Loco's army, as well as some news reports from reporters in the SUSA who are . . . shall we say, sympathetic to our cause?"

Stevens glanced at Millard and King. He'd heard nothing new in his daily intel reports that would justify such a meeting.

"And?" he asked.

"It seems that Ben Raines and some of his closest associates are down in Durango, Mexico, coordinating the fallback and consolidation of the Mexican Army down there."

"So?" Stevens asked, wondering what bee was in Claire's bonnet now.

"Perro Loco and Bruno Bottger both suffered severe setbacks in their last offensive, both due in part to the interference of Raines in Mexico's affairs."

Stevens had to force himself to keep his mouth shut about Claire railing against Raines for interfering in Mexico in a war that was the direct result of some meddling of her own.

"Perro Loco and Bottger are now working in concert and are forming a huge offensive against Durango, coming at the city from both sides with everything they have. It's going to be a do-or-die effort, with maximum effort put forth to crush the Mexican defenders. What they don't know, but I do, is that Raines has at least two battalions of his own coming to his aid. With that setup, who do you think will emerge victorious in the upcoming battle for Durango?" she asked, staring at Stevens and King.

Stevens shrugged, being careful to choose words that would not set Claire off. He didn't dare give Raines and his Army too much praise, though he knew Loco's ill-trained troops and Bottger's hired mercenaries couldn't stand against the highly trained and very loyal troops under Raines's command. "I'd have to give the edge to Raines and the Mexicans," he finally said. "They're much better equipped and the Mexicans are fighting on their home ground, which always counts for something."

King nodded his agreement. "Me too. I'd be surprised if Loco or Bottger come out of the battle with enough troops to ever be a serious force again."

"My thoughts exactly," Claire said, surprising everyone with her agreement. "And, evidently, Bruno Bottger knows he doesn't stand a chance with conventional warfare, because my news sources inform me that three jets bearing BW bombs were launched last evening."

"What?" Stevens said, sitting forward in his chair.

Claire nodded. "That's correct. Bottger has finally launched a BW attack against both Mexico and the SUSA, though his bombers only got as far as Chihuahua and Monterrey before they were forced to drop their plague bombs prematurely."

"Jesus," Harlan Millard said as he took a handkerchief out of his pocket and wiped his face. "It's a good thing Raines shared their vaccine with us, or we'd be facing death and destruction on a major scale."

"Yes, it is," Claire said, still smiling for an unknown reason. "Which brings me to the point of tonight's meeting. Now that the plague is afoot, Mexico is going to be devastated. Even if the SUSA manages to get the vaccine down there, it's going to take a couple of weeks before it's effective. In the meantime, thousands, perhaps millions of Mexicans are going to be infected."

"Do you want us to send some of our medical teams down there?" Millard asked.

Claire looked at him as if he had suddenly gone crazy. "Not exactly," she said. "It appears to me that Ben Raines is going to be extremely busy for the next few weeks, perhaps even months. Even if he wins the upcoming battle for Durango, he's then going to be forced to help the Mexicans treat all their plague-infected peons."

Stevens leaned back in his chair and bit his lip. He had a feeling he knew where this was going.

Claire didn't disappoint him. "I think this would be a perfect time to reassess our decision to pull our troops back from the borders with the SUSA. Raines has already pulled his battalions back, and even sent some of them south to help out on the Mexican border. If we reversed our troop movements and pressed on past the borders, I think it would take Raines by surprise and by the time he could react, we'd have taken control of quite a bit of his territory."

"But, Claire," Millard said, "we can't do that. You said yourself, you gave Raines your word you would pull our troops back and cease the hostilities if he provided us with the anthrax vaccine against Bottger's biological weapons."

"Harlan, you're such a wimp!" Claire said with sudden fervor. "Do you really think I consider myself bound by a promise given under duress? That son of a bitch Raines blackmailed me into promising to pull our troops back, and I don't consider blackmail an honorable way to conduct affairs of state."

Stevens glanced at King and took a deep breath. "Madame President, may I remind you we are rather far along in the pullback process? Our troops are already loaded up, and most have already started to move away from the borders."

"All the better," Claire said, slamming her hand down on her desktop. "If the troops are already loaded up, then all it will take is an order from you for them to turn around and head them back the way they came. The only difference this time is that they won't stop at the borders, but will continue on as far as they can, smashing the token resistance along the way."

"But, Madame President . . ." Stevens began.

"General Stevens," Claire interrupted, her voice as harsh and as hard as he'd ever heard it, "if you are unwilling to give the order, or to support it with all your heart, I am sure I can find another officer who is not afraid to do as I say."

Stevens was defeated and he knew it. "No, ma'am. I'll give the orders immediately."

"And I can count on the full support of you and your other commanding officers in this offensive?" she asked, her eyes dangerously dark.

"Yes, ma'am. You have my word on it, as an officer and a gentleman."

She smiled for the first time in several minutes. "And if

you fail me, Brad, I promise you I'll have your head on it. Understand?"

"Yes, ma'am," he said, putting his hat on and standing up. He gave her a quick salute and left the room, followed closely by Colonel King.

Harlan Millard stood up too. "Claire, once again, I must register my protest. I think you are making a mistake."

"Harlan," Claire said softly, "get your candy ass out of here. I'll deal with you later."

Harlan quickly exited the room without looking back.

Claire turned to Herb, who hadn't said a word during the entire meeting.

"Well, what do you think, Herb?" she asked.

"I think you're a hell of a lady, and that you're gonna kick ass and take names this time," he said.

She stared into his eyes and slowly began to unbutton her blouse. "I love it when you talk like that," she said, letting her glance slide toward her bedroom door.

Herb stood up and walked over to stand behind her desk chair. He leaned over and let both his hands slide over her shoulders and down her chest to cup her breasts under her brassiere.

"Why don't you show me how much you love it?" he said in a low, husky voice, kneading her breasts with his hands until they ached and made her heart race and her mouth turn dry.

She stood up and walked toward the door, glancing back over her shoulder at him seductively.

"I think I will," she said, as she stepped out of her dress and let her blouse slide off her shoulders.

As he followed her through the door, Herb reached up and flipped the light switch off.

Thirty-eight

Mike Post couldn't believe the reports coming in from his intel sources across the SUSA. Claire Osterman had reversed her orders and her troops were now headed back toward their borders at speed.

He got on the radio to Jackie Malone, who was cooling her heels at the Air National Guard base at Peoria, Illinois.

"Malone here," Jackie said into the radio.

"Jackie, this is Mike Post at headquarters."

"Mike, when can I get out of this godforsaken place?" Jackie asked, her voice heavy with disgust. "I'm tired of sitting on my . . . well, sitting around doing nothing while Striginov and McGowen are having all the fun down in Mexico."

"That's why I called, Jackie," Mike said.

"You mean I'm getting my walking orders?" she asked hopefully.

"Not exactly. I've just learned Claire Osterman has changed her orders about withdrawing her troops. She's now got them headed back to attack our borders."

"That bitch!" Jackie said. "I hope Ben kicks her ass from here to there."

"There's a slight problem with that, Jackie," Mike said. "Ben made the mistake of trusting her, so he's pulled most of our battalions down south to help with the Mexican campaign and to give shots to the Mexican citizens."

"You mean the borders are unguarded?" she asked.

"Exactly. Except for token forces, they're completely bare.

They might be able to hold out for a day or two, but unless something is done, and done quickly, we're liable to lose a couple of states to the U.S."

"What can I do?" Jackie asked. "I've only got a couple of hundred men up here. Even if you pull us out, we won't be much help against an entire army."

"I've got an idea, if you're up for it," Mike said.

"Shoot."

"If you can infiltrate Osterman's base there at Indianapolis, perhaps you can talk some sense into her. They'll have all their attention on their offensives against us down south, so the base itself should be at minimum security. They think Ben's too busy down in Mexico to try anything as foolish as attacking her main base."

Jackie didn't answer while she thought about it for a minute. It could be done, she supposed, especially since the troops with her were some of the best scouts in the SUSA's Armed Forces. She keyed the mike. "Got you, Mike. We'll head that way right now. Within a few hours we'll know if it's possible for us to take the base."

"Good luck, Jackie," Mike said. "Call me as soon as you know anything. Meanwhile, I'll do what I can to shore up our defenses along the border."

Jackie knew they'd never make it to the base by aircraft. Since their last attack, the radars had been manned much more diligently. She called her men together and gave them their assignments.

Within hours, every vehicle capable of carrying more than a few men had been rounded up in Peoria and the surrounding towns. Jackie led the way in a large Chevrolet Suburban, with the other two hundred men in over a hundred vehicles of assorted makes and models in a long caravan down Highway 74 south toward Indianapolis. They had almost two hundred miles to travel and they weren't wasting any time.

* * *

It was two in the morning when Jackie pulled to the side of the road less than two miles from Fort Benjamin Harrison in Indianapolis.

She had her men spread out and begin to make their way toward the base. On the northwest quadrant of the base, they came to a long expanse of ten-foot-high wire fence with razor wire curled along the top.

Jackie stepped to the side, and two of her men cut through the fence with wire cutters, leaving a fifteen-foot-wide swath through the fence.

Once inside, Jackie gave quick instructions. One-fourth of the men were assigned to take out the barracks and take the soldiers not on duty prisoner. Half the men were assigned to infiltrate the hangars and guard posts and other administrative buildings to take care of the men on night duty and to gain control of the airplanes and other heavy equipment for future use.

Jackie took the remaining twenty-five scouts with her and made her way toward Claire Osterman's headquarters building, sure it would be the most heavily guarded on the base considering Claire's noted paranoia about her personal safety.

Jackie had warned her men to use their assault knives as much as possible, because any firing of weapons would warn the base it was under attack and would seriously jeopardize their efforts at a complete takeover.

There were guards posted every twenty feet around Osterman's personal quarters, which also served as her office during the day.

Jackie pointed to seven men, who unsheathed their K-Bar assault knives and began to crawl toward the building on their bellies.

Fifteen minutes later, a soft whistle sounded—the signal the outside guards had been taken out. Jackie and the rest of her team of scouts stood up and walked toward the building. So far, there had been not the slightest sign anything was wrong on the base, in spite of the fact that Jackie knew at least half of it had been taken over by now.

Jerry Littletree, a Sioux Indian descendant, stepped out of the darkness, wiping the blade of his K-Bar off on his pants leg. "The door into the building is right there, ma'am," he said, pointing to his left, where a crumpled body could be seen in front of a steel door.

"You didn't scalp him, did you?" Jackie asked with a smile.

Littletree's expression didn't change. "Not yet," he answered, and Jackie shivered, not knowing if he too was teasing or not.

When she got to the door, Littletree handed her a key he'd taken off the night guard. "Be careful, ma'am," he said. "We've taken care of the outside guards, but there're sure to be some on the inside as well."

Jackie reached into her backpack and took out a spray can. Then she put the key in the lock and eased the door open.

Slipping inside, she quickly stepped to the corner and sprayed paint over the lens of the camera hung on the wall there.

She took her Beretta 9mm pistol out of her holster and screwed a silencer onto the barrel, then proceeded up the staircase, her men following directly behind her. She held out her hand at the top of the stairs, and snuck a look around the corner down the corridor.

A lone man was sitting at a bank of video monitors. As she watched, he banged on the side of one of the screens, cursing quietly to himself. When the picture remained black, he picked up a phone and started to dial.

Jackie stepped out into the corridor, her pistol hanging by her side, and walked toward the man, whistling softly to herself as she approached him.

He stopped dialing and looked up, his eyebrows raising in question. "Who the hell are you?" he asked, hanging up the phone and reaching for a holster on his waist.

"Put your hands up, please," Jackie said quietly.

"The hell with you!" the man said harshly, and half rose from his chair, drawing his gun.

Jackie extended her arm straight out and fired, her gun making a *phftt* sound no louder than a soft cough.

The guard's head snapped back as a tiny hole appeared in his forehead and blood and brains exploded out the back of his skull to paint on the wall a grisly portrait of death. His dead body flopped back into his chair and he slumped forward, his head landing with a thump on his desk.

Jackie gave a low whistle and her men poured into the corridor behind her. "Spread out and find me Osterman's quarters, then go in every door and secure whoever's in the other rooms," she ordered.

Minutes later, a sergeant motioned her down the corridor and around a corner to a door marked PRESIDENT OF THE UNITED STATES.

Jackie tried the doorknob. It was locked, so she pulled her K-Bar, stuck the hardened steel point in the keyhole, and twisted. The knife cut through the softer metal of the door as if it were made of butter, and the door swung open.

Jackie raised her Beretta and stepped into Claire's office, swinging her arm around to cover the entire room in one sweep. It was empty, with only a low-wattage night-light on over in a corner.

She turned to the sergeant behind her and motioned to the coffee machine on a side table. "Make us some coffee, would you, Steve?" she asked. "I have a feeling it's gonna be a long night."

"Yes, ma'am," the sergeant said.

Jackie stepped to a door on a side wall and eased it open, pointing her Beretta before her as she walked into the room.

The only light was from a wall clock, which cast a soft light over Claire Osterman's bedroom. Two figures could be seen intertwined, lying on a large bed, half covered with rumpled covers.

Herb Knoff was spooned up against Claire's back, his arm draped over her with his hand cupping her breast. Both of them were completely nude.

Jackie smiled and holstered her Beretta. "How cute," she whispered to the men standing behind her. She reached over and snapped on a light while simultaneously jerking the covers from the bed.

Osterman and Knoff jerked upright, covering their eyes against the harsh light.

"What the hell's the meaning of this?" Claire yelled, sitting up in bed and trying to cover her nakedness and at the same time shield her eyes with her hand.

Knoff rolled quickly to the side and reached for his side arm on the bedside table, only to stop when one of the scouts cocked his M-16 with a loud metallic snap and said, "Uh-uh, podna."

Herb returned to his position next to Claire while the scout picked up the pistol and put it in his pocket.

Regaining some of her composure, Claire glared at Jackie, who was obviously in charge. "Who are you and what is the meaning of this intrusion?" she asked sharply.

"I'm Jackie Malone, commander of the 512 Battalion of the SUSA's Armed Forces," Jackie said.

"What do you want?" Claire asked, glancing at Herb as he put both his hands over his crotch.

"We need to talk, Claire," Jackie said, taking a seat in an easy chair across the room from the bed.

"May I put some clothes on?" Claire asked, reaching for a robe on the side of the bed.

"No, I think not," Jackie said, with just a trace of maliciousness in her tone. "You're fine just the way you are."

Claire looked around at the men with Jackie, who were openly ogling her naked body. "Then could you ask those men to leave the room?"

Jackie shook her head. "Why? From what I've heard, they're

only a few more in a long line of men who've seen you naked, Claire."

Claire leaned back against her headboard and crossed her arms under her breasts, her face defiant. "All right then, get on with it."

"First of all, let me clarify your position, Madame President," Jackie said. "Your base here is under my complete control, and all of your men are either dead or have been taken prisoner."

For the first time, Claire's eyes seemed to show some fear. This was something she hadn't been expecting. "Go on."

The sergeant stuck his head in the door from the other room. "Coffee's ready, Jackie."

Jackie motioned to Claire. "Would you and . . . your friend like a cup?" she asked.

Herb shook his head. Claire said, as cool as a cucumber, "Yes, please. With cream and Sweet 'n Low."

Jackie glanced at the sergeant. "Two cups, please, Steve. Make mine black."

"Yes, ma'am," he said, and disappeared back through the door.

"To continue," Jackie said to Claire, "we understand you've gone back on your word to General Raines and have begun to reposition your troops along our border."

"You are misinformed, Ms. Malone," Claire said. "My troops are merely undergoing training exercises."

Jackie shook her head. "You know, Claire," she said, deliberately using Claire's first name, "as much as you lie, one would think you'd be better at it. Our intel is definite. You plan to attack the SUSA within twenty-four hours."

Claire shrugged, but didn't speak. Her eyes glared hatred at Jackie.

Jackie waited while the sergeant handed her and Claire their cups of coffee. She took a sip. "Ummm, good coffee," she said.

"I'm glad you like it," Claire said. "If I thought you were going to survive this little intrusion, I'd send you some."

Jackie smiled. "Oh, I'll survive, Claire. It's only *your* fate that's in question here tonight."

Claire's eyes widened and her hand shook slightly as she took a drink of her coffee, the only signs she gave that Jackie's words scared her.

"Now, here's the deal," Jackie continued. "If you get on the radio right now and call off your attack, and once again recall your troops, you may . . . I say may . . . get out of this situation alive."

"And if I don't?" Claire said with false bravado.

Jackie shrugged. "Then, first you're going to watch what happens to your little teddy bear there," she said, pointing her head at Herb, whose face paled at the thought of his fate, "and then we'll see just how much pain you can stand before you change your mind."

"I don't believe you'd dare torture a sitting president of the United States," Claire said.

Jackie looked over at the group of men with her. Then she noticed something that made her stomach crawl. She smiled grimly. "Jerry, would you step forward, please?"

Jerry Littletree stepped from the rear of the group to stand before Claire's bed. A bloody scalp was hanging from his belt and his trousers were stained with blood from his K-Bar. "Jerry Littletree here is a Sioux Indian, Claire," Jackie said, watching Claire's eyes fall to the scalp hanging from Littletree's belt. "I don't know how much history you know, Claire, but white settlers used to save a bullet for their womenfolk rather than let them fall into the hands of the Sioux. If you continue to refuse to give the order to pull your troops back, I'm going to let Jerry show you what they were afraid of."

"You wouldn't dare!" Claire said, shrinking back against the headboard.

"Jerry," Jackie said, leaning back in her chair and continuing to sip her coffee.

Littletree grinned savagely and pulled his bloody K-Bar from its scabbard. He stepped toward the bed.

"Claire, for God's sake!" Herb almost screamed, pulling his legs up and crossing them over his privates.

Claire held out her hands. "All right, all right. Call that savage off!"

Littletree looked disappointed as he stepped back among the men around the bed, but he kept his knife out and ran his finger along the blade, staring at Claire through dark eyes.

"Steve, get the radio room on the phone," Jackie said, "and have them transfer the call in here."

A few minutes later, the phone on Claire's bedside table rang and she picked it up.

"Give the man on the phone instructions on how to contact whoever is in charge of your Army," Jackie said, "and if you make a mistake, or happen to say the wrong thing, I won't call Littletree off again."

After Claire had gotten in touch with Stevens and explained that she'd again changed her mind, she told him to call back the troops and have them stand down. After listening to him argue for a few seconds, she screamed into the phone, "This is not a matter for discussion, General Stevens. Either do it right now or face a court-martial and firing squad in the morning." Then she slammed the phone down.

"Are you satisfied now?" Claire asked, again trying to cover her breasts with her arms.

"No, but I'll be satisfied when we get reports the troops are in fact gone from our borders," Jackie said. Then she turned to the sergeant. "Steve, round up the men and have them get a C-130 ready for us. We're going home."

"What about her?" he asked, inclining his head toward Claire.

"She's going to ride with us until we're sure she's keeping

her word this time. If the troops are still gone when we get home, we'll let one of her pilots bring her back."

"And I'm supposed to believe that?" Claire asked.

Jackie shrugged. "Believe what you want, 'cause you really don't have much of a choice in the matter. My orders were to stop the attack on our borders, not to kill you." She grinned. "Otherwise, you'd already be dead."

Thirty-nine

When the C-130 airplane carrying Claire Osterman, Herb Knoff, a U.S. pilot, and Jackie Malone and her band of scouts began its final descent over Base One in Louisiana, Jackie walked over to where Claire and Herb and the pilot sat on the metal benches along the side of the aircraft.

Jackie stared down at Claire and Herb, clad only in military style overcoats to cover their nakedness.

"I have a few things to say to you before we land, Claire," Jackie said in a low voice.

"I think you've said quite enough, Ms. Malone," Claire said in a haughty voice, having regained some of her confidence now that she knew she wasn't going to be killed or kept as a prisoner of war.

"No," Jackie said, shaking her head, "I don't think I have. I think you're planning on trying to go back on your word again, as soon as you're back at your base."

Claire didn't speak, but just stared up into Jackie's eyes.

"I'd like to advise you not to do that, Claire," Jackie said, drawing her K-Bar assault knife.

Herb's eyes widened, and he moved over a bit on the metal seat to distance himself from whatever was about to happen.

Jackie bent down and put her face close to Claire's. "You really should keep your word this time, Claire, because, you see, I own you. I can get to you any time I want to. President Lincoln, the Kennedy brothers, and President Reagan proved that there is no one so guarded they can't be gotten to if someone has the will to do it. Look deep in my eyes, Claire, and realize I have the will and the skill to take you out if you go back on your word this time."

Claire's face paled as she realized this woman was crazy enough to do just that.

"Now," Jackie continued when she saw she had Claire's full attention, "I'm from Texas, and we have a habit of marking things we own, like cattle and sheep. But since I don't have a branding iron handy, I'm gonna do the next best thing."

In a lightning-quick motion, Jackie flicked the knife at Claire's head, cutting a small V-shaped notch in the top of her right ear.

"That's called notching, dear," Jackie explained as Claire gave a short scream and grabbed her bleeding ear. "It's mainly used on cattle, but in your case, I made an exception. Now, every time you look in a mirror, you'll think of me and what will happen to you if you piss me off."

Jackie wiped the point of her knife on Herb's coat, put it back in its scabbard, and strolled back to her seat just as the C-130 touched down for a landing.

Fifteen minutes later, the plane took off again and the pilot made a sweeping turn to the north, heading back to Indianapolis.

Herb sat in the back with Claire, holding her tight against his chest while she sobbed.

"Don't worry, Claire," he said in a soothing voice. "As soon as we get back you can countermand your order to pull the troops back."

She pulled away from him and stared at him, her eyes wild. "Are you crazy?" she almost shouted. "I'll do no such thing."

"You're not afraid of what that bitch said, are you?" Herb asked.

"You didn't see her eyes, Herb. She meant every word of what she said."

"But we can protect you. . . ." he began.

Claire shook her head back and forth. "No . . . no, I don't think anyone could protect me from that . . . woman. She's a demon!"

As dawn lightened the skies to the east, Raines and his team took their places in one of the buildings of the base at Durango. Guerra had his troops spread out along a perimeter spreading in a wide semicircle facing both east and west. The base was protected to the north by a wide river that would prevent any organized motorized attack from that direction.

Bulldozers had worked throughout the night to build berms, high dirt walls, around the base. The troops were arrayed behind these berms with fifty-caliber machine guns spaced evenly along the entire length of the wall of earth.

Snipers, fitted with Heckler and Koch sniper rifles, were placed on the roofs of all the buildings, with orders to concentrate their fire on officers and drivers of any vehicles they could target.

Twenty-millimeter antiaircraft machine guns were stationed on all four quadrants of the base to help keep the helicopters and gunships away from the troops as much as possible.

Ben and General Guerra had done all they could until Georgi Striginov and his Bat 505 arrived to help. Now they just had to hold the enemy off until the cavalry arrived.

As the sun peeked over the horizon, fingers of light illuminated low-lying clouds in the sky with an orange and yellow glow.

Ben glanced over the wall around the roof he and his team were on and said, "Should be any minute now."

Seconds later a whistling drone could be heard and mortar rounds began falling on the grounds of the base. Explosions threw up dirt and dust as the rounds pockmarked the hard-packed dirt of the compound. Guerra and Ben had told the soldiers to hold their fire until the enemy was close, but some of the Mexicans, excited by the sound and fury of the explosions, began to fire their weapons at shadows.

Suddenly, on the horizon, thousands of enemy troops could be seen beginning their advance, walking alongside tanks, half-tracks, armored personnel carriers, and HumVees and old-style jeeps.

Simultaneously with the appearance of the troops, shadowy shapes flitted overhead, coming in low and fast, as Kiowas, Defenders, and even a couple of older-model Cobra helicopters buzzed the base, their machine guns blazing a trail of death toward the defending Mexican troops behind their earthen walls.

Harley had given up his SPAS shotgun for a Browning automatic rifle, which he placed on a tripod on the wall around the roof, a belt of ammunition trailing down to an ammunition box at his feet. He squatted and aimed at one of the Defenders as it made a pass. The BAR danced and jittered in his hands as he pulled the trigger, his teeth gritted and his body shuddering under the recoil of the big rifle as it poured thousands of rounds at the approaching helicopter.

Jersey and Anna and Beth held their fire, their Uzis not long-range enough to be effective yet.

Hammer, on the far corner of the building, held an M-60 machine gun in his huge arms at his waist, Rambo style, and stood up, firing along with Harley at the onrushing helicopter.

The wall along the building top behind which Ben squatted shattered under the impact of the Defender's 20mm Minigun as it screamed overhead.

Harley and Hammer both turned, continuing to pour fire into the rear of the chopper, until smoke began to billow from its turbine engine and it shuddered under the impact of hundreds of fifty- and sixty-caliber shells.

A stream of tracers from Hammer's M-60 danced toward the tail rotor and finally merged with it, chewing it to pieces. The Defender began to gyrate and whip back and forth, out of control, until it finally nosed down and crashed in the middle of the compound with an expanding fireball that roared fifty feet into the air.

Several of the Mexican troops cheered and waved their rifles, evidently thinking they had brought the chopper down with their small-arms fire.

Harley and Hammer ceased firing and grinned at each other, then ducked back down behind the wall and looked for other targets.

The troops advancing across the desert sands toward the base from the east faltered under the withering fire from the berm around the base, and even began to pull back a little, just as another line of troops appeared on the western horizon, also accompanied by a motorized company of light tanks and several Kiowa and Huey helicopters.

"Shit!" Ben exclaimed to Jersey and Coop, who were squatting next to him. "That must be Bottger's troops. Now we're in for it."

A HumVee with a fifty-caliber machine gun on a post in the rear roared close by the berm, raking the troops along the top with rapid fire from its fifty.

Several Mexican soldiers were blown off the back of the wall, to lie twisting and screaming in the dirt, their blood staining the earth as they died.

When the HumVee got within range, Jersey, Anna, Beth, and Coop leaned over the wall and opened up with their Uzis, each firing six hundred rounds per minute into the vehicle as it tried to draw a bead on more soldiers.

The 9mm shells stitched a line of holes in the sides of the HumVee, blowing out the two near-side tires. The driver grabbed his head, blood spurting from his Kevlar helmet, and let go of the wheel. The HumVee veered right, then left on the ruined tires and rolled three times, throwing the dead driver and the rear-seat gunner out of the vehicle.

Three Mexican soldiers stood up behind their wall and pumped round after round into the gunner until he too was dead.

In spite of murderous fire from the Mexican defenders, the troops on both sides began to close the gap, moving forward despite tremendous losses of men and machines in a do-or-die assault.

"It don't look too good, podna," Coop said out of the corner of his mouth to Ben as the troops got within a hundred yards. The number of Mexican soldiers seemed pitifully small in comparison to the forces arrayed against them.

Suddenly, from off to the side, small vehicles began to appear, moving at great speed toward the oncoming troops, spitting fire from 120mm cannons in their noses as they maneuvered in and out of the scattering troops.

"Look," Ben shouted, "it's Vulcans from Striginov's battalion."

As Jersey and Coop and the other members of Ben's team turned to look, other vehicles began to appear. Two huge M-1 Abrams tanks thundered over a distant hill and began to fire at the smaller Sheridans accompanying Loco's troops. The Sheridans tried to return fire, but began to explode one by one under the rapid laser-guided fire of the Abrams.

Two helicopters, a Kiowa and a Huey, turned from their attack on the base and flew toward the Abrams, evidently hoping to take them out with missiles.

From out of the low-lying sun, three Apaches screamed between the Abrams and the two helicopters, their Chain Guns blazing as they arrowed at the hapless choppers.

The Kiowa, much faster than the Huey, managed to turn and run, but the Huey disintegrated under the Chain Guns' fire, dropping like a stone to burn brightly on the desert floor, sending clouds of oily black smoke toward the sky.

The Kiowa tried to gain altitude and make an escape, but the lead Apache let one of its Hellfire missiles go, and it ran right up the exhaust of the Kiowa's turbine, blowing it out of the sky in a thousand pieces that fell like rain on the parched desert below.

Seeing the battle turn, the attacking troops slowed, then

turned to run as more vehicles, including several Bradley Attack Vehicles, appeared from the north. Soon, both attacking armies were in full retreat, running and firing over their shoulders at the Mexican troops, who boiled over the berm and began to chase the attackers back the way they came.

In less than an hour, the field in front of the base was littered with thousands of bodies and hundreds of broken, twisted piles of burning metal, from Jeeps to HumVees to half-tracks, that had been destroyed by Striginov's motorized madmen.

The Mexican troops, enraged and encouraged by the turn of the battle, were taking no prisoners. They mowed the retreating troops down with wild abandon, cheerfully pouring lead into their backs as they rushed forward onto the battlefield.

"Jesus," Beth said, shaking her head. "It's a slaughter."

Ben nodded. "Yeah, exactly what would have happened to us had Georgi been an hour later."

Soon, the troops of Striginov's battalion appeared on the field and began rounding up prisoners, calming the killing rage of the Mexican troops and ending the slaughter of the defeated armies.

Two hours later, General Herman Bundt and General Enrique Gonzalez were brought before Ben, Georgi Striginov, and General Jose Guerra in the officers' wardroom of the base commander's office.

Ben conducted the interrogation. "Where are your leaders, Perro Loco and Bruno Bottger?" he asked the two men standing before him.

"I refuse to answer under the terms of the Geneva Convention," Bundt said sourly. "All you are entitled to are my name, rank, and serial number."

"Is that so?" Ben asked. "Are you aware that under the terms of the Geneva Convention, you are guilty of high war crimes for the manufacture and release of biological weapons?"

Bundt stared fixedly ahead, while General Gonzalez looked at him in horror. "What biological weapons? I have no knowledge of such a thing."

"I believe the penalty for war crimes is a firing squad, at which the Mexican troops are more than proficient," Ben said calmly. "General Guerra?"

Guerra stepped forward to stand in front of Bundt. "I think a firing squad is too good for this one," he said. "I believe I will simply turn him over to my troops after telling them this is the man responsible for the plague which even now is sweeping across our country, killing thousands of their families and friends."

Bundt looked up, showing for the first time fear at what the general was saying. "You wouldn't dare!"

"Take him away," Guerra said to an aide.

"Wait a moment," Bundt said hurriedly. "Field Marshal Bottger and Perro Loco are in the Presidential Palace in Mexico City."

"Are they aware of your defeat?" Ben asked.

Both men shook their heads. "No, there wasn't time to report back to them," Gonzalez said.

Ben looked at Striginov and Guerra. "That means we may still have time to intercept them before they attempt to flee the country."

He thought for a moment, then spoke to Striginov. "I need one of your Chinooks for my team, and a couple of Apaches to accompany us to Mexico City. I have some unfinished business with both of those gentlemen."

Forty

The Apaches came in high and fast toward the Presidential Palace in Mexico City. The soldiers guarding the palace were stationed around the front porch and along the sides of the building, leaning against the wall in the shade, trying to avoid the midday heat of the Mexican sun. They were expecting no trouble, for all the fighting was taking place two hundred miles to the north.

The Apaches separated, diving on the building from opposite sides at over two hundred miles an hour, their Chain Guns chattering thousands of rounds a minute into the hapless, unsuspecting defenders of the palace.

In the first pass, over half the guards were killed or wounded before they knew they were under attack, their bodies shredded and torn apart by the terrible impact of the bullets the Apaches were spitting with such ferocity.

By the time the Apaches banked, turned, and began another pass, most of the remaining guards were running for their lives down the palisade in front of the building. Only a few were brave enough, and dumb enough, to try to return fire.

The helicopters hovered and flitted around the building like angry bees protecting their nest, firing into the guards until there were none left to return fire.

Once they radioed it was safe, the Chinook carrying Ben and his team landed on the tarmac in front of the palace.

Harley and Hammer exited first, cradling their SPAS shotguns in their arms, followed by Coop, Jersey, Anna, Beth, and finally Ben.

They ducked under the blades and ran to take up positions on the front porch, which had been chewed up and splintered by the fire of the Apaches, still hovering overhead, keeping a close lookout for any other threats.

Harley leaned back and kicked the big double doors in the front of the palace open with his foot. Then he and Hammer rushed into the building side by side.

Two shots rang out from guards on the second floor. Harley jumped to the side, leveled his shotgun, and blew them off the balcony, to fall twenty feet to the marble floor, landing with a wet-sounding splat.

Hammer knelt, sweeping the rest of the balcony with his SPAS in case anyone else tried to make a fight of it.

Coop and Jersey were next through the door, running crouched over to ascend the stairs and secure the second floor. Coop carried a SPAS, while Jersey had her Uzi tucked in her arms, her trigger finger itching to find a target.

As Beth and Corrie and Ben entered the building, a door at the end of the corridor burst open and three men charged out, firing M-16's as they ran.

Coop fired three quick rounds with the SPAS, the razor-sharp flechette needles in his shells shredding two of the men where they stood, blowing them back into the room they'd come out of.

The third man managed to get off two shots, one of which hit Coop in the left arm and spun him around, before Jersey unloaded on him with her Uzi on full automatic.

The guard danced and spun and tumbled to the floor under the impact of fifty 9mm rounds that tore him in half before dumping him on the floor in a pool of blood.

The rest of Ben's team went room by room, finding and killing three more guards before Harley declared the second floor secure and empty.

Ben looked up the staircase. "That must mean our men are on the third floor."

Harley nodded. "There's bound to be more guards with 'em."

Ben looked over at Jersey, who was kneeling by Coop's side applying a field dressing to the wound in his arm.

"Jerse, you stay here and take care of Coop," he said.

"Wait a minute," Coop protested, trying to get to his feet. "I'm okay. . . ."

Jersey jerked him back down. "Sit down and shut up, for once in your life, Coop," she said, smiling, "and let me take care of you."

He grinned back. "Now, that's an offer I can't refuse," he said.

She glared at him fiercely. "Not if you want to live!" she said, taking his hand.

Anna stepped next to Harley, covering his back as he and Hammer went up the steps, followed closely by Ben and Corrie and Beth, all holding their weapons at the ready.

Harley peeked around a turn in the corridor and saw the barrels of several weapons sticking out of doors along the corridor.

He pulled a flash-bang grenade from the belt on his chest, pulled the ring, and pitched it down the hall. The phosphorus-filled grenade exploded with a tremendous blast of light and heat and sound.

Several men screamed and ran from their hiding places, their hands over their eyes and ears.

Harley and Hammer's shotguns boomed, knocking the men to the floor and stopping their screaming.

Anna whirled and let go with her Uzi, killing two more men who had come out of a closet behind Harley and Hammer.

Harley glanced around, then down at Anna. "That's one I owe you," he said.

"I'll make sure to collect when we have more time," she said, keeping an eye out for more guards.

Ben eased around Harley and Hammer and made his way down the hall while they covered him. He checked each and every office and room along the way, making sure they were all empty.

Sudden shots rang out and he dived to the side, a furrow of blood appearing along his shoulder and neck from two near misses.

Corrie and Beth stepped into the doorway the shots came from and sprayed the room with their Uzis, not bothering to aim, just waving the machine guns back and forth as if they were watering the grass with a hose.

Harsh guttural screams rang out from two guards that were blown back against the wall, their blood splattering the adobe walls as 9mm bullets pocked the walls and raised a cloud of dust and cordite in the room.

Finally, the third floor was cleared of defenders, each room checked and found to be empty—all except the presidential quarters at the end of the hall. There were large, wooden double doors with a bronze sign on them reading EL PRESIDENTE.

"Looks like the rats are finally trapped in their hole," Harley said to Ben as they surveyed the corridor leading to the last room on the floor.

"Take cover," Ben said as he pulled a fragmentation grenade from his pack. "Time to call the dance."

After everyone was hidden in doorways along the corridor, he pulled the pin, rolled the grenade up against the double doors, and ducked into a room.

The grenade exploded, tearing the doors off their hinges and shattering them into ruin. Jim Strunk and Paco Valdez, who'd evidently been hiding behind the doors, stumbled into the hallway, their skin flayed and bleeding and full of splinters as they sprayed the hallway with machine-guns they held in their hands.

Harley and Hammer leaned out of their doorways and fired their shotguns at point-blank range. The two men's bodies were lifted off their feet and blown ten feet back into the presidential quarters. They landed and rolled into a crumpled heap, dead before they hit the highly polished marble floor.

Through the doorway, several desks could be seen pushed up near the wall to form a barricade. Four men could be seen hiding behind the desks, their heads barely visible in the darkened room.

"You might as well come out," Ben said. "Your armies have been defeated and there is nowhere else for you to run."

"Chinga tu madre!" Perro Loco screamed as he leapt over the desk, a sawed-off pump shotgun in his arms. He fired and pumped and fired, screaming curses in Spanish as he bolted for the door.

Ben stepped out into the corridor, unmindful of the roaring shotgun, and extended his arm. He fired one shot with his Beretta 9mm automatic.

The bullet struck Perro Loco dead center in his forehead, snapping his head back and flinging him to the floor, where he lay with open eyes staring into eternity, his smoking shotgun next to his body.

Jersey stepped to Ben's side. "Nice shot, Boss," she said, holding her Uzi at waist level in case any more madmen appeared.

"Hold your fire! I give up!" a man yelled through the smoke that billowed in the room.

Sergei Bergman walked around the desk and toward the doorway, his hands in the air.

Just before he reached the door, a figure stood up behind him and aimed a pistol at his back. "You coward!" Rudolf Hessner screamed, and fired, hitting Bergman between the shoulder blades and catapulting him onto his face.

Jersey didn't hesitate. Without aiming, she pulled the trigger on her Uzi and spun Hessner around twice before he too was dead, his body draped over the desk.

When the firing stopped, another voice called, "I am coming out. Do not shoot!"

Ben's team gathered in the doorway as Bruno Bottger

stepped around from behind the desk, his hands in the air, his holster at his side empty.

When he was in the center of the room, Ben stood before him. "Bruno Bottger, I'm going to enjoy watching you swing at the end of a rope for the war crimes you've committed."

Ben turned his back and began to walk away.

"Ben, look out!" Jersey screamed, unable to get a clear shot as Bottger reached behind his back, pulled a Luger pistol out of his belt, and aimed it at Ben's back.

"Die, Ben Raines!" Bottger screamed as he began to pull the trigger.

In one fluid motion, Ben jerked his K-Bar assault knife from the scabbard on his belt, whirled, and threw it backhand at Bottger.

The knife buried itself to the hilt in Bottger's neck, severing his spinal cord and killing him instantly. As his body crumpled to the ground, Ben stood over him.

"Never talk when you should be shooting, asshole," he muttered to the dead man.

Forty-one

A month later, General Jose Guerra, now known as El Presidente Guerra, paid a visit to Ben's office in Louisiana.

He entered the office accompanied by Dr. Larry Buck. He stepped directly to Ben's desk and held out his hand. "I am here to thank you on behalf of my people for all you have done, General Raines."

Ben stood up and took his hand. "It was my pleasure, Mr. President."

"The plague is at last under control in Mexico, Ben," Dr. Buck said. "There've been no new cases reported for the past week or so."

"How many did you lose, President Guerra?" Ben asked, sadness in his voice.

The president shrugged. "The total is not known as of yet, but it is a surety that the numbers would have been much greater without the assistance of the medical teams your country sent to aid us."

"We were all lucky," Ben said. "Were it not for the bravery of two of my soldiers, we would all have been caught unawares by the plague."

President Guerra nodded. "I will say a prayer for them at Mass tomorrow." He gave a quick bow of his head and left the room.

Ben glanced at Buck. "Speaking of heroes, how is Coop doing with his wound?" he asked.

Buck laughed. "Quite well, actually. He's got Jersey convinced he has to be hand-fed his meals and requires a back rub at least twice a day."

Ben grinned. "The way I hear it, she won't leave his side because she's afraid he'll make a pass at one of the nurses."

"God help Coop, and the nurse, if that happens," Buck said, shaking his head.

AUTHOR'S NOTE

For those readers interested in facts, the following are the specifications of the weapons and aircraft used in *Warriors from the Ashes:*

Ben carries a CAR (Carbine, Assault Rifle), 5.56 caliber. It is a shortened version of the M-16. Because of the shortened barrel, a Bloop Tube (which fits under the barrel of an M-16 and fires a 40mm rifle grenade) cannot be used on a CAR. His side arm is a Beretta 9mm. Ben will occasionally use an M-14, which he calls his Thunder Lizard. It's a shoulder-pounding bitch on full auto, and is 7.62 mm, which is the equivalent of .308 caliber in civilian ammo. The CAR, just like the M-16 and M-14, uses a 20- or 30-round magazine.

Uzi: aka: Mini-Uzi, Micro Uzi:
Origin: Israel 1952
Caliber: 9x19 mm
Feed device: 20-, 32-, and 40-round detachable box magazine
Action: Recoil, selective fire
Sights: Open
Length: 64 cm (46 cm with stock folded)

Muzzle velocity: 403 M/S
Rate of fire: 650 rounds per minute

Fairchild A-10 Warthog:
Weapons: 30mm cannon in nose, also fires laser- or TV-guided missiles
Length overall: 16.26 m (53 ft 4 in)
Wing span: 17.53 m (57 ft 6 in)
Max. speed at sea level: 381 knots
Combat radius: 463 km (290 miles)
Maximum weapons load: 7257 kg (7 tons, 320 lbs)
Takeoff distance: 1219 m (4000 ft)

Boeing/Bell V-22 Osprey:
Crew: 3 (pilot, copilot, crew chief)
Length: 57 ft 3 in (17.5 m)
Rotor diameter: 38 ft (11.58 m)
Max. speed: 185 knots (helicopter mode), 275 knots (airplane mode)
Range: 2100 nautical miles
Load: 20,000 pounds
Wing span: 45 ft 10 in (13.75 m)

General Dynamics F-111 Aardvark:
Length: 22.4 m (73 ft 6 in)
Wing span: 19.2 m (63 ft)
Max. speed at sea level: 793 knots
Combat radius: 1480 km (920 miles)
Max. weapons load: 11,340 kg (11 tons, 360 lbs)
Takeoff distance: 914 m (3000 ft)

* * *

McDonnel Douglas AH-64 Apache:
Length: 17.76 m (56 ft 3 in)
Rotor diameter: 14.63 m (48 ft)
Max. speed: 155 knots
Range: 482 km (300 miles)
Standard weapon load: M230 30mm Chain Gun; 6 Hellfire antitank missiles

Bell OH-58 Kiowa:
Length: 12.49 m (41 ft)
Rotor diameter: 10.77 m (35 ft 4 in)
Max. speed: 120 knots
Range: 491 km (305 miles)
Standard weapon load: 7.62 or 20mm Minigun plus antitank missiles

Boeing Helicopters Ch-47 Chinook:
Length: 30.18 m (98 ft 11 in)
Rotor diameter: 18.29 m (60 ft)
Max. speed: 138 knots
Range: 370 km (230 miles)
Load: 44+ troops or 12,700 kg (12 tons, 1120 lbs)

Bell AH-1 HueyCobra:
Length: 16.18 m (53 ft)
Rotor diameter: 13.41 m (44 ft)
Max. speed: 123 knots
Range: 507 km (315 miles)
Standard weapon load: 8 TOW antitank missiles; 1 3-barreled 20mm cannon; 2 unguided rocket or cannon pods

* * *

McDonnel Douglas OH-6 Defender:
Length: 9.4 m (30 ft 10 in)
Rotor diameter: 8.03 m (26 ft 4 in)
Max. speed: 119 knots
Range: 428 km (265 miles)
Standard weapon load: 20mm Minigun

Bill Johnstone likes to hear from his readers. You can e-mail him at dogcia@aol.com